# LIVING PROOF
## (that no good deed goes unpunished)
## Neighborlee Book 4

## Michelle L. Levigne

## www.YeOldeDragonBooks.com


Previously released as *Living Proof*, 2018
Revised

Ye Olde Dragon Books
P.O. Box 30802
Middleburg Hts., OH 44130

www.YeOldeDragonBooks.com

2OldeDragons@gmail.com



Published in the United States of America
Publication Date: November 1, 2020

Cover Art Copyright by Ye Olde Dragon Books 2020

## Welcome to Neighborlee, Ohio.

Where? Somewhere on the North Coast of Ohio, south of Cleveland, right off I-71, north of Medina, in the heart of Cuyahoga County.

What is it? That's a little harder to explain.

Neighborlee is a place you need to experience.

The most important thing you need to understand: Neighborlee is *magic*. Some people say the town is alive. It exists to protect the weird and wonderful (and sometimes a little bit scary) from the cold, practical, material world.

More important, Neighborlee protects the outside world from the weird and wonderful that come to visit … and sometimes come to stay.

First stop: Divine's Emporium, a four-story Victorian house sitting on a hill overlooking the Metroparks. Whatever you really need, you can find at Divine's. Even if you don't know what you're looking for when you walk in the door. The shop is often bigger inside than it is outside. Angela is the proprietor. Please stay on the first floor. You don't want to find out what is hidden and locked safely away upstairs. Like Aslan, Angela is good, but that doesn't mean she's safe. And neither are the secrets and wonders and doorways to other worlds that she protects … and keeps securely locked.

Come in and explore. Meet the people who help Angela guard Neighborlee. Share their adventures of magic and wonder, danger and sacrifice. You never know who or what you'll run into as you walk the streets and listen to the stories of their lives.

# Chapter One

No good deed goes unpunished. I'm living proof.

Just ask any superhero. Does Spider-Man get to swing off into the sunset with a happy ending? Hardly! And what about Superman? The happily-ever-after factor is conspicuously missing from most superheroes' lives.

My strongest evidence lies in the events of four years ago on Senior Prank Night. I was performing my duties, as a teacher at Neighborlee High School and a guardian of Neighborlee. Some of us Lost Kids have, for reasons we still haven't figured out, been given semi-pseudo-superhero powers. Mine were half-baked at best because, as I proved that June night, my hero package didn't include invulnerability.

Kurt, Felicity and I still went out on patrol despite the stormy weather. When we heard two trucks were stolen from the service department lot, logic took us to the quarries, north and west of town, as the best place to park the stolen trucks, to be easily found. After all, what was the use of pulling the prank if nobody knew what you did?

The lack of lighting at the quarries wouldn't have been a problem, if it hadn't been raining.

Rain might have made things tricky, but not fatal. Except that the enemies of Neighborlee, inimical forces from other dimensions of reality, took advantage of the situation to attack. The storm was brutally heavy and blinding. The boy driving one of the trucks got lost and crashed through the barriers to keep people away from steep slopes and cliffs. Then the brakes died. When the boy tried to jump to safety, his coat got caught.

What's a high school track, basketball and journalism teacher to do when one of her students is about to go flying off a cliff in a killer storm at midnight? Especially when said teacher kinda-sorta has the ability to fly?

Yep. I got up on the truck and released Toby and got us both off the truck before it went over the cliff.

However, something nasty was guiding that runaway truck.

My back had a couple too-close encounters with a stone wall and the heavy, old-fashioned bumper of the truck.

We're talking gravel where my spine used to be. The protective field around Neighborlee kept me alive, but our enemy was interfering, just like the day Stephanie Miller, another guardian, died. I healed, but only partially. I could walk, a little. Best to save my sporadic mobility for certain semi-embarrassing hygiene tasks. Most of the time, my legs were tingly-numb and my joints had a tendency to do the opposite of what I wanted. The smart move was for me to go through the rest of my life with semi-natural four-wheel drive.

That's snark-speak for "wheelchair."

I shouldn't complain, because I should have ended up paralyzed from the shoulders down, depending on ventilators and the kindness of medical personnel for the rest of my life. Thanks to the prayers of my church and the otherworldly, if diluted magic of Neighborlee, I was a walking — or should I say rolling — miracle.

I also lost most of my kinda-sorta flying ability. Kurt was already used to taking over that part of my talent and putting boosters and controls on it. This let our team continue to fly to perform our guardian duties. I still had my telekinesis, and sometimes I got cryptic glimpses of the future. Sometimes when I touched people I could tell if they were lying or telling the truth, and got images that let me see into their character.

Thanks to the broken back, I gave up teaching and went to work full-time at the local paper, the *Neighborlee Tattler*. I had been working there as a stringer, handling the school sports beat, since high school. I expanded my snarky sense of humor. My friends who aced college psychology class would say that humor is a self-defense mechanism, and they would probably be right. All I know is that within a few years of landing in my chair (manual, not electric), I had a decent side job as a comedian, performing at comedy clubs and doing parties or half-time entertainment at local events. I had a reputation for being able to verbally slice-and-dice anybody who made the mistake of assuming that a broken body equaled a broken mind.

*Do not mess with the physically handicapped, because we don't need motorized wheelchairs to leave tread marks all over you.*

*Just saying...*

At the holidays four years later, everything seemed to come full circle. I had three comedy CDs under my belt. My wheelchair basketball team, the Ezekiel's Wheels, had a loyal following. Mum and Pop were out of town on a research trip to the Bermuda Triangle.

And my life started coming apart all around me.

The unraveling began maybe a week or so before Thanksgiving. There was so much going on in our lives, I missed some of the clues at first.

Mum and Pop had missed their regular check-in phone call. Pete and Harry and I weren't too worried, because our folks were always doing that. They'd get involved in a story, investigating something fascinating or following up on a lead, and get so tightly focused they would forget about time or even location. For example: the research trip where they started out interviewing bushmen in Australia and ended up driving a dogsled in Siberia.

There was the usual flutter and fuss of the holidays approaching. Both my brothers were living with me. Harry had his own small trucking company, including a contract to deliver papers to carriers for the *Neighborlee Tattler*. He had sold the latest condo he had been renovating and the deal for his new place fell through at the last minute, so he was literally out in the cold with nowhere to go. I had room, even with Pete bunking with me long-term. I always got along well with both my brothers. They made useful roadies handling my wheelchair, in situations when it wouldn't be smart for people to realize I had telekinetic powers.

Problems and distractions were increasing at this point, the most prominent and visible: losing my job.

Technically, I was still working for the paper, but that Friday after Thanksgiving, our entire world got rearranged.

Our silent, nearly invisible owner arrived without warning.

For generations the Severidge family had owned the *Tattler*. However, over time the stock had been inherited and re-inherited, until more people outside of Neighborlee owned pieces of the newspaper than those who still lived here. We had never heard of Waldo Sloane because he was the perfect silent partner and majority owner of the *Neighborlee Tattler*.

Back in the 1950s, Waldo Sloane's father had amused himself by tracking down and buying up shares in our newspaper. Hey, rich people have weird hobbies. Just before his own death, Waldo Sloane had all the shares not owned by Conrad Severidge and his father. He was entirely happy to be a silent owner, letting the Severidges run the paper as they saw fit, and collecting his share of the profits on a regular basis.

In August, he died, and left behind a widow who was the original Gold-Digger Barbie. Widow Sloane had no use for newspapers. I found out much later that she made only one demand for Conrad to buy out her shares of the *Tattler*. When he didn't give her an immediate answer, she went hunting for a buyer.

The Friday after Thanksgiving, Widow Sloane slithered into the office. She commanded Conrad to call a meeting of everyone in the building, and introduced Daniel Sheridan to the general staff. Then she announced the sale of three-fourths ownership of the *Neighborlee Tattler* to the Sheridan Corporation, a multi-state conglomerate of newspapers (think the Borg collective). This announcement was followed by the new majority owner, Daniel Sheridan, announcing the immediate reorganization of our staff.

She led up to the announcement by letting us know just what a hassle she had been going through, clearing up her late husband's estate. If she was trying to make us feel like we'd been relegated to the bargain basement, she succeeded. It didn't put us into the best mood even before we found out about the reorganization.

Exit the Wicked Witch. Enter the Evil Overlord.

It wasn't quite the destructive effect of the bomb dropping on Hiroshima, but close. People who had worked their beats for years, decades even, got reassigned. I tried to look on the positive side: No one was fired.

Then Sheridan took the academic sports beat away from me. My beloved sports beat, which I had been covering since high school, which had stayed my property even when I landed in my wheelchair. He took it away from me without more than a brief glance in my direction. Like maybe he would catch some gimp germs if he looked at me too long?

Or maybe he could see the fury in my eyes.

Maybe he thought that retaining me in my duties as a copy editor would console me? My new assignment, the *Talk to Terry* column (and who the hey-ha was Terry, anyway?), certainly was no consolation. More along the lines of a booby prize.

Too bad Kurt, Felicity and I had a rule about not displaying our semi-pseudo-superhero powers in public, and most especially not in front of people who didn't live in Neighborlee. I would have had a lot of satisfaction with giving the new despot the heave-ho through the front window of the *Tattler* and into the late-model sports car quickly being buried by that afternoon's snowstorm. I had no proof it was his, but if it had been Widow Sloane's witch-mobile, the emotional catharsis would have been just as satisfying.

So I seethed from the moment the new owner left our office, as I slalomed my way across the parking lot. I got into my Jeep, and drove home to pick up Pete and Harry, before driving to the comedy club where I had a dinner show. I was able to think about something besides wishing I really did have access to a starship armed with photon torpedoes, by the time I rolled through the back door of the comedy club. Hey, I had a show to do, after all.

Then I looked out through the flimsy curtains that separated the negligible backstage area from the tables, and realized we had a new problem.

"Where's my ramp?"

"It was there ten minutes ago." Ramon, the owner, looked about as relaxed as a 300-pound former bouncer could look with a full house just before the first show of the night.

He didn't look so relaxed five minutes later, when his two go-fers verified the ramp to let my wheelchair get up onto the stage had evaporated into thin air. We had exactly five more minutes until I had to get out there and do my routine. It took us three minutes to decide we couldn't get a board in time that was long enough, thick enough, and wide enough to improvise a ramp. It wasn't like I could back out at the last minute. This was my fifth performance at Ramon's club, and I had worked my way up to actually having my name on the mobile marquee out front. Chances were good at least a dozen of the people out there had come specifically to see me perform. And anyway, the understanding was that after five or six return performances, Ramon offered a contract of some kind. I *needed* that ego boost after the wretched day I had.

That left the only other option: roadies.

Honestly, I had been joking when I referred to Pete and Harry as my roadies, because I was mobile enough to get myself in and out of my Jeep, even without my telekinesis. But tonight, there was no way in the world I could get myself up onto that stage without visible, physical help. I was here to do a comedy routine and that contract for regular performances and some steady money was close enough I could taste it. Very attractive, now that I wanted badly to bail on my job at the *Tattler*. I certainly wasn't there to audition for a revival of the *X-Files*.

So Harry and Pete lifted me, wheelchair and all.

Halfway through what should have been a smooth maneuver, I saw this swirling flash of a dozen tiny sparks of light, circling my head. My fingers tingled, just for a second. It was how Kurt described the sensation he always got when he felt other Lost Kids use their semi-pseudo-superhero powers.

All that fled my brain, because for a split second, I could have sworn I saw Sylvia Grandstone standing in the doorway, glaring at me. She pointed at me. There was something in her hand. I wouldn't have been surprised if it turned out to be a gun. The darkness behind her took on a dull sheen like a dirty oil slick, and it spun counterclockwise.

That tingle turned painful, like wintertime dry air static, cubed in intensity. The sparks darted across the seating area, toward the door. Sylvia vanished — if that was Sylvia, because honestly, what would she be doing back in town after all these years?

And my loving brothers dropped me.

Have you ever seen a wheelchair-bound woman fall out of her chair from nearly five feet up in the air (two-and-a-half feet from the floor and another two-plus feet between the bottom of the wheels and the seat, for those who are counting) going sideways, with a "Take me now, Lord!" look on her face?

Ain't pretty.

The comedy club audience inhaled on cue, a packed house, with the suction power that rivaled my super-duper-deluxe vacuum cleaner when it was brand new. Too bad I couldn't harness all that sucking power and turn it into profit. I needed some extra money, with Christmas approaching. And wanting to quit my job.

The guys fumbled and stammered and basically got in my way as I climbed back into my chair. Thank goodness for upper-body strength developed from years of pushing my own chair everywhere in town. The boys were useless, thanks to stage fright.

In those few seconds when my misspent life flashed before my eyes, the most dominant thought was, "Someone is definitely out to get me." In the last couple of weeks, I'd had two flat tires, a dozen prank calls at the office, and just as many middle-of-the-night hang-up calls on my cell phone and the landline at home. And now someone had stolen the ramp up onto the stage. What else was I supposed to think?

Someone was out to get me!

The silence, once the guys stepped out of the spotlight, was profound enough to hear a pin drop from across the street. Without super hearing. This was the type of moment in a struggling performer's career when you either called it a night, permanently, or you took the equivalent of a bloodbath on the next smart-alec line that popped out between your teeth. I flashed those bug-eyed, horrified people my best Pac-Man grin, buying a few seconds to think.

I swear, the only inspiration that came to me was Kermit's line from *The Muppet Movie.*

"I hope you all appreciate the fact that I do my own stunts."

*Silence.*

Oh…heck. What I wouldn't give for the power of invisibility, or to turn time backwards a whole day.

Laughter roared. Loud enough to shake the rafters. And bring down a few decades' worth of accumulated dirt that I didn't want to examine too closely, thanks very much.

The audience was mine for the rest of my allotted twenty-five minutes.

"Hi, I'm Lanie Zephyr, World's Greatest Sit-Down Comic. And now, before the rumors start up again, let me make it clear that I am not Ironside's illegitimate daughter."

*Snickers.*

Okay, that was fine. They laughed at my unplanned line. Mustn't be greedy.

"Actually, I'm the only comedian I know of who needs roadies. Umm, anyone looking for a job?"

That got lots of laughter, and some dirty looks from my brothers. Maybe I deserved getting dropped, bringing my brothers into a former-strip-club-turned-comedy-club, but they needed an excuse not to go shopping on Black Friday with Felicity just as desperately as I did. After all this time, they knew anything they did was fodder for my routine. And to be totally fair, they had drawn attention to themselves by dropping me.

"Can you believe we're sitting here in a strip club? Excuuuuse me—former strip club." I pretended to wipe sweat off my forehead. "Man, this is the last place I ever thought I'd be. Not that I'm in bad shape." I flexed my arms, showing off my biceps by tugging on my sweater to outline what, I had to admit, were pretty well defined muscles. "But honey, my bikini days are waaaay behind me. Scars just aren't pretty—and I want to stay way far away from guys who think scars are attractive, if you know what I mean."

That didn't hit anywhere close to target. A few snickers from the back of the room. Well, that was what I got for using material I thought of between the pseudo-dressing room and the stage.

"And face it, a wheelchair just doesn't go with a strip-tease routine, y'know?" I pivoted back on my wheels for a few seconds, waggling my footrests in the air. The spotlights glinted off the chrome. "Where would you put the dollar bills? In my spokes?"

That got more laughter. Relief. I hadn't lost the audience before I actually got started.

From there, I segued to talking about rotten jobs. I had plenty of ammunition, thanks to the surprise announcement we got at the *Tattler* that afternoon. Was it any wonder that I spent most of my time on stage using my "so dumb" one-liners, and picturing Sheridan's too-handsome, smug face with every line?

"He's so dumb, he thinks that the international dateline is a surefire way to pick up foreign babes."

Lots of female laughter. Good.

"He thought about getting a mail-order bride, but he ran out of postage."

Daniel Sheridan was on my dirt list, and I considered asking Felicity to generate an EM storm while sitting on the hood of his car. Not that she had any more control over her electrical storms than she did when we were kids, but I could talk to her about what happened to her friends on the *Tattler*'s staff until she had a snit fit and then let nature take its course.

Until she got back from her yearly pilgrimage to credit card nirvana, putting most retailers in northeast Ohio into the black, I had to soothe my bruised feelings by mocking Sheridan in my imagination.

"And as I close tonight, I want to leave you with this highly philosophical and depressing thought: Maybe Led Zeppelin was right, and there really is a *Stairway to Heaven*."

Silence for a heartbeat, then a roar of laughter and applause, a few whistles, and half the audience got to their feet as I backed up to the edge of the stage. Ramon helped the guys get me down. Going backwards and down was always easier than going up, anyway. And if I made sure things stayed steady by using a little mental control, who was going to tattle on me?

The high of a successful gig stayed with me for nearly an hour. Ramon paid me and asked me to come back on alternating Friday and Saturday nights starting in January. That was good. When I hesitated, thinking of my wheelchair basketball schedule, he added a share of the entry fee to the pot. When I explained that I might have basketball games on Friday and Saturday nights, he got that stunned, jaw-dropping look on his face that I loved to inspire in people. Why did they find it so hard to visualize a woman playing basketball in a wheelchair? The Ezekiel's Wheels, my team, wasn't as popular as the Cavaliers, and we certainly didn't make the money they did, but we had a loyal following. We got in the papers. Not the front page, though. I wondered if I would have to bring my scrapbook or one of our league trophies to my next gig, to prove my athletic tendencies. Then Ramon shrugged and said we could schedule around my games. As long as I got on stage by nine, that was fine with him. That worked for me.

Too bad the comedy scene in northern Ohio was almost as depressed as I felt after getting my sports beat taken away. Otherwise, I might have been tempted to quit my day job and pursue comedy.

Remembering the bomb that hit me that afternoon succeeded in dragging my spirits down as the boys and I crossed the slushy back parking lot to my Jeep. I got into the front seat while Pete took care of cleaning the windows of the crusty slush that had accumulated while we were indoors. Harry got my chair into the back of the Jeep.

"Okay, Lanie, what's the problem?" Harry's demand was accented by the thud of the hatch closing.

"Problem?" I fluttered my eyelashes at him as he slid into the front passenger seat. Anybody who didn't know us might have thought I was flirting with this gorgeous Latina guy—who was seven years younger than me. Harry was my brother. Didn't matter if all three of us were adopted, we were tighter than blood.

For those who jumped onto this crazy ride of my memoirs after the first hill, and haven't formally met us yet, let me give some background.

Our parents, Charlie and Rainbow Zephyr, were escapees from the Hippie era. With all the weird things that happened, regular as clockwork in Neighborlee, no one even blinked when they joked about falling into a time-warp and ending up twenty years into the future. They ran into me during a church project when I was a little rug-rat, causing havoc at the Neighborlee Children's Home, fell in love, and brought me home. They must have decided I was housebroken, because they agreed to help some research friends by adopting Harry. Actually, he was born Jeraldo, with the Latin good looks to match the name, but everyone called him Harry, even though he wasn't. Hairy, that is. Pete was also adopted under similar circumstances, when I was already teaching high school.

Pete was the blondie in the family. Pop had been gray-turning-white for as long as I could remember, and Mum, with Asian features, dyed her hair a different color every few weeks. Me, I was something of a mutt, with brunette hair, hazel eyes, and a threat of freckles. Pete would probably be the tallest one in the family, when he finished growing. I nearly had to tie him to the back of my chair to force him to go shopping two weeks earlier, because he had gone through yet another growth spurt. Mum was the shortest one in the family, even with me permanently fixed at a doorknob-level view of the world. So we were a pretty evenly mixed grab bag. That was what family was supposed to be, right?

"Yeah, problem," Pete said, as he gave the windshield wiper blades one last thud to clear ice off them. He stuck his tongue out at me for good measure.

I sighed for the good old days, when I could talk him into putting his tongue on icy metal.

"What makes you guys think—"

"You can't lie to us," Harry said. "Something was off when you picked us up to head here, but we both thought it was just you gearing up for tonight. What let the air out of your tires?"

"Yeah, and don't try giving us some fake story," Pete added as he got into the back seat. "We aren't living lie detectors like you — "

"That's on the fritz, remember?" I crossed my eyes at him in the rearview mirror.

Truthfully, that particular talent usually meant getting an image in my head that contradicted what the person said, and always needed interpretation. I would have preferred to be invincible. Flying and the ability to bounce off walls and have bullets bounce off me just sort of seemed to belong together. Obviously, given my permanent four-wheel-drive situation, God hadn't made me bulletproof. There was a reason. There had to be a reason. I just hadn't discovered it yet.

Such thoughts didn't help me now, when my brothers were gearing up to grill me on why I wasn't still high on satisfaction after my successful comedy gig. That, and the relief of escaping the horrors of the after-Thanksgiving shopping crush with Felicity.

"I thought you were happy the Pikes smeared the Bulldogs," Harry added. "When I stopped in the office this afternoon, Conrad said your take on the whole season was the best thing you've ever written. So what happened at work after I left?"

The problem with living in a small town like Neighborlee (besides the rotten name for the high school sports teams, because who really wants to win when you're named after a *fish*?) is that chances were good you worked with relatives. Harry's contract to pick up papers from the big printing plant over in Valleyview meant he was in and out of the office a dozen times a week. He was there when Conrad raved about my story on the Neighborlee Pikes and announced it had already been picked up on the wire by a few national magazines.

He wasn't there when Mrs. Sloane and Sheridan invaded the office and rearranged our lives.

"You're looking at the new writer of the *Talk to Terry* column." I concentrated on pulling out of the parking lot into the dwindling traffic around the club. "You guys want to stop at Mac's on the way home?"

"Uh oh. It's the junk food defense," Pete sing-songed. He ducked before I could consider reaching back between the seats to slap him, so I didn't try. Besides, I was driving.

"So that's not a good thing? Never heard of it, but it sounds like a gossip column or something. Conrad's adding it to the paper?" Harry said.

"The column runs in four papers and is being added to eight, including ours. We have a new owner." No way was I going to say the name of the Evil Overlord and pollute the interior of my beloved Jeep. "We're getting lumped together with all the other papers he just bought, and a bunch of the columns are getting picked up in all the papers."

"So, *Terry*, what do you write about?" Harry leaned into the door on his side of the Jeep and turned sideways to grin at me as we reached a red light.

"It's mostly an advice column." I swallowed hard and wished I had a big can of ginger ale to wash the bad taste out of my mouth and settle my stomach. "Mostly lovelorn junk."

"Ick. Gross. Mental deterioration of the — " Pete ended on a yelp as my fist connected with his knee. My radar worked as faithfully as always, letting me swing back between the seats without looking. His leg jerked, hitting the back of Harry's seat. Two birds with one wallop.

"It's not like you can't handle something like that with your sports reporting and copy editing," Harry offered.

"Someone else is doing the sports reporting. Big-shot new owner has a whole staff to cover four counties, so he doesn't want to inconvenience poor little me. Make me go to sporting events where I might be so depressed, seeing all those athletes in action while confined to my wheelchair. Can we say *Tiny Tim syndrome?*"

"So… Are we going to get any new material about the boss from h-e-double-hockey-sticks?" he murmured, and very carefully didn't look at me.

"You might. If I don't invest in voodoo dolls or a Mafia contract, first." I caught sight of the Golden Arches too late to get into the curb lane to pull in. The guys didn't seem to notice.

"So the bozo took away your sports column. Not a smart move. Having you write romantic advice is like — " Pete snickered and slid over in his seat, to protect his knees.

"Like having me for a track coach? I've been a track coach. And even though I haven't had a date since… Okay, longer than I want to remember. I can still give advice to idiots who think a stranger can help them when they can't seem to find their common sense with both hands!" I narrowly missed pounding the horn, sparing the guy in the rustbucket Ford in front of us a heart attack.

"So tell us what you really think." Harry dug in his pocket for his phone. "Mancuso's for pickup?"

"You got it. The usual, please."

Now that I had gotten the bad news out in the open, and the guys gave me their usual teasing sympathy, my appetite was coming back. Extra-thick pizza, onions, olives, marinara sauce and garlic, with cheesecake on the side. It might not give me a good night's sleep, but it would go a long way toward soothing the ache in my soul.

I had a good record on the track and on the basketball court in high school and college, and had proven myself as a part-time sports stringer for the *Tattler*. It hadn't been pity that prompted Conrad Severidge to give me the sports beat. Or let me keep it after I turned my back into modern art. I had proven myself. (Okay, it also helped that I introduced him to his wife. And let him marry her. Hey, she was my college roommate.) So why did it look like pity in Daniel Sheridan's eyes, when he gave me my unwanted new assignment?

I wanted to strangle someone. I wanted to leave tire tracks up the back of his designer suit and skid marks across his too-handsome face. I entertained myself with thoughts of what Felicity and Kurt could do to make Sheridan's life miserable, once they found out about this afternoon's development. A certain rich boy might soon find himself in some pretty unhappy, peculiar, embarrassing situations. It was good to have friends who knew what would make me happy, even though I didn't have the guts to defy how my parents raised me and do it for myself.

Amazing what having friends and a good pizza could do to make the world a friendlier place.

Felicity's dogs were going nuts, or rather, more nuts than usual, when we pulled into the driveway an hour later. (For those joining the confession late in the game, Felicity lived in my three-car garage, which had been turned into an apartment, and had a bunch of dogs. We're talking rescued strays. Big, drooly, smelly mutts. Felicity was a dog person, part of her semi-pseudo-superhero talent, along with uncontrollable EM bursts.) Between the usual letdown after a performance high and the knots of hunger in my stomach from the smell of that heavenly pizza, I wasn't in the sweetest mood. The big fence around my property kept the dogs relatively contained, but it didn't keep them quiet. When they were noisy, it meant someone had tried to break into my property.

Too bad security was often noisy. No lights were coming on in the houses around us, up and down the street. Translation: those dogs had been yammering and throwing themselves at the fence long enough for everyone to go back to whatever they had been doing before the alarm went off. Which meant, oh joy, the cops would show up any time now.

"Save a slice for Gordon," I warned Pete.

He slid out of the back seat and headed for the ramp to the kitchen door, holding the pizza boxes with all the care such treasure deserved. It was more important to get the food inside and keep it hot in this weather, than it was to get me and my wheelchair inside, after all.

The dog clamor meant Felicity hadn't come home yet. Big surprise. As soon as Harry swung my wheelchair out of the back of the Jeep and unfolded it, they shut up. For all their noise and smell, those dogs were smart. They knew I was the boss. It was my house, and they knew who was the alpha when Felicity wasn't there. Too bad my brothers hadn't learned that lesson yet.

I got to the top of the ramp and paused to use the towel hanging by the door to wipe the ice-melt grit off my wheels before going inside. The big black-and-white truck belonging to Neighborlee PD pulled up before I could go in. The dogs yapped once, then slunk around the side of the house to their kennels. They understood what police were for.

"Hey, Lanie." Gordon unfolded himself from the cab. There was a reason why the PD kept the truck they'd confiscated from some idiots who thought they'd set up a meth lab on the outskirts of Neighborlee. Gordon didn't fit into regular issue vehicles. In fact, he made this heavy-duty machine look a little delicate when he stood beside it. And over it. One of these days, I knew I had to ask him who made his uniforms. Had to be special order.

# Chapter Two

"Hey, Gordon. Who reported us?" I tipped back, pivoted to face him, and balanced on my back wheels for a few seconds.

"Mr. Poldruhy." He stepped over to the railing at the bottom of the ramp and leaned on it. The two-inch pipe groaned in protest.

"He's three blocks over. Man, those dogs have lungs."

"Joyce says she saw somebody creeping around the fence just before the dogs woke up. All this snow reflection, even with the lights out, it's hard to find a dark spot." He hooked his thumb over his shoulder at my neighbor across the street and one door down.

I would have to wheel over to Joyce's place tomorrow with a plate of cookies and thank her. Problem was, I hadn't even started my holiday baking. The combination of my folks being in the vicinity of the Bermuda Triangle and missing their last two check-in phone calls took a lot of the steam out of me.

Harry came outside and retrieved the big spotlight from under the passenger seat of the Jeep. Pop had insisted that I needed to have one, just in case I had car trouble in the middle of the night, in the middle of nowhere. What was I going to do? Turn it into a klieg light and wave it at the sky until the Mounties showed up? Well, Pop would have been laughing now, as Harry helped Gordon look around the perimeter of the fence for footprints.

Problem was, between the melting and freezing of old snow and the blowing of new snow for the last three hours, it was hard to tell what footprints all over the yard were new and what were old, what belonged there and what didn't, and what had been covered up already. Gordon loved to play with his CSI toys, but he didn't even make a half-hearted offer to take footprint casts and try to match the soles with famous brands in the national registry. I knew that had to depress him, so I made sure he took two pieces of pizza when he left. From the boys' meat-lovers box, of course.

"So, who was poking around, do you think?" Pete said, when we finally settled down in the kitchen. He flipped the lid open on the top pizza box and didn't go through his routine of inhaling loudly and smacking his lips. The boy was distracted, for sure.

"If the security cameras Kurt installed in the fence posts were working..." I shook my head. Felicity felt bad enough about breaking Kurt's newest toys. I didn't want to rub it in, even though she wasn't even in the house.

"Whoever it is will come back, eventually." Harry opened his mouth and turned the pizza around so he could devour it crust first. The glitter in his big, dark eyes challenged me.

"Pete, say the blessing this time?"

He hadn't even gotten his pizza onto his plate, let alone lifted it to his mouth. He groaned, let his two slices drop, and licked sauce off his fingers before folding his hands together to pray.

I barely listened to him recite the standard lines he had been using since he was seven. My mind switched back and forth between the rotten turn my day had taken, and the mystery that greeted us when we got home. Sure, we had some weird characters in Neighborlee, but on the whole even the weirdos were friendly, and mostly harmless. Other than the Grandstones, and some of the wackos who ignored the subliminal "go away, we don't like you" vibe the town gave off.

For someone to be skulking around outside anyone's house was odd enough to be creepy. A lot of the older generation still didn't bother to lock their doors. If someone came to visit, they would have left a note, or walked next door to ask Makenzie on the left or Joe on the right to tell us they had stopped by. Skulking and setting off Felicity's dogs added up to something that just didn't belong in our town.

Maybe it was someone from out of town?

I almost didn't hear Pete bark "amen," but survival instincts overrode my temporary paranoia. I snagged three slices of pizza before I got my eyes open.

Odd thing: I didn't think about that flash of impressions, the sparks in the air and tingle in my fingers and seeing Sylvia and the dirty oil slick in the air, until I was nearly asleep. It was like something had been blocking my memories until I started sliding down into sleep.

I didn't have a chance to think too long about it, but the impressions affected my dreams. At least, when I woke up the next morning, I hoped they were just ordinary dreams, trying to interpret the stress of the day before. My other option was that my dreams were warning me of something about to happen. I did not want that. My life was already stressful enough. Christmas shopping season had officially started, and I hated shopping.

~~~~~

Saturday morning, Felicity came over to show me all the loot she had dragged home from shopping. When she was in super-shopper mode (not one of her superpowers, no matter how amazingly fast she moved) she was definitely a Felicity, rather than what we sometimes called her: Zap. Thinking of her as Zap, unable to control her powers, helped me ignore the fact she was gorgeous and looked like she was in terminal ditz mode, with those big, Bambi-wide eyes, coffee-and-cream skin, and all that curly hair. Currently she had it tinted amber, but it could be jet black tomorrow and platinum blond the day after, without her resorting to a bottle of dye.

I groaned, but didn't even think of complaining, when she spilled all her shopping bags on the kitchen table. And into the TV room. *Mi casa es su casa.*

I had to bite my tongue while she enthused about all the bargains and treasures, and contradicted herself every three or four sentences about who would get what gift. There were an even dozen presents in the pile of loot she had bought for me, to give to people. Gotta love having a shopaholic at my beck and call. Especially when I hated shopping. And not just because I loathed going into crowded malls when I couldn't see over people to navigate. The malls generally struck me as a ski slope obstacle course. The problem was that the poles moved without warning, and they had a tendency to scream when I hit them.

"How about this for your mom?" Felicity held up a neon green-and-purple sarong with matching foam-rubber sandals. "They're still in Bermuda, aren't they?"

"Probably." I caught myself twitching, trying to reach back and scratch that tender spot between my shoulder blades that always seemed hyper-sensitive when there was something wrong with the person I had just been thinking about.

*Uh oh.*

"What's wrong?" She paused in folding the sarong to put back into the gift box. Felicity might have looked like Lobotomy Barbie, but she regularly out-thought the Prime Time TV detectives and
~~~~~

would have been a millionaire if she ever auditioned for *Jeopardy*.

"They missed their last two check-in calls." I shrugged. "You know how Mum and Pop are when they're tracking down the strange and unique. They forget there are people back home who want to make sure they're still alive. But it's not like we're little kids, left home with the babysitter."

"They never left you home with a babysitter when they went hunting down the inexplicable. Remember those pictures, jumping over Stonehenge? You always had the best family vacations." She giggled. "You could make a mint getting impossible photos, getting past all those no-fly zone restrictions."

"Could have. Past tense." I grinned, remembering all the stunts I had pulled as a kid, thoughtless tricks that even Superboy wouldn't have thought of. I had done them just because I knew I could, or wanted to find out if I could.

Back when I was a kid, I hadn't realized that I broke just as easily as any ordinary mortal.

"Hey, you can still fly, with Kurt's help. Thank goodness he's the Handyman." She slipped the lid on the box with Mum's sarong and tossed it to me.

I caught it with brainpower and tossed it down the hall and around the corner to my office. I couldn't see where it landed, but since I didn't hear a crash, chances were good it hadn't knocked over any stacks of papers or CDs or books.

"One down, a dozen to go," I muttered, and mentally marked present number one off my list.

"Speaking of Kurt..." She flipped an ominously plain brown plastic bag upside down, emptying a half-dozen sorting-and-storage boxes onto the floor. "What do you think? He can adjust the sizes of the compartments."

"Just right."

The perfect gifts for Kurt had always been mechanical, in one form or another. I admired the sorting boxes she had chosen, in varying depths and widths, and promised to help her wrap the presents.

"Have you heard from Kurt?" she asked, when the present ended up on the table, designating it as a keeper.

"Nope. Nothing either way."

"Did you think he'd have some success this time?" Her face

seemed to melt into that somber, little-girl-worried expression that I had always hated.

Kurt was out of town, following yet another lead on Lost Kids who had left Neighborlee while they were still minors. Lost Kids were the abandoned children who appeared on the outskirts of town, usually toddler age, no language skills, no identification, and despite the best searching methods available, no one ever claimed them and they never appeared in missing persons reports. At least, no one claimed them until strange things happened around Neighborlee Children's Home, and then suddenly people swooped in with paperwork proving they were long-lost relatives. And those Lost Kids vanished. As far as we knew, Felicity, Kurt and I were the only ones with unusual talents who'd stayed in Neighborlee. Sure, lots of Lost Kids had stayed in town, made lives for themselves, and became upstanding and sometimes integral parts of the community. The ones who didn't show any unusual abilities, or who weren't in the vicinity when odd things happened.

That was the pattern we assembled since we decided to investigate why we were the way we were, and why or how we had ended up at Neighborlee Children's Home. Once we had those answers, or at least hints at those answers, maybe we could get closer to solving the really big question: where were we from and why weren't we there anymore?

There were a lot of whispered stories and fragments of rumors to investigate. We had discovered an interesting and pretty consistently frustrating tendency for memories to be hazy when it came to the Lost Kids who vanished. Always around adolescence. According to the comic books and science fiction encyclopedias, and all the books of supernatural phenomena that my parents regularly debunked, psychic and superhuman powers usually manifested in adolescence. Mixed in with the stories of the just plain weird, amusing, or frightening things that happened in Neighborlee, there were true stories of children discovering their abilities.

Mysterious people in dark cars were usually seen loitering in the vicinity of Neighborlee Children's Home just before the Lost Kids vanished. Those people knew enough to watch the children's home for odd talents to show up in the Lost Kids. They knew how to make official records vanish, so those of us trying to pick up the trail years later came up against dead ends. So far, anyway. We knew as much about these mysterious people and the vanished Lost Kids as we knew about the enemy forces who tried to break through to Earth from other dimensions of reality. Neighborlee served as a patch on a weak spot in the fabric of the cosmos, or a lock on the gate. Lost Kids, whether we had semi-pseudo-superhero powers or not, often ended up as guardians, holding the door closed, slapping reinforcements on the weak spot.

The three of us were grateful that we hadn't been discovered and snatched away, because Neighborlee needed us. We were also kind of ticked that more Lost Kids hadn't been left to help carry the burden. That was part of why we were looking for others like us.

About the time I broke my back, we decided it was time to expand our search beyond the borders of our town. Were there other towns in the U.S. and scattered throughout the world where other abandoned children showed up and did the Superboy routine? Who made those other potential semi-pseudo-superhero kids vanish?

Not to start sounding like a sulky little brat who didn't get chosen for the school play, but how come they didn't take *us*?

True, Kurt's gift for mechanical wizardry wasn't splashy, and Felicity's talents with dogs, changing her appearance, and killing electronics were easily hidden with believable explanations. I had always been careful to do my flying/gliding where most people wouldn't see me. But if someone had the power and connections to snatch other kids away, how come they'd never noticed us?

Maybe we felt more than a little left out.

"Who knows?" I said to Felicity, who was rearranging her loot. About then I thought I heard movement coming from my brothers' rooms, and took a look down the hall. No signs of life yet. Well, it was only 9:30, and we had been up late with pizza, and it wasn't like anyone had homework to worry about until Sunday night.

Correction: I had homework. My first *Talk to Terry* column.

*Lord, now would be a good time for the Rapture. Please? I'd settle for an alien invasion.*

Remembering the roller coaster of good and bad news from the day before, I brought Felicity up-to-date while we dove into examining the rest of her loot. I got as far as describing the first request for lovelorn advice, when the landline phone rang. I headed for the shelves holding the phone and answering machine. Naturally, the outgoing message played before I got to it.

"Lanie, this is Col. Hayward." It was a gravely male voice. "Please pick up the phone. This isn't something I want to leave on an answering machine."

I yanked with brainpower when I was still two feet away from the phone, and nearly clocked myself across the cheekbone with the receiver before I could grab the handle.

"Hi, Colonel." My voice shook for half a second. Hearing from the military, even if that particular officer was a good friend of my folks, could not be a good thing. "What's up?"

"You're getting a registered letter today. I thought I'd prepare you. As a friend. Unofficially."

"Officially," I said, forcing ice into my voice, "my folks aren't working with the military this time."

"Things don't always work out the way we want them to."

"What does the government want with my folks' investigation of electromagnetic fluctuations around the Bermuda Triangle?"

"We won't know until we figure out what we saw."

"Meaning what?"

"Exactly that. No one is sure what happened. All I can tell you is that your folks…vanished. They're officially listed as missing, reason unknown."

"What were they doing?"

"No one knows yet. There's nothing to analyze."

"What do you mean, nothing?" My voice got loud enough to trigger a thud from down the hall. About five seconds later, Harry stumbled into the kitchen, holding up his sweatpants with the broken drawstring and trying to pull a Willis-Brooks College T-shirt down into place. He must have remembered that Felicity had threatened to invade, first thing this morning.

"They weren't measuring anything. No equipment. Nothing indicated in the notebooks we found in their room at the hotel." The frustration in Hayward's voice cut through the churning in my head and gut. "Those on-site are trying to blame the stormy seas and freak weather patterns. Considering your parents weren't anywhere near the water, that doesn't do us much good."

"No signs of a struggle? No explosion? What were they working on?"

"As far as I knew, they hadn't started working yet."

I slumped in my chair, feeling like someone had pulled a plug and I was deflating like a punctured waterbed. "How long have they been missing?"

"I'm sorry."

"How long?"

"What's up?" Pete demanded, joining us. He saw Felicity two seconds after he stumbled in, dressed in threadbare boxers with purple hearts on them. He shrieked and dashed into the laundry room, just off the kitchen, and emerged a few seconds later with a bath towel wrapped around his hips. To add insult to injury, Felicity was too busy watching me to notice Pete's condition.

"How long have my parents been missing?" I demanded again, choking on the words.

"Two weeks," he admitted on a sigh.

"And you've been looking for them all this time?"

"If Mum and Pop didn't want anybody to find them for some reason, nobody could find them," Harry growled. He glared at me when I signaled him for silence, then sank into the nearest available chair. Fortunately, it didn't have any of Felicity's loot on the seat.

"When I have more information, I'll contact you," Hayward said. "Don't stir up any more trouble than there already is by calling here or the hotel they were last at. Understand?"

"Oh, I understand far more than you might imagine."

"Lanie… I'm sorry. They're my friends." Another sigh. "I didn't even know the military was trying to ride on the coattails of their research until after they were reported as missing."

"If that's a ploy to try to find out what we know —"

"Your parents are my friends. Trust me, all right?" He waited, while I tried to find words, and swallow down the sharp-edged block that filled my throat. "Lanie?"

"We don't really have any choice, do we?"

"I'll contact you as soon as I can." Then he hung up before I could respond.

Harry's usual response to a lot of stress in our family was to cook something. He got that from Mum, who reasoned that food was the best medicine. Considering that one of her best-selling books was on healing through nutrition, that made sense. So before I finished relaying to the boys what Col. Hayward had said, Harry started making a massive breakfast.

The only blessing in all this was that I could gorge and not worry about outgrowing my wheelchair. I still had a superhero metabolism, even if I spent most of my life sitting down.

We talked about the news from Hayward. We tried to remember what Mum and Pop had told us about their research. We couldn't remember. That bothered me more than learning our folks had been missing two weeks and we hadn't known it. Other than worrying because they missed their check-in. And how come that hadn't set off bigger, louder alarms?

"So," Pete said, when we had cleared all the plates, and even the smell of Harry's cooking had faded from the air, "who's calling the church?"

"What good will that do?" Felicity asked.

She was willing to admit there was a higher power, something beyond the touchable, but she didn't believe in God as we had learned about Him from the Bible and Sunday school. She didn't razz me (too often) about my spiritual "co-dependency," as she called it, and I refrained from thumping her with my Bible.

"Prayer makes a lot of difference," Harry said. "If we get the whole church to pray... who knows?"

"You think you'll get loud enough for God to hear?" She sounded kind of wistful. That was an improvement.

"God hears when we want Him to hear," I said. That didn't come across quite as profound as I would have wanted. "Harry, you call Pastor Rocky."

~~~~~

If Mum and Harry turned to cooking to soothe a lot of hurts, Felicity turned to shopping. She knew I wasn't up to a trip to the mall on the day after Black Friday (Charcoal Saturday?) to distract me from worrying about Mum and Pop.

She could distract me, though, with a trip to Divine's Emporium.

Among all the truly weird and wonderful features of Neighborlee, Divine's Emporium is the centerpiece. The testing point, the dividing line between insiders and outsiders. Those who loved Divine's, who saw the treasures there, the potential for amazing things and delightful discoveries, were the people who belonged in Neighborlee. Anybody who didn't like the place, who
~~~~~

walked out with a negative, confused expression, rather than a delighted, confused expression… Let's just say they either drifted to the edges of town or they avoided the dead-end street where Divine's sat, and did all their shopping and socializing in another town. There were some who fell through the cracks, so to speak. They didn't get the "we don't want you here, go away" vibe, so it didn't drive them away. They were welcome in Neighborlee, and made good neighbors, but they just didn't synch with the *otherness* that was a strong component of town.

Then there were those who ignored the vibe and were so contrary and flat-out crazy that they chose to interpret "go away" as a plea for them to run everyone else's life.

Such as the Grandstone clan. With every failed attempt to rule Neighborlee, they just got nastier. If it had just been the Grandstones themselves, it wouldn't have been so bad, but they always managed in elementary school to pick up a handful of nasties and idiots for henchmen. Those henchmen acted as buffers, getting hurt or taking the fall for the Grandstones when their schemes failed or they were caught in illegal activities. Usually by the time college came around, those henchmen left town permanently, one way or another.

My generation had produced a bumper crop of Grandstones: Reggie, the lawyer; his brother Freddie, the architect; and their cousin, Sylvia, who was making B-grade movies and trying to convince Hollywood she was somebody important. She had proven more benevolent than the rest of her family because she stayed away and her career didn't yet include the main occupation of female Grandstones: becoming wealthy widows.

If I really wanted to punish the Evil Overlord for taking over the *Tattler*, I would try to fix him up with Sylvia. The two of them deserved each other.

I liked Divine's, even though it could freak me out at times. That was saying a lot, considering just how much weirdness was embedded in my blood and bones, and the fact that when something bizarre hit town, I was right there on the front lines with Angela. Maybe the reason was Angela herself. She had always been there, practically unchanged, for as long as I could remember. She had one of those faces that could be any age, ageless and serene and alive with joy, and often a twinkle of mischief. She always had this air of knowing a little more than the person standing in front of the counter at her store. Often she knew what someone wanted before they figured it out.

Divine's Emporium always had the perfect gift, the perfect treasure and surprise, even if it wasn't what shoppers had in mind when they walked through the door. Plus there always seemed to be more room, and more rooms, inside the shop than the outside indicated. I knew for a fact that the ceilings elevated at Christmas, to accommodate the traditionally enormous tree. Doors occasionally appeared where there hadn't been doors before, leading to new rooms. The shop was crammed with "neat junk," as Felicity referred to it, but the aisles were always more than wide enough for my chair and for someone to pass me. How often did that happen in the chain stores?

Angela was our anchor spot, and our power charging station, the one who heard our strange stories of what we encountered as guardians, even when we couldn't tell anyone else. Especially when we couldn't tell anyone else.

Besides, that Saturday was the decorating party at Divine's. It alternated every year between the Saturday after Thanksgiving and the first Saturday in December. When Felicity suggested we go visit and help with the yearly ritual, I wasn't fooled and I didn't remind her that we always went. She wanted to see what Angela had to say about Mum and Pop vanishing. She probably wanted to get me out of the house, so I wouldn't be there when Col. Hayward's registered letter arrived. What good would that do? It would still be there when I got home. I appreciated the effort to distract me, though.

The decorating efforts were in full swing when we arrived. Ken Jenkins brought the tree this year. He was an all-around good guy stuck in a truly wretched marriage. The only problem was, he hadn't discovered it yet. Still in the newlywed bliss stage. His wife of one month was the ultimate Gold-Digger Barbie, with fangs for sucking all the joy and money from a man's life. Ken hadn't awakened to that fact and still had a lot of joy and life left in him. I kept praying someone would drop a house on her before he realized what kind of a mistake he had made.

The usual gang was there, grubby from helping to haul all the boxes of antique decorations from the cellar. I remembered when I had been among the crew doing the hauling and taking peeks into the dark storage rooms under the house, trying to get a hint to what kind of treasures Angela had waiting to emerge into the light of day. I was convinced that part of Angela's cellar only appeared at certain times of the year. Kind of like null-space storage in science fiction stories.

I had to sit on the sidelines a few times, out of the traffic zone, and wait, which gave me more time to really look around and see. For a few seconds, I flashed back to my dreams, and through them to that odd mash-up of impressions at the comedy club the night before.

No, those sparks weren't my imagination. Tiny, sharp-edged blips of pink and green and blue-white and gold. They were like fireflies, but at sonic speed. For half a second I thought I saw something alive moving at the center of them, and the other half of the second they were just lights.

When they noticed me watching them, swirling through the air, pushing on the ceiling of the main room of the shop and raising it a few more inches … that's when things got interesting. For half a second, I had the impression of looking through all those eyes, looking down at me. A blast of tickling, cold lightning touched the edges of my mind, followed by surprise and then amusement and then giddy happiness. Those sparks swirled down from the ceiling and swarmed around me. I held my breath, terrified for a second or two that I would inhale one or a dozen of them.

Angela stepped through the cloud of multi-colored sparks, both hands waving them away. She looked far too somber for decorating Saturday, and she wrapped her arms around herself, as if she were cold.

"Did you … see?" she said, her voice pitched soft, so nobody could have heard even if they were standing next to me. With all the happy chaos and chatter in the shop as several of the guys helped Ken adjust the bucket of dirt that would hold the tree, it was amazing I heard her.

"Sparks? Aware and they kind of like me?" I said after a few seconds of thought.

"Oh, Lanie, they very much like you. They think you're wonderful and a self-sacrificing idiot at the same time." Angela's somber expression brightened. "They're called winkies…" Her smile faded as she looked upward.

I looked up too, and saw the swarms of lights pushing at the ceiling again. Well, that finally explained how the dimensions of the shop changed. I had always theorized the building adjusted itself to accommodate needs, but somehow it made more sense that the sparkly winkies did the adjusting for Angela.

"And you shouldn't be able to see them," she said on a sigh. "It is as I have feared for several months now. The ebbing power of the shop's defensive shield reflects the fading defenses around our town, slowly but steadily since …"

That bit of shadow and pain I hated seeing in Angela's eyes darkened them. I knew what she meant. The slow failure of the shield that nurtured guardians and helped us bounce back from the strain of defending Neighborlee, had been happening since before Stephanie Miller had died. Stephanie had died because the power had been drained so low. My back had broken, and I hadn't healed as completely as I should have, because the energy of the defensive field had fallen so low.

"They're usually invisible, but they don't have the energy to do that anymore?" I guessed. "How come nobody else is freaking out seeing them?"

"Oh, winkies will always be invisible to the ordinary, average Human." That bit of humor returned to her eyes, the corners of her mouth. "I daresay that even most guardians won't see them. For a while, at least." She shrugged.

I knew what she meant. The other guardians wouldn't see the winkies until the power had fallen even further, and the energy they needed to stay unseen would have to go to defending our town.

"So … do we need to be on the alert for …?" I tipped my head and glanced downward. As if I could see through the floor of the shop. Through all the layers of cellars. To the theorized resting place where the snake, as we called the enemy of Neighborlee, waited in an interdimensional passageway. Waiting for its strength to build up to allow it to attack us again.

"Oh, my dear, not at Christmas. The holidays protect us, if only through the high spirits and the joy and hope and holiness of the season. Ordinary Humans have a strong magic all their own. Our batteries will be charged and our defenses reinforced. Relax and enjoy the holidays." She brushed my cheek with her fingertips, like she used to do when I was a child.

Angela's smile faded a little. She tipped her head to one side and really studied me.

"We're going to need to talk after everyone goes home, aren't we?"

"Enjoy the party," I said.

Angela nodded slowly, then turned and was ready when someone ran up to her with yet another questions about where a box of decorations went.

Finally, the tree was up. Angela handed out ornaments that were miniatures of the Wishing Ball, and encouraged specifically chosen people to make wishes. I felt relieved, actually, when she didn't hand me an ornament. If I didn't need the boost of magic from wishing, then the situation with Mum and Pop wasn't that bad. Angela would have sensed if my folks were in real danger and needed extra help. Even from as far away as the Bermuda Triangle.

What were the chances that within the Bermuda Triangle was another doorway like the ones I sometimes sensed in Divine's, and it had taken my folks so far away they couldn't be sensed?

Not a good thought. Why did I have to let my imagination get out of hand like that? Maybe it was time to step down as captain of my Star Trek club.

People made their wishes. Several people who had been working on speeches since last year's party stepped up and made silly and wistful toasts with eggnog and spiced cider. Then faster than I thought possible, the decorating party was over, and everyone trickled out of the shop to go home. Snow was falling like a classic Christmas card scene. I wouldn't have put it past Angela to have somehow arranged it. The sparkle and glow of the lights and ornaments filled the shop with magic. Even without the help of the winkies. Seasonal magic, expanding on the regular, year-round kind.

My chest got heavy when it hit me that Mum and Pop might not be home for Christmas like we had planned. I could take having my brothers camping out with me indefinitely. I could take the thought of strangers living in my folks' farmhouse, renting it until they came back. We had survived such arrangements before, for other long-term research trips.

But Christmas in my place, instead of our farmhouse on the

edge of town? Christmas without Mum's cheese Danish and chai tea for breakfast? Without Harry whipping up a gourmet feast on the industrial-size cast iron stove Pop salvaged from an old church when I was eight? That wouldn't be Christmas.

*Please, God, all I want for Christmas is Mum and Pop safely home. I know You can do it. But will You?*

Angela stepped back into the main room after seeing the last person out. "Something's troubling you."

"That's an understatement." Felicity leaned against the counter where Angela had rows of old-fashioned penny candy jars — always full, no matter how many children came skipping through with their handfuls of pennies. The Wishing Ball sat nearby in softly glowing splendor.

Felicity looked at it with a little frown, like she always did, raised a hand as if she would touch it, like she always did, and backed up about two feet, like she always did. Other people could run their fingertips over the bowling ball-sized, metallic rainbow-streaked globe, sitting in a holder shaped like a coiled dragon. They got a sizzle of static electricity in their fingertips, at the most. Felicity said when she got too close, sometimes it made the roots of her teeth itch, like subliminal harmonics creating dissonance with something inside her. Maybe whatever it was that let her zap electronics clashed with the energy radiated by the ball?

"I didn't think you'd come here to do your Christmas shopping." Angela winked at me, her head turned just enough Felicity couldn't see.

It was a running joke among us that I was a shop-a-phobic. The Internet was created by people who were afraid of mall parking lots, I always said.

"Just need someone to talk to. It's about Mum and Pop."

"Charlie and Rainbow are in trouble?" She pulled up one of the dainty white wrought iron chairs from a matching bistro table in the corner.

"We just got the official word. Vanished without a trace. No clues, no suspects."

"What do your dreams tell you?"

"Not to give up my day job." All right, that joke fell flat, in light of my current miserable situation at work. Honestly, all my dreams lately had been about my comedy gigs, and trying to create some new strategy for the Ezekiel's Wheels. Until last night.

"The fact you haven't dreamed of your parents in any danger might be an indication that all is well. They're not in trouble so much as…misplaced, maybe?"

"Is that your final answer?" Felicity chuckled when Angela just raised an elegant eyebrow and shook her head.

We really hadn't expected Angela to give us definite answers, as if she could turn the Wishing Ball into a crystal ball and home in on Mum and Pop. Or maybe even magically teleport them home. Angela was one of the few people in Neighborlee, besides Kurt, who we could talk to about the "situation" without endangering some unspoken rules of national security.

Mum and Pop worked with or for various tentacles of the government a whole lot more often than was believable for two former Hippies. We tended to keep quiet about the extracurricular things that happened in the course of their investigations into the just plain weird and wonderful. Angela could be trusted not to brush us off as having wild imaginations.

# Chapter Three

By the time we left, I felt a little better about Mum and Pop. We hadn't found any answers or solved any problems, but I felt more assured that we had done everything we could do, and my folks knew how to take care of themselves. Angela suggested we call Athena Longfellow, granddaughter of Ford, who was another guardian. Athena wasn't out of college yet, but she and her gang of computer geniuses might be able to find out something that had happened around my parents' hotel, catch some detail maybe the military hadn't caught. Or they weren't sharing with us.

Felicity used my phone to call Longfellows. Athena was at a computer convention with her team, promoting the software they had developed. Charlotte took the message and said she would have Athena call when she came home.

"Dang …" she said, as she put the phone back in my backpack on the console between our seats. "I swear that red pickup has been tailing us since we pulled away from Divine's."

I was making a left turn into my neighborhood and couldn't check the rearview mirror. By the time I could look, there was no one behind me. I kept checking, down three streets and three turns. No red anything, let alone a pickup.

We agreed that since I lived in the center of the largest residential block in Neighborlee, a lot of people drove the same route through town, so someone could just as easily say I was driving in front of the red truck. Until the driver turned onto his street. Still, Felicity was good with details, and she was sure she had never seen that particular red pickup truck before.

~~~~~

I must have really been missing Kurt, wanting him to show up so we could talk about Col. Hayward's call, because I dreamed about flying that night. The only way I could fly anymore, once my back shattered, was with his help.

In my dream, I flew by myself. Real flying, not just the aimed-rocket-at-low-altitude flying that I used to do.

*I spread my arms like wings and did loops and corkscrews. It was*
~~~~~

*glorious.*

*Until that truck appeared out of the darkness, just a blocky black shape with headlights that blinded me and dragged me closer like that tractor-beam in the first Star Wars movie. I reached and grabbed and clawed, but thin air wasn't much to hold onto. No matter how hard I pushed with my flying ability, I couldn't get away. Invisible weights wrapped around my arms and legs, spreading me flat so my back slammed into the grill of the truck. I hung there, pinned by the truck's velocity, ice streaking through my blood.*

*Then the truck fell, and I couldn't move to break free. It took a nosedive, and there was nothing I could do. Then at the last minute, I slid free — right under the wheels as it landed, so it rolled right over me and vanished into the darkness, leaving nothing behind but the growl of its engine and the rumble-crunch of its wheels on the gravel quarry road.*

I woke up in a sweat, hearing the rumble of those wheels. My body ached with bruises and a feeling like my bones had been crushed into splinters.

*Okay, God, so what was that for? Are You warning me about something?*

My flashes of foresight weren't always reliable or regular. Sometimes I had dreams that, in retrospect, could have been warnings. I didn't have enough experience to discern what was warning and what was just a result of too much gummy candy and popcorn before bed. I knew better than to have a movie-and-junk-food-marathon on Saturday night, when I had to get up early to work my rug-rat Sunday school class. So was my dream just a result of my own bad choices, or was God warning me? Or scolding me to avoid high-fructose corn syrup and artificial flavors and colors?

~~~~~

*Dear Terry--*

*I just don't know what to do with my boyfriend. He comes over almost every night, cleans out my refrigerator, then complains about my cooking. That's about all he says to me before he goes downstairs to play video games with my brothers until about eleven. Then, just when I think we're finally going to get some alone time, he grabs his laundry and heads for home. He does have to get up early for his mechanics job, but you'd think he'd schedule things a little better for his girlfriend, right? He never says anything about all the things I do for him, except when he complains about the way I do his laundry. I fold his shirts wrong,*
~~~~~

*or he hates my lilac fabric softener. I want him to think about me while he's at work. What's wrong with that? I'm having second thoughts about asking him to move in with us, so we can spend more time together. What do you think?*

*The Little Woman*

~~

*Dear Little Woman —*
*Repeat after me:*
*He is not my boyfriend.*
*He is using me.*
*Real boyfriends spend time with you before they spend time with your brothers. Boyfriends take you out for dinner, they don't expect you to have dinner ready for them. Without contributing for groceries. (He isn't, is he?) Boyfriends at least provide their own scent-free fabric softener.*

*Who told you he was your boyfriend? You or him? Did he ever take you out, or did he start showing up at your house every day and figure you were an easy touch for food and laundry? Do your brothers know he's your boyfriend?*

*If those were my brothers, I'd dump them at the same time I dump that loser boyfriend. God gave you brothers to defend you, and make sure nobody uses you for maid service. Including them. And shame on you for not raising them to do their own laundry and make their own PB&J.*

*Real romance is when two people compete to see who can make the other happier. Dump the loser, and then go on strike until your brothers wise up.*

*Medicine tastes awful, but it's good for you in the end.*

*Terry*

I showed my first advice column to Felicity that Monday afternoon, snickering the whole time she was reading it. The snickers got louder every time her eyes got a little wider.

"You're trying to get fired, aren't you? Conrad isn't about to publish this." She stepped back from my computer desk and nudged aside one of her mutts so I could wheel back up in front of the keyboard.

"Conrad has no input on this column. New rules, new owner." I slid my gaze down the column one last time before saving. "This goes to all the papers in the chain, through central editorial."

"Then you're going to get fired from every small town paper within fifty miles. You can't hack off your new boss your first week. Word like that gets around, y'know?" She raked her fingers through the rainbow stripes she had put into her hair during a fit of boredom that morning.

"Conrad has control over his local staff. He still needs me for copy editing and proofreading. I just want off the lovelorn column beat, that's all. You'd think with all his business smarts, Sheridan would know that's not where my talents lie." I saved my column in RTF for upload. "Besides, there's no time to rewrite. It's due at the site in like…six minutes." I clicked on the tab to bring up the upload window for the Evil Conglomerate's FTP site.

"You're not bulletproof, y'know?"

"Don't have to be. I'm faster than any speeding bullet this town can produce. Natural four-wheel drive." I patted the left-hand wheel and caught her reflection in the monitor, rolling her eyes. "You want to step back before you do a power surge?"

"Oops. Sorry." She grinned and scooted backwards to the blue electrical tape marking off the safe zone on the tile floor.

Felicity didn't mean to do it, and most of the time she had her electrical current under control, but every once in a while she slipped and zapped important things. Like the microwave, my computer, and the alarm system. Her garage apartment kept her out of the danger zone most of the time. We had learned to mark off the safe zone around important pieces of technology we didn't want to replace on a regular basis.

In a few seconds, the deed was done, and my first (and hopefully last) column as *Terry* sat in the mailbox of the editor-in-chief of the Evil Conglomerate.

"So, what should we do for the rest of the day?" I turned my chair around, narrowly missing the oversized paws of whichever slobber machine had crept up behind my chair before lying down to take a nap. For some reason, Felicity's dogs liked me enough to try to park all around me whenever they got a chance. Wheels and paws generally did not combine for pleasant results.

"We could go Christmas shopping." Felicity's big eyes gleamed with the excitement that only a shopaholic looking for a fix could understand.

"Already did this morning. Online. Earned bonus points on my credit card, got free shipping, and I didn't have to do the slalom down the aisles of any stores. Man, it's rough when the poles move, and they scream when you run into them."

"You are so booooring." She didn't even wince at the very old line, which I used so often it was threadbare.

She snapped her fingers, waking up the three dogs, and gestured for them to leave the office. One thing I had to say for Felicity: she had those mongrels of hers under control. If only she could teach her secret to spineless mush-brains like *The Little Woman,* so they could learn to control the men in their lives.

Then again, she didn't have much success with Pete or Harry, so maybe her superpowers in that regard only worked on animals.

We settled for three episodes of *Beauty and the Beast* (Honey, Vincent could read poetry to me all day) while we did laundry and made a shopping list for my annual baking extravaganza.

Kurt called to let us know he was back in town, and wanted to make the rounds with us that evening while he filled us in on what he'd found out. From the tone of his voice, it wasn't encouraging. My first reaction after getting off the phone was to zip into my office and check the weather for the area. When Kurt wanted to make the rounds of the town, he wasn't talking about dinner, a movie, and talking in a coffee shop until midnight. We would run a security sweep of the perimeter from two hundred feet up. I didn't want to get airborne and end up coated with ice and snow or whatever other surprises nature decided to throw at us.

The phone rang just as Felicity had gone out to pull the Jeep up to the ramp so we could go grocery shopping. I seriously considered letting the machine pick up and answer, but this was the call I had been waiting eagerly for, ever since I hit the *send* button on my journalistic bomb. With a mental yank, the receiver leaped off the hook and into my hand.

"Zephyrs."

"Lanie Zephyr, please."

That smooth baritone wasn't Conrad, ready to ream me second-hand in his official capacity as my boss, and then laugh at my snarky column. For half a second, I contemplated hanging up, but my cursed curiosity got the better of me. Our phone was unlisted for a reason, and Kurt had rigged a handy little computerized gizmo that read the number of the incoming caller.

Thanks to a program designed by Athena's partner-in-crime, Wallace, the gizmo had the ability to learn which numbers we wanted to hear from, and blocked the ones we didn't. Even better, it reported to the proper authorities anyone who kept calling to the point of irritation. (Such as the liars who asked for "Theresa," and while I was still saying, "Sorry, wrong number," jumped in with, "Then maybe you can help me." Ah, no. Start a conversation with deception, I'm not going to give money to your fake charity.)

I couldn't see the display, but I would have bet my seat cushion and footrests that my caller was from the Evil Conglomerate.

"This is Lanie. Who's this?"

"Daniel Sheridan." He sounded amused that I hadn't recognized his voice. Well, duh, I had only been exposed to that voice for an hour last week, why should it stick with me? Even if it did sound like melted dark chocolate, with caramel swirls. Not that I liked caramel.

Okay, so the big boss himself was calling to scold me and take away my new column (shucky darn) and warn me about my attitude. How did I rate?

"I guess you've seen my *Terry* column. That's the only way I can respond to twits like that. She's begging to be —"

"That's why I gave the column to you, and that's exactly what I was looking for."

"Huh?" Fortunately, I didn't zap the world when my emotions spiked. Otherwise, I would have blown the answering machine, the clock on the stove, the microwave, and that ridiculous espresso machine Harry brought when he moved in with me.

"You were hoping I would can you, weren't you?" He laughed. If I hadn't loathed the man already, I might have fallen in love with the luscious sound of his voice.

For about five seconds.

Before common sense took over and rescued me.

"Look, I am a sports writer, even though I'm a girl."

"Giving you the column had nothing to do with you being a girl."

"You don't want to hack off —" I stopped short, almost choking as I realized I was about to threaten to run him over with my wheelchair. Several times. With snow chains on my wheels. Not a good idea, when he had me so off balance already. Maybe, just maybe, he wasn't about to say that someone in a wheelchair couldn't possibly be a decent sports reporter. Was he?

Anyway, there were times I had to learn to keep my comedy routine and snarky attitude separate from my so-called real life.

Felicity came in, jangling the keys. When she saw me on the phone, she frowned, visibly questioning. I tucked the phone between ear and shoulder and pretended to type. She grinned, and I could only hope she understood that I was talking to someone from work. Then she ruined things by skipping over to the shelf and hitting the speaker button on the base of the phone.

"It's a matter of economics. I have more than enough sports reporters to cover all the newspapers and all the high school and college sporting events in the surrounding counties we serve," Sheridan was saying. "I'd end up with two reporters at every event, if I kept the staff unchanged at all the papers I took over."

"Why do you feel the need to explain this to me?" I asked in the sweetest voice I could muster. That earned a groan from Felicity, who knew all too well what kind of trouble came when I felt compelled to use that *sweet little ol' helpless me* voice.

"I'm in the communication business, Miss Zephyr. I've found that like charity, communication needs to start at home."

"I'm in deep doo-doo, when you use my last name all formal like that, ain't I?"

He laughed, the sound echoing through my kitchen. It was kind of nice, for about three seconds. Then I realized it might be a mistake to make nice with the Evil Conqueror.

"I want to use your brother's cartoon for the column, to give people a visual warning that we've lost the sugar-coated, I'm-okay-you're-okay Terry. That woman could put a diabetic into a coma."

"Cartoon?" I felt like the race had started and I hadn't even heard the starter's pistol.

"The one from your CD. The one about school and jobs. We're willing to pay for the right to run it with your column, but we're not going to claim exclusive rights. Your brother did copyright it, didn't he? Although, you might just run into some trouble if someone gets bright enough to link you, the comedienne, with the columnist."

"Oh, that cartoon." Movement from the corner of my eye had me turning, to see Felicity bounce back into the kitchen. She waved the drawing Pete had done in art class, and then turned into a CD cover and stickers and other promotional paraphernalia.

The cartoon showed a frizz-haired, overweight woman with a five o'clock shadow, dressed in a plaid robe and bunny slippers, holding a rod pretzel (coated in salt crystals) like a cigar, and trying to light it with a candle. She leaned one elbow on a tilted computer desk, with a mountain of paperwork and books and take-out cartons ready to slide off, glaring bleary-eyed at a keyboard, while the computer monitor displayed a bomb with a short fuse. Underneath was the caption, "Deadlines amuse me," with underscoring emphasizing *dead*.

"At least it isn't the one of me in my wheelchair, on the roller coaster," I offered. Half a second later, I looked around for a convenient wall to slam my forehead into. What was I doing, joking with the enemy?

"I have that CD, but I haven't listened to it yet."

The horrified thought came to me that he might have been in the audience last Friday, as I worked off a good chunk of my frustration. Well, even if he had been, I hadn't said anything about bosses from h-e-hockey sticks, so he couldn't know I imagined *him* every time I did one of my "he's so dumb" jokes.

Unless he could read minds?

Just my luck. Another semi-pseudo-superhero in town, and he ended up being the last person I'd want to be friends with.

Somehow, I managed to pay a reasonable amount of attention to the business discussion that followed, and agreed to look over the contract that would come in a few days. Pete had to sign it, anyway, since he owned all rights. Daniel Sheridan sounded like an ordinary, semi-decent businessman as he finished the conversation. I said thanks, good-bye, and hung up. All the while looking for the shortest route to a wall to bash my forehead into.

"Okay, this is going to be good," Felicity said. "But can we get on the road? If we're going to make the rounds tonight, I have a mess of laundry and homework to do before I can go out and play."

By "homework," she meant the medical coding work she did as an independent contractor. Did I mention sometimes I really hated her for finding a work-from-home job that let her set her own schedule? To top that all off, she met her current boyfriend, Jake, through the medical coding job, when she took a course on disaster management innovations. Jake was gor-gee-ous, a combination of Nick Fury and Stingray, and ran a security firm.

And no, I was neither coveting my best friend's property, nor lusting. More like appreciating God's handiwork with extra gusto.

"Play, my left foot," I muttered. I caught the pea coat she tossed me, and snatched up my saddlebag before wheeling to the front door and down the ramp. Just my luck, it started snowing when I hit the driveway.

Pete came home from school right then. He slid up the driveway on his antique moped, which Kurt kept running despite every scientific law. It continued sliding when he hit the brakes. No one needed the ability to see the future to know he was going to crash into the hedge. Before I could yell warning, he put his feet down and stood up, still holding onto the handlebars, and came to a hard, fast stop with his hiking boots digging into the slush. My arms ached in sympathy as he struggled with the still-moving moped. The rotten kid just laughed and killed the engine.

Just for that, I decided not to tell him about the contract, and the nice chunk of money that would come his way, until *after* we got back from shopping. I seriously considered making him come shopping with us, but then who would cook dinner? Baking was my forte, and cooking without recipes was Pete's. Our mama didn't raise fools. I promised Pete a batch of cheating fudge for dessert if he'd do something wonderful with all the leftovers trying to evolve into semi-sentient life in the refrigerator.

~~~~~

Harry was back from a last-minute hauling job when Felicity and I returned with enough groceries for an army. Admittedly, an army with a killer sweet tooth. She loaded the carrier on the back of my wheelchair with grocery bags and I started up the ramp to the kitchen door. Harry didn't need asking, just filled his arms with the last four bags and started up after me. Mum had trained him good, after all. Felicity parked the Jeep, tossed the keys to Harry, and hurried into her garage apartment to get to work. She had about four hours of coding to do, or in her way of reckoning, the electric and gas bill to work off.

"I stopped by to talk with John Stanzer today," Harry announced halfway through stashing all the groceries.

"What's he hiring you to— No." I wasn't prepared for the chill
~~~~~

down my spine and tickling my scalp as certainty spoke to me. "You're hiring him. To start looking for Mum and Pop."

"Just talking to him about how to start looking. I know Athena is doing her thing, but he's got connections she doesn't, you know? Yes, they've vanished before without meaning to, running off on a hot trail. They always come back with a crazy story, but this time feels different. Why wouldn't there be any trace unless they were trying to hide their trail? But if they did that, they'd let us know what was up, so we could find them, at least. They aren't thoughtless flakes, you know?" He sighed, visibly forcing all that tension out of his body. "You have to agree something's wrong."

"Weird. Off. But not… Well, you know how Mum and Pop are when they're tracking something. They get forgetful." I took a deep breath and consciously unclenched my hands from the economy-sized bag of candied fruit. "The military aren't into sharing when it comes to what they consider national security. I prefer to believe somebody is hiding something and Hayward doesn't know it. I'd know if something was wrong, if they were hurt."

"Or dead?" Pete said from the stove, pausing in pouring fresh, steamed veggies into a sauce so full of spices it looked black.

"I'd know." *Please, God, don't let this freaky gift You've given me fail now, when I need it most.*

"I just want to be sure where they are, in case your radar goes off and they do need help." Harry shrugged. "Stanzer is just going to send out feelers, ask around, see if anyone has heard anything. He says he specializes in weird."

"Then that should help, considering where he lives." I finished stashing my share of the groceries and pulled up in front of the stove. "That smells good. Is it ready?"

"You're not going to argue over it?" Pete didn't slap my hand when I slid a spoon out of the drawer and reached to scoop up some of the steaming mixture in the big Dutch oven. "That scares me more than our folks being gone."

"They haven't contacted us when they said they would. Twice. And it's too early in their investigation for something freaky or dangerous to happen. Of course I'm worried. I know they're okay, but…it's not knowing anything more than sensing they're okay. That's what gets me.

"We've got plenty of money set aside," I said after a few

minutes of those two giving me the poor-pitiful-puppy-dog-eyes treatment. "We can take Stanzer's fee out of the psychological health part of the budget, how about that?"

"Yeah, like we *never* use the money from there," Pete muttered. When I scowled at him, he guffawed and snatched up some hot pads to take the pot to the table.

The psychological health portion of the budget was for anything that relieved stress. For example, a movie marathon. A pizza feast. Concocting the weirdest homemade slushy flavors. Enough Chia Pets to fill the windowsills in the living room. Silly things and fun things. Innocent fun.

If we could lump hiring a P.I. to investigate our parents' disappearance into the budget item usually designated for silliness, that took some of the sting out of admitting we needed some help. Didn't it?

~~~~~

Kurt grew up on the Marvel Comics training plan for superheroes: *With great power comes great responsibility.* My theory: behind his sense of "I have a gift, so I must use it to protect the world," lay a hope that one of these days he would run into some babe who looked great in multi-colored Spandex. A babe who thought that a guy who could echo everyone else's powers was just what she was looking for, and fall madly in love with him.

Sometimes I wondered why Felicity and I put up with him. I mean, we were both relatively good-looking, despite some slight handicaps. Besides my chair. And Felicity's tendency to color her hair a different shade and change the length or texture every other week. Without going to the salon. Why did he always look at us as pals, practically sisters, and never as romantic interests?

Then again, having grown up with him, we both knew him a little too well to slip on the fuzzy pink glasses of romance. In a sense, we were at an impasse. Kurt dated occasionally, and Felicity had been pretty consistent with Jake for eight months now, a new record for her. As for me, after a bunch of lukewarm dates in high school and college, and that pedophile who tried to use me to get access to fresh victims, I hadn't dated. I couldn't blame my wheelchair for creating a barrier most guys couldn't leap over, could I?

Two kids were whisked away from Neighborlee Children's
~~~~~

Home when we were kids, but other than them, no one else had showed any signs of developing semi-pseudo-superhero powers. There were lots of Lost Kids living in Neighborlee, and their descendants, and some, like the Longfellows, had enough sensitivity to join the ranks of the guardians. However, none of the Lost Kids who had vanished had returned. Kurt's plans to become patriarch of a new race of superheroes were pretty much dead in the water. Felicity and I would razz him every once in a while, and then leave the topic of dating, romance, and procreation safely under its rock where it belonged, thanks very much.

I had time to kill between dinner and Kurt showing up to take us on patrol. I made the mistake of checking my email and found that dreaded contract for the licensing of Pete's cartoon, plus four more *Terry* letters that the Evil Overlord wanted me to answer.

Yes, I had fun with my first letter, even as I let my inner snark run loose, but could I keep that up? There was always the chance that people would get tired of *Terry* pointing out everyone's stupidity and they would stop writing letters altogether.

There was also the chance that I would get even stranger letters, the local equivalent of the Jerry Springer syndrome, with loonies wanting their fifteen minutes of fame.

I was so rattled by that idea, I nearly deleted the entire email, along with Pete's contract. I couldn't claim I never got it. I had logged into the corporate email system, which meant the Evil Overlord could tell when I had opened his email and when I deleted it. No way of covering my tracks without enlisting Athena's help. I had been her babysitter, and then her teacher. I didn't want to look stupid and helpless, or be a bad role model.

I wished I had gone into computer science. It would certainly be handy to be able to hack into the corporate system and insert a worm program to keep the Evil Overlord from sending me anything ever again. But did I need any knowledge of programming? After all, I had been visited a few times by London Holiday, our friendly Artificial Intelligence who had come to life thanks to a magical video camera and Athena's computing talents. Maybe London would do sabotage for me? If I could figure out how to contact her. I couldn't ask Athena to make the request, because there was the bad role model dilemma again.

# Chapter Four

Plus, Mum and Pop had raised us to try to be honest as much as possible. Even if nobody on Earth knew what I had done, God would know. Eventually, Mum would know, and she would tell Pop, and they would both give me these disappointed, sad, "Didn't we raise you better than that?" looks. Even lost in the Bermuda Triangle, my folks had that kind of an influence on me. Even if they were on the other side of a dimensional gateway, they would know what I had done.

So, I swallowed my pride, said a quick prayer for strength and creativity (forget patience, because anyone who asks God to grant patience is just asking for trouble) and yelled for Pete to check his email, because I was forwarding something to him.

Pete's excitement over the contract helped me feel a little better. Then both my brothers wanted to read my inaugural *Terry* column. Their laughter raised my spirits a few more notches. I was able to snatch up my coat when Kurt showed up, and wheel outside without much reinforcement. That, and a bag of jelly spearmint leaves and dark chocolate morsels, would get me through the night.

Our pattern for patrol was to drive out to the edge of town, park deep in the shadows where no one could see us, then take to the skies. If it had been a bad day and my legs were prickly-numb, or worse, the equivalent of cooked spaghetti, Felicity would help me slide out until I could stand up by leaning against the door. Otherwise I could get out on my own and stand, still holding onto the door, until we were ready to fly. We would then put on our flying harness to link us all together, and hooked arms with Kurt, who was in the middle. I would push up as much as my legs allowed, and in those few seconds, Kurt would borrow the shredded remains of my kinda-sorta flying ability, and wrap us in an energy field that let us all share that immunity to gravity. Then we would head straight up into the black night sky and fly a grid pattern over the town.

Kurt's ability to make us all fly helped cover over a lot of irritations we might have had with him. When I broke my back and turned my blue ribbon track star legs into tingling numb, spastic noodles, I lost the ability to fly. I could still levitate myself up to observation balloon height, but I couldn't do anything but go up and down. What use was that? Maybe it was the need to take a running start that affected the horizontal and speed control. Kurt had loved being able to fly together, since our orphanage days. He had been controlling our flying expeditions since elementary school. When he activated my flying ability, there was no more need for the running leap. No more aiming, either. His talent for fixing things, even superhero powers, let him rig a steering wheel into the formula. So to speak.

When Kurt wanted to go on patrol, I didn't tease him that he only wanted to borrow my flying ability. I missed it just as much as he did.

That night, we got a late start on our regular pattern of patrol above Neighborlee. We sat in the truck and talked for nearly an hour beforehand. Kurt had to hear all about the changes at the newspaper, thanks to the Evil Conglomerate taking over the *Tattler*. Not that I wanted to tell him, but Felicity was all excited about my first column and the fact that I hadn't managed to get myself fired from being *Terry*.

Kurt laughed and commiserated with me, and threatened to find a way to short-circuit Felicity if she continued killing his inventions. He wasn't too serious about his threats. The security system was all prototype and experimentation. He would have kept working on it, fiddling and improving and adding things, even if Felicity didn't occasionally do one of her EM bursts and wipe it out. When he got it working right, he would sell it to a big corporation.

"So, how did the hunt go?" Felicity asked, when we finished covering everything that happened while he was out of town.

"No luck," he said with a shrug that we all felt, jammed shoulder-to-shoulder on the front bench seat of Kurt's very old truck. "Which just supports our theory."

Every Lost Kid who had left Neighborlee Children's Home after odd events happened had all been claimed by distant relatives. The kind who miraculously appeared out of thin air with all the appropriate, necessary paperwork of proof. Not a single one had been adopted. And every single one of them had entirely vanished. Their document trail simply ended. That meant someone knew how to create new identities for them and then make them disappear into that thin air with them.

Kurt's latest trip had been to follow up on some faint trails that Athena and her computerized friends had found for us. He confirmed what we had been theorizing for a few years now.

"So, we aren't any better off than we were before," Felicity said.

"We have solid proof now that someone did a professional job of erasing records," Kurt said. "They just didn't know that Mrs. Silvestri was as allergic to computers as you, and she kept her own records."

Mrs. Silvestri, former head of the orphanage, had retired two years ago at the ripe old age of 103. She claimed she was only eighty-eight. My personal belief was that she was the first Lost Kid and stayed right in Neighborlee to watch out for all the others who came through. She had kept careful records of every child under her care, with photos and locks of hair, fingerprints, lost teeth carefully saved, report cards, and other bits and pieces of lives.

Kurt and Harry had been called out to the orphanage two weeks after she retired, to haul "private memorabilia" to her cottage in the assisted living village in Sylvan Heights. A couple old boxes had fallen nearly into dust when they picked them up. Those boxes held the proof we had been seeking: kids nobody remembered actually did exist and inhabit the orphanage at one time. That was the break we had been looking for, since we got the idea to look for other Lost Kids. Specifically, to find other mutants. The strange and uniquely gifted freaks of un-nature, as Felicity called us.

Kurt had borrowed some of Mrs. Silvestri's memorabilia, read through it, returned it and took more, read through it, returned it and took more. For four months. With extreme caution and stealth. Aided by the fact that he gave his handyman services to the assisted living village at a huge discount. That meant he could go anywhere without stirring up any questions, because he was there quite often on legitimate business. Then he found out she knew all along what he was doing. She'd let him think he was getting away with it because she liked watching him work, and had thrown little challenges at him to make the game more interesting. It turned out she was just as interested as we were in the children who had been taken out of her care. We had her blessing, as long as we kept her informed of our progress.

Only it seemed now someone was not only sweeping up the trail of breadcrumbs, but planting trees in the forest trail to totally obliterate the path.

"Maybe Mrs. S will have an idea when we go to report to her," I said. "How about some sub-zero wind in our faces to clear our brains?"

"Sounds good. Only ..." He rubbed at his face. "I followed up on a couple theories while I was out there. Sherwood's been watching me, and he picked up on what I was trying to piece together and ... It's bad."

Sherwood, for those who have come into the story late, was the Artificial Intelligence boyfriend of London Holiday. Both of them checked up on us from time to time, through texts or emails. Kurt and Sherwood seemed to have hit it off, working on programming for some of Kurt's gizmos.

"How bad?" I asked, and braced myself for something along the lines of finding out the Grandstones had actually told the truth for once. Some important landmark or historical property in Neighborlee was legitimately theirs, and they were going to yank it out from underneath everyone and charge us several centuries' worth of interest and fees for the use of that property.

I had Sylvia Grandstone on my mind ever since that weird night at the comedy club. Honestly, when we were out shopping, I thought I glimpsed her, just for a second there.

"All the other Lost Kids. Sherwood figured out the statistics for me. Maybe about two-thirds of the Lost Kids don't do anything special. The other third are pretty much divided up, two-thirds who have sensitivity, or they have kids who end up with talents, or their grandchildren have talents that make them guardians."

"Like the Longfellows and the girls," Felicity said slowly.

"Right."

"The other one-third is us? Lost Kids who have real, freak-'em-out talents?" I guessed.

"Let's focus on the un-freaky Lost Kids." Kurt gripped the steering wheel and looked out into the darkness. He exhaled long and loud. "It looks like the first Grandstone was a Lost Kid. Back before there was a Neighborlee Children's Home. He got tossed with a bunch of other orphans into a workhouse situation, and had a legitimate us-against-the-world thing going, because the county authorities weren't real nice people back then. The Willis twins tried to help, but by then, Grandstone and his original band of thieves had already decided to punish the rest of the world because things didn't go their way."

"What's so awful about that? I mean, yeah, it's bad they got a raw deal, but it just reinforces what we've already known. They blame everybody else all the time."

"The thing is … okay, the short version is that Grandstones focus on Lost Kids, down through the years. They recruit all the Lost Kids they can. It looks like some of them were involved in helping the talented ones vanish. And the really scary part is that the ones who end up working for the Grandstones, they don't go anywhere, they don't do anything. They don't get married and they sure don't have kids. So any talents, any superpower that might help protect Neighborlee, it never gets passed on or has a chance to show up in the next generation."

"So … we'd have a lot more guardians if those Lost Kids didn't get turned to the Dark Side, basically?" Felicity said.

"The only ones who turn out good or their kids or grandkids do, are the ones who stay free of the Grandstones."

"And the ones who don't get themselves noticed, and claimed by long-lost relatives who might have been sent by the Grandstones all along," I added, feeling kind of like the truck was spinning around underneath me.

"How many Lost Kids who never amount to anything are there?" Felicity asked.

"I'll have to ask Sherwood for the numbers." Kurt tried to shrug. "Do we really want to know?"

After a few seconds of thought, we both shook our heads.

"Let's get some fresh air," I said.

We flew our usual grid over Neighborlee that night, enjoying the chilly air against our faces, and watched the pattern of lights changing as people turned in for the night, and those on the midnight shift got up and went to work in the factories in other towns. Since it was a cloudless night, we flew out over the park and watched our silhouettes in the ice-free patches on the lakes, among the stars that seemed to hide in the depths. We had fun swooping down to tap the uppermost branches of trees and knock the few stubborn globs of snow down. Even Felicity liked that.

We irritated a few squirrels in their thick nests of leaves tucked among the topmost branches, and Kurt speculated aloud for the umpteenth time on just how the varmints got those leaves and other forest trash to stick together. Felicity dared him for the umpteenth time to take a squirrel's nest back to his workshop to take it apart and find his answers, and stop boring us with his wondering. Kurt growled at her, and I laughed, as usual.

The problem wasn't Kurt letting go of us to grab hold of the nest, because we were using our flying harness. The challenge was keeping those squirrels contained once the nest left the tree. They were, after all, rodents. None of us wanted one or several racing up and down our backs, scratching and biting and letting their irritation be known.

One of these days, Kurt would figure out how to get a nest down and keep the critters inside contained. Until then, we were safe.

~~~~~

The *Neighborlee Tattler* was housed in a connected series of renovated buildings on the south end of the shopping and business district we referred to as the Mall. The *Tattler* had grown through its long life, expanding from one old house into the next building and then another, down the connected row of houses. I liked the changing ambiance, from one "house" of the newspaper to another. Especially since Conrad's grandfather and father had installed ramps between sections, where floors didn't meet at the same height, instead of making people go up and down three or four steps. That section of the street was on a slope, so nothing was on the same level. It made navigating the workspace interesting.

Wednesday was my half-day. All the preparation work for the next edition had been done and everybody else was either catching up on sleep, tracking down the next story, or standing guard over our print run at the plant in Valleyview. I left the office about 1:30-ish, timed just right for when all the traffic through the center of town had calmed. I could be sure the parking lot was empty of the bozos who ignored the "no parking zone" signs. Or when the pavement wasn't covered with snow, those diagonal yellow lines that meant "no parking." There was always someone who reasoned that their emergency, which always turned into an hour-long
~~~~~

shopping trip, excused them from obeying the law. They always seemed to park close to the driver's side of my Jeep, making it hard to swing the door open all the way, balance against the door, and heave my chair one-handed into the back seat before my legs decided to fold, and I landed face-first on the pavement.

Of course, if no one was around, I had no problem lifting that chair with my telekinetic powers.

Sometimes I wondered if God gave me that particular talent *because* He knew I'd need it once I got my driver's license back.

The parking lot was practically deserted when I got outside that afternoon. Just me and my Jeep and ruts in the snow averaging about four inches deep. What was wrong with people that they couldn't drive in straight lines? It would have been so much easier getting from the nicely shoveled sidewalk, down the ramp (three parking slots *away* from handicapped parking) and across to my car, if I could have driven in straight slots someone else had dug out ahead of me.

I thought about my worn-thin joke about needing chain mail gloves if I put chains on my wheelchair tires in the winter.

Not funny anymore.

I got to my Jeep, opened the door, and pulled myself out of my chair, hanging onto the door with three times the upper-body strength I had in high school, thank you very much. Then instinct made me pause as I reached for my chair, to fold it up.

My left rear tire was flat.

I just held onto the door and stared for about ten seconds before I dropped back into my chair. When the realization of what I saw finally penetrated my tired brain, my first thought was to wish I had taken that conversational Klingon class with Pete the summer before. It would have been immensely satisfying to shout something in a language nobody but Trekkers could understand. While I said something innocuous, it would sound horrific to anyone who heard me. Not that anyone was outdoors at that moment, but it still would have been emotionally satisfying.

Sighing, I scooted backwards to get a better look at the damage. And buy myself some thinking time as I tried to figure out who I could call in the middle of the day to come help me. I could do a lot of things, but wheelchairs weren't built at the right angle and height to change tires. Kurt had a big, all-day job helping install some equipment over in Euclid, and Felicity didn't have a cell phone, for obvious reasons. Harry? Where was he? I couldn't remember his delivery route that day.

It took me a few seconds of sitting there at the hind end of my Jeep before I realized that the other rear tire was flat.

What were the chances of *two* tires going flat at the same time?

I hadn't been a math genius or a gambler, but I could make a good guess on the odds.

Then I noticed the deep footprints next to each tire. They looked like someone had stood there long enough to sink into the slushy snow. Why would those same boots stand a noticeable length of time behind both tires? Unless someone was checking out my Jeep?

With a sinking feeling in my gut, I followed the footprints. Oh, joy — it looked like the guy with the big boots went up the passenger side of my Jeep. I didn't need a vision of near future events to know what I would see when I wheeled my chair around and up the passenger side.

Yep, a third flat tire.

What were the chances of such a thing happening on one car in one day, without some help?

Practically nonexistent. Even if I had run over a crate of tacks, I should have escaped with fewer flats.

That creepy feeling I always associated with a sense of danger slithered into the thick scars along my spine. I knew better than to look around. I was sure someone was watching me. Common sense suggested that the person who had attacked three of my four tires was probably preparing to do something even nastier to me. If he, she, or they hadn't attacked the moment I realized the tires were flat, it meant the un-jolly jokester liked to inflict some psychological torture. I wasn't about to give him the satisfaction.

I figured pulling out my cell phone to call for help might be a trigger, so I used a good, strong mental push to get my chair through the snow at twice the usual speed. This put me conveniently within sight of the people working in the big picture windows at the front of the newspaper office. I waved to them, and they waved back. The presence of witnesses would slow down anyone who intended me bodily harm. At least, that was the theory. If the person harassing me was totally nutso, all bets were off.

The creepy feeling went away by the time I got safely back into the main doorway of the office. I stayed there, pulled out my cell phone, and called AAA. My head hurt a little from the effort of the extra boost I'd used to get out of the parking lot. The smells of the office on Wednesday would only make the ache turn into nausea. Fresh air for me.

I had a ninety-minute wait until someone could give me a tow and a lift to the nearest garage that would fix or replace my tires. Maybe if I had told them that I was a woman in a wheelchair, someone might have come out faster. It wasn't like I was stranded in Downtown Cleveland with snow falling, ten below zero, at eleven at night. I could wait, loitering in the office to stay warm, or I could get a ride home from someone and then come back to meet my rescuer.

What do the tough do in situations like this?

As a desperation move, to be a harder-to-hit target, I went shopping.

I hated shopping. Then again, I did like rolling around Neighborlee whenever I got the chance. And I was just peeved enough over what had happened to inconvenience myself for the sake of irritating someone else.

Now, someone might think that staying out in the open when I had definitely felt a threat was a stupid thing to do. They would probably be right. But the thing I loved about Neighborlee was that someone was always around. Traffic might have died until the evening commute started, but all the shops were in old-fashioned buildings with big picture windows. There was plenty of foot traffic no matter what the weather. Plenty of witnesses if anyone tried anything. Besides, chances were pretty good I would hack off my enemy if I didn't look afraid.

It was a lot easier to navigate Neighborlee's sidewalks in the summer, granted. At this time of the day, I probably could have stayed in the street and not had any trouble. Of course, I still had snow to contend with, both on the sidewalks and in the street, and the effects of all that slush and salt and grit, rubbing off my wheels onto my nice leather gloves.

What was I saying about chain mail gloves and chains on my tires?

My grumbles died an abrupt death when I wheeled past the

building where Spindelmutter's used to be. For just a few seconds, my physical vision wavered. The killer icicles hanging off the gutters vanished. The gutters lost their sag and turned from rust-spotted white to black that contrasted nicely with the glowing red of the bricks. If there really was red brick under all those layers of grime and moss. Instead of those empty bay windows lined with rotting brown paper, I saw displays of all sorts of natural beauty products and advertisements for massages and facials, manicures, pedicures and waxing, herbal teas and home spa treatments. I couldn't see anyone inside the shop, to give me a sneak peek at the future owner, but from the lack of ice in my vision, I deduced it would be transformed from abandoned shop into spa by spring.

*Please, God, this coming spring? I could use a good massage, and some herbal teas and other good stuff.*

I must have prayed too loud or too hard. The vision vanished, replaced with the icicles and dirty paper and dingy bricks. I sighed and continued down the bumpy sidewalk. I didn't have enough time to get all the way down the block, to the edge of the commercial district of Neighborlee, to visit Divine's Emporium. Well, I did have time, but as soon as I got inside the front door and tempted myself with a whiff of those cappuccino candles I swore Angela stocked just for me, it would be time to turn around and head back to the *Tattler* to meet AAA. I settled for stopping in at Papyrus People to drool over colored filler paper and gel pens, and pick out some totally obnoxious Christmas cards for my brothers and friends.

Besides, those three flat tires had me off balance. Someone had sabotaged my Jeep. Why, I couldn't even begin to theorize. Once the guy from AAA checked out my tires, I would know how they had gone flat, and that would give me an idea of the type of person who had done it, and whether I should report the incident to the police. I mean, there had to be a difference between someone who used a knife to kill my tires, and someone who stabbed them with a big nail or something else sharp. Right? The difference between someone who had deliberately hunted for me and was prepared, or just someone in a foul mood who used whatever tool he could find at hand, to cause damage just for the sake of making someone else's day as lousy as his.

For all I knew, someone who hated the *Tattler* was out for

vengeance over a story. Maybe he started with my Jeep and then got scared away. Or maybe he was one of those wackos who felt that the physically handicapped didn't deserve to have reserved parking spots, so he went after the first car he saw, sitting in front of that blue wheelchair sign. The thing is, how come nobody looking out the front windows of the paper saw someone skulking around my Jeep? So maybe it was an inside job? Somebody went after me because I was a friend of Conrad, and they were ticked to the extreme… And that was where my theorizing fell apart.

If this was a deliberate attack on me, I couldn't figure out the reason. Yes, I had participated in frustrating some pretty nasty characters in the past, as a guardian of Neighborlee, but most of the time we managed to keep our identities hidden when we performed our duties. We didn't need masks or costumes to keep our ordinary personas secret. Which was kind of depressing, because face it, superhero costumes are pretty cool.

I was still chewing on the whole conundrum by the time I finished drooling over writerly goodies at Papyrus People and wheeled back down the street to the *Tattler*'s office and parking lot. Maybe we could talk the Evil Overlord into investing in some security cameras? Not that I would ever admit anything good came out of being sold into durance vile by that slithery Mrs. Sloane.

~~~~~

The verdict from the AAA guy was that my tires had been slashed. With a knife. A big, sharp knife. It was no accident. *Well, duh.* Three tires at once and those deep footprints around my Jeep kind of gave me the clue that it was deliberate.

The fact that it was deliberate damage, and pretty nasty, prompted the AAA guy to call the police. I was sitting in the front of Mulcahy's Garage, making a list of all the baking to do over the weekend, and trying to remember what gift boxes I had and what sizes I needed, so I could replenish my supply. In walked Gordon. Of course. Sometimes I felt like Gordon was my private cop.

Not that I minded. Better to have a friend looking after me, rather than someone who subconsciously equated a broken body with a broken brain. The kind of bozo who treated the physically handicapped as if we didn't know how to shut our mouths to keep from drooling.

"Who did you hack off?" Gordon leaned against the counter.
~~~~~

The chairs in the dingy, cement-floored waiting room at Mulcahy's qualified as antiques and didn't fit him.

"Me?" I just grinned and didn't even try for an innocent expression.

"Somebody had to be pretty mad, to go after three tires. The puncture where the knife went in makes me think it was a thick blade. Like a hunting knife. Most hunters I know wouldn't use their blades on tires. They've got respect for their tools."

"I'll keep that in mind."

"Lanie—"

"My first choice is the lunatic fringe who don't think handicapped people should have special parking spots or other privileges."

"So he ignores the cars parked illegally in the handicapped spots—"

"Car. Singular. There are only two handicapped spots in that lot. I had my permit tag hanging from the window. Easy enough to see. If it was an anti-gimp loony, that'd mark me as a target."

"So, nothing personal. I don't buy it. Kind of extreme for an anonymous kind of attack."

"You don't keep up with the news, Gordon. There's some radical fringe element trying to build up steam in Washington to do away with the Americans with Disabilities Act. They equate it with reverse discrimination."

"Man, sometimes I wish we could just put a big dome over Neighborlee and lock the rest of the world out."

Little did he know how close he came to the truth. The protective field around Neighborlee was either crumbling, fading, or malfunctioning. Still, the "go away, we don't like you" effect continued to drive away most troublemakers. However, that inconvenient span of time between when troublemakers crossed into Neighborlee and when the protective field drove them away was increasing every year.

Which meant more work for the guardians to do. Too bad Kurt's ability to fix things didn't extend to the protective field.

# Chapter Five

"What's wrong with people?" Gordon continued. Not that he would have known about the fizzing and grumbling going on in my brain right that moment. "No charity, no common sense." He shook his head and yanked his cap off to scrub his hand through his hair for a few seconds. Then he got that considering look, narrowing his eyes at me for a few seconds.

"What'd I do now? Hey, Gordon, remember, I'm the victim this time around."

"Yeah. This time." One corner of his mouth crooked up. "Let me give you a warning, as a friend. Don't go putting this in your next comedy routine."

"I don't know, might be good material if I put enough of a spin on it. If you make your enemy laugh, he calms down enough to listen and be reasonable."

"Yeah, but people whacked enough to attack a handicapped driver's car, seems to me they're way beyond reasonable. They'll just get angrier, and maybe justify what they were doing."

I laughed and pretended to be reluctant to take his advice, but inside I shivered. I had imagined the tire-slasher as one person. With Gordon's words, all of a sudden I had a crowd of enemies. Kind of like the mob that went after Dr. Frankenstein in his lab. I'd always felt some sympathy for the monster. He was a gimp, too, in the final analysis. It wasn't his choice to be put together with spare parts and brought to life, to limp around and worry that the bolts holding his head on might come loose.

Needless to say (but I'm going to say it anyway), the boys weren't too happy when they got home that night and heard what happened. We talked about it and couldn't come up with any reasonable (or unreasonable) suspects. Even the lunatics in Neighborlee were friendly. Other than the Grandstones and their single-digit-I.Q. henchmen. Kind of depressing to think that the jerks we had despised growing up were Lost Kids who might have been allies, if they hadn't been warped by Grandstones. It made Sylvia and Reggie's overtures of friendship all the more frightening. If I hadn't seen them in action before they decided I might be useful, would I have fallen for their lines and lies, and come under their influence?

~~~~~

Thursday night was practice with the Ezekiel's Wheels at the community center in Darbyville. We were registered in the Wheelchair Basketball League as a Darbyville team, since five of our fifteen players lived there. That was a clear majority, since the rest of us were the only players from our respective towns.

We were good; we were hot. We had a lot of fun. Until the next team showed up to practice and nudged us out of the gym. The manager for the gym had double-booked the teams practicing. Again. If it didn't happen with such regularity, I might have blamed the mix-up that night on whatever handicapped-hating loony had targeted me. Would that be arrogance? Getting our two-hour practices trimmed to an hour happened at least twice a month. The community center manager had a reputation as a sexist idiot who didn't think women had any business playing sports, period.

So, we were outside on a snowy night, slightly sweaty and revved from our practice, but nowhere near ready to go home. Three-quarters of the team's members had formed a heavy metal band, and they decided to go to Peg-leg's garage to practice. I was invited, but I decided to be virtuous and go home to work on my next *Terry* column.

The parking lot outside the community center was a little too quiet. Snow fell with that muffling sensation that made me think of isolated clearings in big, dark forests, with the parking lot lights casting multiple shadows from every vehicle. I reached the edge of the sidewalk and paused to try to spot my Jeep. There was no use trying to find a handicapped accessible parking spot with ten eligible vehicles competing for each one, so I hadn't even tried. Of course, that meant I couldn't quite remember where I parked. It was a bad habit, to always expect to park in the spot closest to any building.

I looked down and noticed how the falling snow had partially erased the newest footprints. That sent a shiver up my spine that had nothing to do with the good sweat I had built up.

"Hey, guys. Hold up a second."

Needlenose and Janice stopped in mid-glide down the ramp.
~~~~~

Peg-leg, the third in line, didn't react quite as fast (she had that problem on the basketball court, too) and slid into the back of Janice's chair.

"Whazzup?" Needlenose turned her chair and tilted back on her wheels. Not a smart move, considering the fresh snow on the ramp, but she had always been a daredevil.

"I got three tires slashed yesterday. Just in case some of those anti-gimp bozos are lurking, be careful, okay?"

"That's all we need," Ellen groaned, but she grinned at me and eased her chair down the curb instead of waiting for the traffic jam on the ramp to clear. That impatience was what got her in her chair in the first place, damaging one leg, then the other, and trying to get back up to supersonic speed in her life before her injuries were healed. "Thanks for the warning."

The others kept up their chatter as they spread out across the parking lot, revved about our upcoming game against an out-of-state team, the Hot Rods. I couldn't quite join in the exaggeration and speculation, as I waited for someone to turn up as the next victim. Quite frankly, Darbyville was a more likely spot for a tire-slasher than Neighborlee. I wasn't exactly reassured when no one found any damage to their cars. We crisscrossed the parking lot with our brushes and scrapers, those with longer reaches or the ability to partially stand helping the others clear ice and blown snow off car windows. We talked as we worked, and agreed that since the game was at Neighborlee High School the next night, we'd meet for dinner at the Sipping Post before the game.

Without intending it, I was the last one to climb into my Jeep. I sat behind the wheel, watching in the rearview mirror as the red taillights exited the parking lot, and felt colder than could be explained by the slowly growing gusts of wind. After all, my heater was going full blast and I could still feel the sweat caught under my T-shirt, sweatshirt and parka. In fact, I was sweating right that moment. I yanked my stocking cap off and raked my fingers through my hair.

I froze, hands on my head, as the one-story office wing of the Darbyville community center in front of me vanished, to be replaced by a gravel road, barely visible on a stormy, wet night. Headlights came at me, but I was aware enough to realize the headlights didn't touch anything beyond the gravel road of the vision. Light bounced off the deep puddles along the side of that road, giving me glimpses of red paint on a pickup truck.

Then the gravel road vanished into darkness and the pickup tipped sideways as it went over the edge. I heard the *rattle-roar-crash* of a garbage truck going into the quarry, clear through the haze of pain that had shrouded all my senses that rainy summer night when my back was shattered.

"Okay, God, that wasn't enlightening in the least," I muttered, my voice a rasp because my throat was so dry.

I really wished sometimes God would give me some controls for this unreliable, sporadic gift of foresight. Or an owner's manual. Was that too much to ask? I never got big enough glimpses to use what I saw, until it was almost too late to do any good. I knew better than to complain. Mum and Pop always said that God limited us to make us stronger, and to learn to rely on Him more. If I got shreds of clues in my visions, it was to prompt me to think and to figure things out on my own. I had a brain, a gift from God, so I should use it.

~~~~~

"What does that mean?"

I got that question often enough when I went out in my super-light wheelchair made for speed, I knew the slightly congested voice coming from the bleachers behind me was referring to my bumper sticker: *Living Proof that the Good Times Roll*. Complete with a wheelchair tipped back into the "shuttle position," and that *swoosh* mark indicating high speed.

Pete had made it for me in the creative arts class at Neighborlee High School. He got an "A" in the class, until Mr. Schuberkowski found out angel-faced Pete was making a mint selling them to everyone on my basketball team, the teams we played against, and all our fans.

I turned around, nearly bashing my footrests on the bleachers next to me, and looked up at the gangly, wide-eyed girl studying me. She wore a letterman sweater with pins for basketball, baseball and football, making me wonder just how many jocks she dated at one time. That couldn't be her sweater. Probably it was a gift from the guy she dated. Yeah, girls who looked like her, all skinny and perky and wide-eyed from a lack of oxygen, got lots of dates. Then I got a good look at the school jacket on the bench next to her, which
~~~~~

stated she belonged to the Huber Heights Swim Team. So, did that make her a jock… Jock-ess? Considering the collective I.Q. of our rival school system barely broke three digits, I came up on the spot with four jokes about chlorine damage on gray matter, and nearly choked keeping them to myself, saved for later use. I had learned never to let a snark go to waste.

"What do you think it means?" I finished peeling off my second sweatshirt, to reveal my basketball uniform underneath.

Those makeup-clogged eyes got wider and she shook her head. I popped a wheelie and pivoted, doing a little sashay in my electric blue wheelchair.

"Roll." I demonstrated, putting the front wheels down again and sliding back and forth a few times.

"But how can you have a good time in a wheelchair?" She gave me a look like I was the dumb one here.

"See them?" I pointed to the rest of my team, warming up out on the floor. The Ezekiel's Wheels, if I do say so myself, were about the best women's wheelchair basketball team on the North Coast. "They're having fun, aren't they?"

"Well, that's just goofing around until the *real* basketball game starts." Again, the "you're so dumb" look.

Sometimes I had to agree with the eugenics extremists, who wanted to make it mandatory to pass I.Q. tests before people could procreate. Some genes just should not be passed on.

I was sure now that the letterman sweater belonged to her date, a basketball player who was either a fan of the Wheels, or had been given an assignment from his coach to come watch how we did our magic without any fancy footwork. I wondered if she listened when he said it was a *wheelchair* basketball game, or she just blindly followed wherever he led. Poor kid was in for a boring evening.

"Honey, you got a long wait." I popped back in my chair, pivoted to face forward again, and zoomed out onto the floor.

Needlenose shot the ball to me and I went for a zooming glide up under the basket and popped it in for a swish, nothing-but-net shot.

If there were a professional league for wheelchair basketball, I could play full-time, make a million, and retire at age forty to live the easy life. And no worry about arthritis in my knees and ankles or any other health problems that "normal" basketball players had to contend with as they aged.

*Define "normal," other than a city outside Bloomington, please?*

Tonight, we played the Hot Rods, a women's team from Indiana. Their best player was this tiny, square-shaped girl with the confusing name of Hooter. When Kurt heard the name a few weeks ago, he started to make a crude comment about her figure. When Felicity got up off the floor, after trying to make him sing soprano with a judo kick and missing the mark yet again, I showed him the team photo. Hooter didn't have a figure to speak of. She was all torso, flat and square, with skinny arms and legs that almost vanished in the folds of her uniform. I thought maybe she had an ooga-horn attached to her wheelchair, but was proven wrong when the team rolled out onto the floor that night. Hooter was as quiet as she was tiny, but those breadstick arms could shoot the basketball across the court from the half-court line with pinpoint accuracy.

At the half-time break, the Hot Rods did some fancy wheelchair ballet moves, and when Hooter took her bow, she leaned forward enough that we could see her name on the back of her shirt. It turned out, that was her real name: Cathy Hooter.

*Well, duh.*

I didn't have time to look for a reaction from Kurt, sitting next to me. I was the rest of the half-time show.

Protestors streamed out onto the floor before I could pull my Cleveland Indians sweats on over my basketball uniform and wheel out there. They shouted words like "Unfair," and "Reverse discrimination," and "Let real athletes have a chance," before the gym security force—all three of them—herded the eight noisy, badly dressed protesters off the floor. Honestly, just because it was winter was no reason to mix plaids with polka dots, and maroon marabou-trimmed socks with neon orange cross-trainers. One of them tried to whack a security guard with her picket sign, but she missed. When it hit the floor, the cardboard separated from the stick and the crowd roared, deciding it was funny instead of obnoxious. People shouted for her and her buddies to sit down. Someone offered to make it legal for her to use handicapped parking. Someone else shouted that the handicapped parking spots were for physical handicaps, not emotional or mental.

*Hey, that bozo stole one of my lines!*

She turned bright red, which clashed horribly with her violet spangled jogging outfit. Of course, that was assuming that someone with hips and thighs to make a rhino jealous even knew how to spell "jogging," much less do it.

"What are they protesting, exactly?" I asked MarySue, who had elected not to go into the locker room during the break, so she could hear my routine. For the thousandth time.

"They've been harassing the Hot Rods for two months now, ever since some twits who got kicked off their college team for drinking decided they had the right to be Hot Rods. First they got upset that tryouts were closed until next August, but there wasn't anything they could do about it. Turns out the Hot Rods have a rule requiring a doctor's certification that you need a wheelchair, to be on the team. One of them found out and has been trying to take them to court ever since. The ACLU in their town can't make up their mind if they want to take the case. Picking on the poor crippled girls like that, dontcha know? One of the local papers has decided that anyone who gets their license yanked for drunk driving doesn't have the right to be in control of any wheels. Whether they have an engine attached or not. They've been crucifying them in the press on a regular basis."

"And the twits and their supporters are in too deep to just drop the whole thing," I guessed. Sometimes pride made people do stupid things, and get even more stupid by refusing to admit they were wrong. "Did they think people in Ohio could force a team in Indiana to let them play? Why would they want to play with people who probably can't stand the sight of them by now?"

The crowd had quieted only a little, now that the unplanned halftime show had ended. I had spent enough time in my career trying to warm up an audience who had been bored or offended by the act ahead of me, I knew a good opportunity when it landed in my lap. This crowd was ready to laugh. I nodded to MarySue, popped a wheelie, and zipped out into the middle of the floor. I did a few twists and turns and shimmies while the court manager trotted out with my microphone, effectively grabbing everyone's attention and using up some time. The poor guy was busy cleaning up all that marabou dropped by those ugly socks.

"Remember," I said, as everyone quieted down enough I could hear the ventilation system bang two stories above me, "sanity is just a group norm, and the majority has been wrong before."

Not even half a second of pause before the audience caught on and laughed. Okay, this was going to be a good night.

"Protesters. Gotta love them. No matter how…weird they are. Hey, is that politically correct? You know, I always thought it was dumb that in the 60s and then again in the 90s, protestors always wore those tie-dye T-shirts, because--I don't know about you--they look like bull's-eyes. Shouldn't they wear camouflage, instead?"

From the corner of my eye, I saw two Hot Rods slide out from the locker room. Wheelchair people were among my harshest critics. I could never figure out why some of them couldn't laugh at themselves. It helped avoid a lot of other problems, and shut up a lot of people who could only relate to us if they got to act like heroes and wipe the drool off our faces.

Best way to handle potential attackers? Put them on stage with me.

"Okay, I'm in trouble. Here come a couple Hot Rods to watch the show. If I don't make them laugh, they'll break my legs!"

Good laughter. From them, which was more important.

"But you know, being in a wheelchair has a lot of advantages. Shoes, for instance. A friend at work asked me if my shoes were brand new. I said no, ten years old. I'd had them so long, they came back into fashion. But there are those shoes that, no matter how long you have them, they just will not make sense. What is with those shoes with the lights in the heels? What are they for? To blind cockroaches?"

The protestors used up some of my time, so I was still trying to decide what to trim from my routine when I got the five-minute signal from the manager. That was okay. I got paid already.

"Now, me, I don't drink or do drugs, because if I get wasted and start walking funny, I would lose my parking space. And with that confession, I must prepare to leave you with this bit of wisdom:

"If you want to make a big impression in the world, try skydiving without a parachute."

The half-time buzzer went off, signaling the start of the second half of the game. I gave myself a good shove backwards toward my team's bench--guided by a little judicious mental steering--and ended up with Kurt guiding me to where I could peel off my sweats.

It was a good evening. We won by five, Pete sold thirty copies of my two comedy CDs, and four people asked me to contact them about doing my routine for their meetings and parties.

I was flying, feeling like I floated about six inches above my seat cushion, as we headed out to the half-empty parking lot. Most of the Wheels were gone, and all the Hot Rods had already loaded onto their lift-bus to head back to their hotel. I was a long way from coming down, and planning where we could stop for a junk-food infusion, so we could invite some people back to the house. The night was still young, only nine-thirty.

Then Toby Malone's sulky face appeared in the spill from the parking lot light, and the rest of his big, slouching body followed suit. He just stood there, staring at me with those vacant, chocolate eyes of his, no emotion, not much in the way of awareness.

How come people like that are scarier than a whole battlecruiser full of Klingons enraged by that cloud creature from *Day of the Dove* in Classic Trek?

The worst part of it? Knowing I had no reason to be scared.

Toby didn't hate me. I knew he had no reason to want to hurt me. Last year when he had been home from the Marine Corps, we had spent four hours and nearly $20 in quarters on the video games at Eden, challenging each other over *Tempest* and *Centipede*.

No memory of that fun, sweaty night of laughter remained in his eyes. That was scary. It reminded me of the Terminator; no emotions, no thoughts beyond his programming for destruction. Toby looked like all the joy in life had been drained out of him.

What was wrong with that kid? What had he been doing with the Marines? If Toby had been hurt, if he had been brain-damaged or was on drugs, wouldn't his parents have mentioned it?

"Lanie! Great job tonight." Tom Malone came tearing out of the darkness, his grin as big as ever, his enormous hands reaching out to shake mine. "You were amazing tonight." He hunched his shoulders in his decades-old Neighborlee High letterman jacket, grinning and red-faced, the quintessential small town boy who loved it too much to live or work anywhere else. Neighborlee was in good hands with Tom Malone taking care of the Service Department.

It just showed how nice the whole town was, that Tom didn't lose his job when Toby stole his keys so he and Steve Muldoon and Jay Parker could steal those two trucks for Senior Prank Night. Tom visited me every day I was in the hospital, until the nurses thought he was my boyfriend.

The contrast between father and son, the extremes in impressions I got looking from one to the other, almost made me dizzy. What was wrong with Toby? Had he gone back to those sullen days between the accident and heading off to boot camp, when his buddies had tried to blame me, Kurt and Felicity for what happened at the quarry that night?

Wait a minute. Tom had said something a few weeks ago about Toby getting out of the Corps and going to college. Finally. Maybe Toby was just feeling unbalanced, adjusting to civilian life.

"Yeah, the Wheels just keep getting better," Pete said

"Wasn't that a great game?" Tom slapped Toby's arm, probably his subtle way of getting his son to join the conversation.

Toby grunted and finally looked away. I noticed during the short exchange of how-are-you, we're-good-how-are-you, started-your-Christmas-shopping-yet, rotten-weather-predicted, Toby's gaze slid everywhere, avoiding any direct contact with my chair. Interesting. I had heard through the grapevine, back when I was still waiting for my jigsaw puzzle back to reassemble, when his buddies blamed Kurt, Felicity and me, Toby had been pretty silent about it. The outrage that erupted through the town sealed the fate of the trio. They never thought when they decided to "borrow" Tom's keys and take the city's equipment, that their plans for the fall and college would be changed forever. Essentially, the three had been exiled from Neighborlee, through military service.

Now Toby was back. Since he was supposed to be going to college now, I asked what he would major in.

"Criminal studies," Tom said, grinning as proudly as he probably had the day Toby was born. "My boy's going to be a detective one of these days. Maybe a profiler. Work for the FBI. The sky's the limit."

"That's great. Your training will be a big help," I offered.

"Go for something that'll let you use your brain over your brawn," Kurt offered. He hadn't smiled during the entire conversation, and I wondered what sort of vibes he was getting, to make him so somber. "Brain lasts a lot longer than brawn."

"Yeah. Maybe," Toby said.

I barely bit back a quip about the stone speaking. Common

sense fought with my fading sense of trouble and threat from Toby. After all, if I was in danger, if my quivers had any validity, I would have had some kind of vision, a glimpse of trouble, of Toby gunning for me. I really couldn't read people's minds. But sometimes, when strong emotions were involved, it was like I caught momentary glimpses of the things filling their brains. Nothing came from Toby, so at least he wasn't plotting my demise while he stood there, studying the toes of his big boots.

All this peace and quiet, no interference from my sporadic gift of foresight, convinced me that I had just been edgy from all the stupid, nasty tricks someone had been pulling on me. I had no vision of warning, no glimpses of the future to tell me about trouble waiting for me. God wouldn't leave me in the lurch, blind and unwarned, would He? Despite that silence, I knew now wasn't a time for joking. Toby obviously wasn't happy to be there in the parking lot. Whatever friendliness had existed between us the last time he was in town had vanished. I found it hard to imagine Tom, who seemed to shrink a little more every year, physically dragging big bruiser ex-Marine Toby to the game that night, but it had happened. What was going on?

"Nice to see you're home. How long are you visiting?" I said.

"I thought you went to see Lanie when you got home." Tom frowned. Funny, how Toby cringed at the disappointment in his father's eyes. Not anger, not threats, just disappointment. He didn't like to disappoint his father. That was a good sign. It meant the good boy I knew in high school was still in there.

"Forgot," Toby mumbled, and looked off across the parking lot. Like he would be out of there half an hour ago, if he had his choice.

"You said you ran into her last month."

"I did?" He shrugged and kicked at a lump of slush at his feet.

"Sorry, Lanie. I thought Toby told you. He's starting at WB in the new year." Tom shook his head, giving his son another sorrowful, slightly confused look.

I shivered, and it had nothing to do with the arctic gust that whipped through the parking lot at that moment. Why had Toby lied about talking to me? How come he had been in town for a month and I hadn't heard about it? Or sensed it? Of course, not sensing anything was a good sign there was no trouble waiting to pounce. But why expect trouble from Toby in the first place?

Time to replenish my blood sugar. Kurt must have sensed I was getting wigged out. He made our excuses and got us sliding across the parking lot to his truck. But not before commenting that Toby should hook up with Gordon, who had gotten his law enforcement coursework from Willis-Brooks. That got a momentary wide-eyed look of panic. Just for about two heartbeats. Then Toby resumed his dull expression. It was enough to make me doubt what I had seen, the change was so complete. I looked back once before we got in Kurt's truck, and caught Toby staring at me with a stony, resigned, not-angry-not-hurt, but definitely unsettling expression in his eyes.

# Chapter Six

"Toby's got some big problems," Pete announced, once we were heading out of the parking lot. "What was with him? You'd think Lanie hurt him, instead of her getting hurt saving his neck."

"Guilt does weird things to a guy's brain," Kurt said. "The guy who is most to blame in a car wreck usually makes the most noise."

"You don't think—" I shut up, but the image of my three flat tires kept popping into my head. Bottom line: Toby got into trouble on Senior Prank Night. Just because he had gone into the Marines didn't mean he had outgrown the stupidity that changed his life.

All that military training just meant if he wanted to be nasty, he could.

"What?" Pete said, when we had gone another block down the street and neither Kurt nor I had said anything in all that time. Unusual, after such a great night.

"You think he's out to get you?" Kurt said.

"Dumb idea?" I shrugged. "The thing is ... someone smart wouldn't start his nasty tricks with his return to town. He'd wait a few months before doing anything. Or start the nasty tricks before he officially returns. If he was out to get me. Which I really doubt," I added, feeling a little breathless.

"I'll keep an eye on him," was all Kurt said.

Col. Hayward was waiting at the house, talking with Harry, when we arrived with the deluxe, guaranteed-to-serve-ten dinner package from House of Wang. With my brothers and Kurt to feed, the package was more like serving six. Our switch in plans, from pizza to Chinese, just proved how badly that encounter with Tom and Toby had jangled all of us. I recognized Hayward's car before I saw the discrete little military sticker in the window, and my post-game appetite took another nosedive.

For about five seconds, I debated asking Kurt to turn his truck around and take us to his place to eat in peace. That wouldn't be fair to Harry, who probably hoped we'd bring something home. Col. Hayward was a friend. He wouldn't come unless he had good news, or information he thought we needed to hear.

More important than being a friend, the Colonel was Mum and Pop's liaison with the military. In all their travels and investigations into the just plain weird and fantastical, they sometimes uncovered items, events, phenomena, or even people, of interest to national security. Hayward grew up in Neighborlee, a Lost Kid, so he understood the weirdness and he had a stake in protecting the people who lived here. He made sure Mum and Pop were protected, rather than hauled in for questioning every time a warning they passed along turned out to be a little too true for comfort.

After Hayward had called us last week, I remembered some things that hadn't seemed significant when they happened. He had found some classified information Pop needed, last spring. What if that information took our folks to the Bermuda Triangle? They'd said their research trip was personal this time, though they hadn't really said what the subject of their next book would be. Even though there was no military connection, we knew from experience the military had a talent for inviting themselves along. Charlie and Rainbow Zephyr had an impressive enough track record that the military probably checked up on them regularly, even when their lives were boring and quiet.

Maybe *especially* when their lives were boring and quiet.

Hayward gave my folks information or conferred with them on a regular basis. Sometimes the information related to protecting Neighborlee, rather than research our folks did for the military, or for their books. Since nothing had happened right away after the last time Hayward had contact with them, I just assumed … right that moment, I wasn't sure what I had been thinking last spring. A funny-sick feeling twisted through my gut. What if our folks had kept this development secret from us to protect us, or protect Neighborlee, or simply because they knew nearly a year ago that this particular path might turn out dangerous?

"What are you thinking?" Kurt murmured.

"The snake has been a little too quiet lately," I said, even more softly. We had Pete with us, after all. Yes, my little brother was a sophomore, but I still needed to protect him, even if he was taller than me. Sometimes I still saw the little boy who got thrown off the balcony over the river, by the guy who broke into his parents' flat in England, right after they died.

"You don't think it had anything to do with your folks ..." He sighed and gave me his apologetic little shrug.

"With the sabotage?" I sighed. I wasn't sure what sabotage I was thinking about. The recent nasty tricks inconveniencing me, or the slow, steady drain of energy from the protective field that surrounded Neighborlee? I was wishing we had a real dome, like Gordon had talked about. Wouldn't it be nice to just lock out the rest of the world, on a permanent basis? Funny thing, but even in that Stephen King TV show, the seal hadn't completely enclosed the town. The snake could still get at us. Its favorite tactic was to come up from below, after all.

I was just borrowing trouble, maybe? Low blood sugar, tired from the game, coming down from the high of performing my comedy, and all the weirdness piling up on me. Lots of things to blame for my funky feelings and thoughts as we finished pulling into the driveway.

Bottom line: when it came to my folks vanishing without any warning, or any threats or harm to or mystery surrounding the people I loved, I wasn't quite reasonable.

Of course, Pete and Harry would be the first to tell anyone who asked, and sometimes even people who didn't ask: I wasn't reasonable that often, anyway.

"Oh, heck," Pete groaned, after he got out of the truck and got close enough to the car to see that military sticker.

"My sentiments exactly."

"What?" Kurt slung my wheelchair out of the back and brought it over for me.

"The Colonel."

Kurt knew who I meant. He had met Hayward years ago. When we were kids, trying to contact our alien parents, on the off chance we really happened to be lost *alien* kids.

"He has some kind of news," I added, even though he hadn't asked for an explanation.

"You don't expect it to be good?"

"If it was good news," I said as I slid down into my chair, "Mum and Pop would be here themselves, not sending an advance man."

"Ah. Right." He pulled me backwards to navigate around a couple ridges of slush that had frozen solid again. "I don't suppose you'd consider the three of us taking a little flight down there ourselves, just to look around?"

"Unless you have some kind of stealth technology in your bag of tricks that Felicity can't zap, so we don't get shot down by the military of a couple different countries, I don't think that'd be a good idea. Besides, we've never tried long-distance flying. I don't want to find out what your limits are when we're over water."

"You've thought about this a lot, then." He walked backwards ahead of me as we went up the ramp. Pete had gone into the house already with his arms full of food. The order of priority was always hot food first, gimp second. My rules.

"Darn right."

Col. Hayward was in the family room with Harry when we came in through the kitchen door. He looked like anybody's very fit, active grandfather, with his iron-gray hair mussed by the stocking cap he'd left on the kitchen table. He wore a red plaid flannel shirt, baggy jeans, and hiking boots. He was sitting in the ratty, olive green recliner that only Felicity's dogs ever used. I wondered if Harry had thought to warn him, then decided he'd probably directed our guest into that chair. My brother had even less tolerance for the military than the rest of us.

Sometimes I suspected he carried a grudge that he wasn't conscious of, thanks to losing his parents through the work they did for the military. We still weren't sure if Harry's parents were dead or deep undercover or prisoners somewhere. Hayward had asked my folks to take Harry when he was seven and I was fourteen. Just like he had asked our family to take Pete, when his parents were killed ten years later.

The fact that Hayward wasn't in uniform meant he was here unofficially. Meaning either he came with information that wasn't supposed to be shared, or he intended to give us some comfort. News coming from a friend was easier to take than news from an official, or some such theory like that. Not that I subscribed to it. I wanted my bad news fast and short, like ripping a bandage off a wound.

"Good game," Hayward said, when we were all inside. He slid out of the recliner and paused to brush dog hair off the backs of his legs. Meaning he did know dogs used it. Maybe the joke was on us?

"You came to watch and decided to wait until now to talk?" I guessed.

"A gym full of screaming fans isn't the best place for an exchange of news." The warmth left his eyes, making me wonder if it had all been pretense a moment before.

"Exchange implies we have something you want to know," Kurt said.

Hayward's eyes narrowed, and I could almost hear him considering asking Kurt to leave, that this was a family matter, but he knew better. Kurt and Felicity were just as much a part of everything as Harry and Pete.

"The official story on your parents' disappearance is very different from the bits and pieces I've been allowed to tell you," he began, after a long, deep sigh he barely kept from being audible.

"Well, yeah," Harry muttered. He flashed Hayward a big, cheesy smile, stepped into the kitchen, and dropped down at the table. "Who's starved?"

"Did they go to the Bermuda Triangle, or was that a story they told us to distract someone who might be following them?" I had to ask. Blame the newspaper reporter in me.

"The Triangle has become such a cliché, it's one of the best cover stories anyone could ever come up with." He rubbed his face with his big, grandfatherly wide hands, and seemed to lose about ten degrees of tension.

When Pete shoved a plate across the table to an empty chair, by way of invitation, he nodded thanks and sat. Pete liked Hayward. I wondered sometimes if he knew that Hayward's wife was a relative of his mother, and that was why Hayward sent us to claim him, when his parents died. Family meant a lot to us Lost Kids, because the ones who belonged to us had been taken away so early. Kurt and Felicity considered my folks their parents, too, though I suspected they had never consciously thought of it. Bottom line: when my folks adopted me, they got Kurt and Felicity in the deal.

"Do you know why something becomes a cliché or an old wives' tale?" Hayward continued. "Because there's an element of truth in it. Something solid and real is at the bottom of it. Something that rings true." He shrugged. "There are enough verifiable cases of weirdness, for lack of a better term, attached to the Bermuda Triangle, to make it worthy of its reputation. At the same time, that reputation deflects most reporters and those suspicious folks who consider themselves too sophisticated to believe in such things."

"Which means?" I prompted, as I opened the nearest carton of food.

"Yes, they were investigating the Bermuda Triangle. The funny thing is, they were still miles away from what they determined was the 'active zone' when they vanished."

"So do we blame the Triangle, or someone who thought they were getting too close to something nasty?" Kurt said, his tone soft as he concentrated on spreading just the right thickness of hot mustard on his egg roll.

"I need to know what Charlie and Rainbow told you about their search, anything that they might have left out of their research papers we found at the site."

"We thought they were joking when they said where they were going." Harry looked back and forth between Pete and me. "We've talked about what we remember from those last two weeks before they left, but they were so busy arranging things, they didn't say much."

Pete and I made the required noises of affirmation. We weren't dummies; we were eating while the food was still nice and hot.

"So they never talked about a link between Neighborlee's Lost Kids and theoretical power grids spotted around the planet?"

Fortunately, I had already swallowed my mouthful of Kung Pao chicken, or I might have done a Mount Vesuvius across his nice plaid shirt. Considering he was on the other end of the table from me, the force required was just an indication of how his words startled me. The timing of this unexpected subject was a little too convenient, after the latest research trip Kurt had taken to find other abandoned children. He and I very carefully didn't look at each other.

"What about power grids?" Kurt asked.

Wouldn't it have been ironic, I mused, if the military and my parents were all working on the same questions that Kurt, Felicity and I had? What kept me silent about our search, or offering the information we had found so far, and our theories, was the certainty that we were coming at the question from different angles and had completely different uses for the information.

"Hot spots. Energy spikes at regular intervals. We've only been able to detect them in the last decade because we've only had the right equipment, sensitive enough, for that long. It's a long-term project, backtracking other possible energy spikes by coordinating occurrences of the meteorological phenomena patterns that seem to accompany them."

"So…there have been these spikes in Neighborlee?" Harry said slowly.

"Not a single spike. But interestingly — " Hayward tortured us by pausing to fill his plate. He had our attention enough that we slowed down eating while we waited. "The spikes have been charted at recurring spots often enough to detect a pattern. They're almost mathematically exact in their placement, and equidistant from a blank, circular territory almost two hundred miles in diameter." He tipped his head to one side, sliding into that cool, bemused expression that reminded me of Hannibal Lecter the first time he met Clarice. "Neighborlee sits in the exact center of that circle. Makes you think?"

"Fascinating," Harry drawled, doing his best imitation of Spock.

"So, what does that have to do with the Bermuda Triangle?" I had to ask. "Why would our folks go there, out of all the spots where the spikes occur? Except maybe they wanted to work on their tans at the same time?"

"There have been numerous theories that the Triangle is a gateway from another dimension. It has the strongest readings of all the energy spikes, consistently."

"So all the kids that show up in Neighborlee, you think they're from another planet, and they come through the Bermuda Triangle?" Pete snorted some more and slouched over his plate. He was one of the few people I knew who could laugh and shovel food down his throat simultaneously, and not choke.

"There's still not enough proof to convince me there's life on other planets. However, I've seen enough strangeness to believe in other explanations. All these lost children could have been caught up in a spike that occurred somewhere else on the planet," Hayward said with a calmness that nearly reached boredom. Like a well-rehearsed or often-considered explanation. Rehearsed why? To cover up something even more bizarre? "They could have been shuttled forward through time, for all we know. Some speculate time occurs in waves, not in a straight linear fashion."

"The spikes tear holes through the space-time continuum," Kurt offered.

"And the children fall through, to a place far in the future. Yes." Hayward actually looked pleased that someone had caught onto his idea. Maybe he was just pleased someone didn't mock it, first, before giving it serious consideration. "Even if 'far in the future' is only ten years or so, it would make identifying these displaced children nearly impossible. They would be the wrong age, younger than what searchers would expect, and in a place no one would expect them to be. Especially halfway around the planet."

"Is it possible for them to be yanked backwards in time?" I asked.

"Law of physics," Pete said, shaking his head. "Matter can't be two places at one time. The molecules that make up you, right now, were somewhere else fifty years ago." He grinned as he half-rose to snatch at the carton of pork fried rice and refill his plate. "Kind of gross when you try to make stuff co-exist in two different places at the same time."

"Oh, Mr. Science, you've seen it happen?" I gladly played along with the half-joking, half-serious talk. It gave me a chance to digest my most excellent dinner and let the theories Hayward had proposed sink in a little bit.

"Video games. In books. We were talking about it in science class last week." He shrugged, and managed to talk and eat without grossing us out or spraying across the table. Multi-talented, my little brother.

"Interesting science class. Or maybe more interesting teacher," Hayward said.

"Mrs. Shufflebaum was a Trekker since the first episode," Harry said. "She liked to get us to expand our minds, any way she could. She used to say, if you can't expand, you'll blow up someday, and that's a waste of a lot of potential. Or something like that. Then she'd go into a lecture about what a small percentage of the brain Humans actually use." He laughed. "You could add her to your think tank. Bet she'd get a kick out of it."

"Maybe." Hayward applied himself to his dinner, and there was blessed silence for about five minutes.

Well, as much silence as there can be with five adults eating really good, spicy Chinese with chopsticks.

"If you can remember anything your parents might have mentioned, if you can think of any other place they might have stored notes or research, we'd all appreciate it," Hayward said.

The duck sauce turned sour in my mouth as I silently groaned at the return to the subject that had brought him to our door in the first place. "Let me guess. You already searched their office at home." I put my chopsticks down before I broke one from clutching too tight.

They were my favorites, cobalt blue with Klingon symbols. Pop had bought them for me at a really big, eclectic Trek convention, a high school graduation present. Fans were capable of making anything and everything in honor of their passion, and the really smart ones made thing that were both useful and beautiful.

"The renters weren't too happy about our foray." He actually looked uncomfortable for a few seconds. "They didn't know the office was even there. We had to use three different keys that your parents had left in my care, to unlock the sliding panel. We decided the renters were a little too interested, so we emptied the room. As a precaution, of course."

"Of course."

"But why would they have left behind anything relevant to their investigation?" Kurt asked slowly, just as slowly raising his frowning gaze from a spot in the center of the table to meet Hayward's gaze. "Why wouldn't they have taken all their notes with them?"

"A smart man makes backups of any important information or research," the Colonel said with a shrug. "Charlie Zephyr is one of the smartest men I know. The only person smarter is Rainbow."

"People that smart are usually called insane," Pete grumbled. That got grins from us, but not the laughter I could tell he wanted. Too much tension had already built up to allow that, despite the lingering aromas of Chinese and the post-game exhaustion catching up with us all.

"Do you want us to look through those files?" I asked, unsure if he was going to ask us to do it. Unsure if we wanted to do it.

Well, it was an excuse not to write my *Terry* column for next week. *Sorry, Evil Overlord, I'm busy with a job for the government. Hush-hush. If I tell you what it is, I have to kill you.*

Oh, if only…

"When we're done. A lot of it is review of things they've done for us, or in conjunction with us. We might find some clues to this new theory of theirs. Letting you sit and think for a few weeks — "

"Months," Harry offered softly, his grin sharp-edged, daring Hayward to prove him wrong.

"The delay before you look at it might give you a new perspective," Hayward said, nodding. "You could very well find something we missed. Fresh eyes."

"Just because they're our folks doesn't mean we understand them," Pete offered. "Hey, for all we know, their joke isn't a joke at all, but the truth. Wouldn't that be cool? Maybe they were out in the Bermuda Triangle in the 60s and got hit with a time spike or energy spike or whatever, and ended up in the quarries here in Neighborlee, twenty years into the future. Maybe they're trying to find their way home again?"

"Maybe they're from another planet," Harry said.

"We won't really know until we find their research notes, will we? Or they show up and we can ask them."

For some reason, he looked at me when he said it. What made him think I had the answers?

~~~~~

I couldn't put it off anymore. Saturday morning, I went to see John Stanzer, Neighborlee's resident private investigator. He attended our church, helped coach the summer sports leagues, and had bought and was renovating the six-story building where he had his office. Nice, but not too remarkable. That just about summed him up: nice, but not remarkable. I could never decide if that amused me or irritated me. Shouldn't a private investigator be unusual in some way, have some quirks? At the very least, skulk around town in a trench coat and dark glasses? Stanzer was an average guy, nice-looking with his dark, curly hair and dark hazel eyes. He blended into crowds, probably what made him so successful. How could someone spy and get information and find out things people wanted hidden, if he made an impression of any kind? I imagined it could get kind of dangerous to be memorable, in his line of work.

The closest parking spot was around the corner on the opposite side of the street. Traffic had tripled in the retail/business district of Neighborlee, thanks to Christmas shopping season in full swing.
~~~~~

The long approach gave me time to think some more and study his building as I rolled up the sidewalk. The front room of his office was visibly empty from the street that morning. I rolled through the melting slush to cross the street to the sidewalk that he kept neatly shoveled and salted. A good landlord had to be responsible, right? I entered his office by rolling up the shallow cement slope that replaced the usual steps in front of store doorways in the rest of the town. Other store owners had installed basically plywood sheets on half of the wide, shallow steps to their doorways, as a token of compliance with the ADA. Stanzer going above and beyond had to say something about him. I smelled fresh coffee and heard saxophones playing softly somewhere at the back of the office, but no Stanzer.

From the corner of my eye, I saw *something* move. A blue and black flash, there and gone again. That reminded me of the winkies I had seen at Divine's, but nowhere else in town. Angela said they liked me, and they were watching out for me, even if they couldn't really do anything. Outside of Divine's, they had no power other than to watch. Knowing I was being watched … well, honestly, I had other things on my mind. Knowing something friendly was watching, yeah, that made me feel good. Even though they couldn't really do anything, if I was in trouble.

In that moment when I thought about it, I decided the feeling that came with the flash was very different from the spark of the winkies. I looked around, trying to feel for some sense of energy, though most of the time that awareness of energy was more Kurt's thing than mine. I had been running a little on edge with the weirdness of the last week. More than the usual background weirdness of Neighborlee.

Nothing and no one there. The office was empty of all people except for me. I shivered, with that sense of having been looked at, just momentarily, by something big and dangerous and amused. Definitely not the winkies. I had learned back in the orphanage, before I realized I was different, to trust my instincts. God had given me some sense, some ability to read the mental and emotional atmosphere, even before I could pick up glimpses into people's thoughts.

When my gut instinct said something was there in Stanzer's office, something big and dangerous, something that *liked* me, I didn't argue with those impressions. I didn't have to like what my gut instincts were telling me, but that didn't mean they weren't reliable. After all, who wants to know they *amuse* something big and strong, with pointy teeth?

Respect, please. Don't look at me like I'm a cute little kid, knee-high, with bandaged knees and jelly on one cheek.

It crystallized for me in that moment: this was why Stanzer's office, and sometimes his presence, made me itch where nothing could scratch. This was that subliminal something that made me hesitate to even consider asking him for help with my folks, now that they were officially missing. This sense that he had his weird, unnatural secrets, too.

I know. It didn't really make sense, all of us "strange and unique" folks, keeping our secrets and having friendly truces, but never asking the necessary questions and joining forces.

Maybe the problem was that Kurt and Felicity and I had learned early, without needing to be told, that we should hold our differences close to the chest, so to speak, and not confide in anyone outside of the small circle of the guardians. Different was dangerous, even when there were other "different" folks around who might just be valuable allies. Other than Angela, of course. Only someone with a death-wish discounted Angela and Divine's Emporium, and tried to work around them.

Maybe I had seen too many B movies about dangerous, psychotic freaks from parallel universes and far distant planets. If I found out I really was from another planet, sent to hide on Earth, I probably wouldn't trust myself anymore, either.

Another barricade was knowing that Stanzer wasn't from Neighborlee. Not in the same sense we Lost Kids were "natives" since our earliest memories. Stanzer had moved to our town about five years before.

"Hey, Lanie." Stanzer came out of the back room with two oversized mugs. Both steamed, one jet black and the other foamy brown.

He probably saw me coming down the street, but it still surprised me that he had made hot chocolate for me, without even asking. Nice surprises were just fine in my book. Mostly because I had had so few of them lately.

"My hero." I peeled off my slightly slushy gloves and stuck

them in the mesh pocket on the side of my chair, where they could drip and dry a little before I put them in my backpack and put on another dry pair. Every year, I swore I would get industrial strength, water-repellent winter gloves that wouldn't go to shreds after a little rough handling. Every year, I stuck with the same tough-but-absorbent brand. They protected my hands from the ice and salt of Neighborlee's streets and sidewalks in the winter, and that mattered more than being dry, quite frankly. Besides, I usually carried four pairs in my saddlebag or backpack when I left the house. It wasn't like I was inconvenienced.

Able-bodied people never fully appreciated the convenience of shoes to handle the gunk and wet on the ground during the winter. Maybe they would if they had to walk on their hands all day.

Stanzer gave me the mug, and we sat and sipped in comfortable silence for a few moments.

"Harry called again, said you had a visitor Friday. Good game, by the way." He didn't quite wear a smirk, but that sparkle in his eyes showed that I had reacted a little to his comment. Actually, it startled me more that he had been to the game, not that he knew about Hayward's visit. I never said I was logical, did I?

"He didn't tell you what our visitor wanted?"

"Said he was already in enough dirt for hiring me in the first place." Stanzer put his mug down and shoved his old-fashioned wooden swivel chair back a few creaky inches, then put his feet up on that pull-out board that had become useless once computers replaced typewriters.

"The thing about Harry is that he's usually right. He just doesn't go about it the right way all the time." I cradled my mug under my chin, warming my hands and giving myself a chocolate steam facial at the same time. It felt good after the chilly, damp wind that blew straight into my face on the way to Stanzer's door.

"So, Bermuda Triangle. Truth or dodge?"

"Unbelievably, it might just be the truth. We're talking a SyFy expose. Mum and Pop… they've connected some meteorological or electro-magnetic or whatever phenomenon to the mystery of abandoned children appearing in Neighborlee."

Stanzer lost his relaxed, friendly look. Not in a blink, but rapidly enough I saw his eyes widen and his neck straighten and his shoulders pull back. A little color seeped from his cheeks and around his mouth, not that easy to detect under several days' worth of stubble. He wasn't following the unkempt stereotype of the rough-and-tumble P.I. He was growing a beard for the Christmas play at our church. I pulled back mentally and catalogued everything I saw.

"How do you fit into the mystery of all the kids who appear here?" I said, when only a few seconds had passed and we just sat there, looking at each other while jazz played from the back room. "Speaking as one of the Lost Kids, I kind of have a right to know." I bared my teeth in a teasing grin, to take away some of the threat.

Yeah, as if showing all my teeth *wasn't* a threat? Too late, I wondered if I had anything stuck in my teeth, to ruin the impression.

"I don't. But I'm doing an ongoing investigation that has similar characteristics." He ended with a crooked little twist of his lips. "If I can learn something from what's been going on in Neighborlee for the last hundred years, maybe it'll help my own investigation."

"Uh huh."

"Don't you go all reporter on me, Lanie." He relaxed back to his former slouch with a chuckle. "You and I have just as much invested in keeping this thing quiet until we get the information we want. Harry told me your military connection can be trusted, but not too far. Neither of us wants powerful, unfriendly forces to get involved in the mystery, do we?"

"So, coming at this from your own investigation, you think there might be some validity to tying the Bermuda Triangle into my folks' disappearance?"

"Why the Bermuda Triangle? Why not Stonehenge or the temple pyramids at Chichen Itza?"

"We don't have their notes, so we can only guess. Something tied into the regular bursts of the electromagnetic-whatsis phenomena." I shrugged and took a big gulp of the chocolate, now at the perfect temperature for drinking. Stanzer invested in the good chocolate, not the pseudo-chocolate powder in little paper packets, more sugar and food coloring than anything else.

"You know anything you say here is fully confidential. I even have a white noise machine I can turn on, if you're worried about being recorded."

"Hail, hail, James Bond."

"Please. I prefer Q. Or better yet, that inventor monk from *Van Helsing*."

We shared a grin. I took another big gulp of chocolate, then a deep breath, and proceeded to tell him about our visit from the military on Friday night. Halfway through, Stanzer raised a hand for me to stop, and went into the back room to make us more coffee and chocolate. His attention to little details like that convinced me that Harry was right to involve him. We could trust Stanzer to find our folks and not turn it into a media circus.

"On a mission to prove wonder and mystery remain in the world, without violating a belief in God," he mused, after I had finished by giving him thumbnails of all the different research projects that had taken my folks into trouble and adventure for the last forty years.

"They've had their lives and ours threatened by weirdoes trying to recruit them as high priests or as supporters of their high-tech cons, or stop them debunking whatever is making them rich or powerful or both. This time—" My voice caught, which surprised me. "This time I'm worried they've really gone over the edge, into something more real than usual. And because it possibly involves the Lost Kids, I feel like it's my fault. Even though they'd be the first to laugh and then scold me for being vain."

"The biggest mysteries are the ones that are closest to us, that we can't solve no matter how much we know," he said, his voice going soft, his eyes losing focus. I knew he referred more to his particular investigation than mine. Despite being just a sports reporter—and ugh, yes, a lovelorn advice columnist—the reporter in me itched to get at the story he hid.

"What if it turns out we *are* from another planet, that it's not just a joke to explain something pretty nasty and cold? What are we, the place where every endangered planet sends their kids?"

Something flashed blue in the corner of my eye again, and this time I turned fast enough to see something like an electric spark, like the after-image of something big vanishing. I turned my head in time to see Stanzer staring at the same corner of the room where I thought I had seen that something. He kept staring, with his lips pressed together so tightly, the skin was white around them. He hadn't laughed at my unusually lame joke.

I reached across the desk and touched the back of his hand. A blue spark shot between us, but despite the zing, his skin felt cold. I lost my breath as an image smacked through my head, leaving a headache in its wake. That rarely happened anymore. I saw *blue lightning and enormous black dogs with silver and blue sparks for eyes, and rows of sharp, sparkling teeth.* I saw *children falling through darkness, guarded or herded by the dogs.* I saw the thin lines of scars on Stanzer's wrists spark blue, just for a moment. With gut-tightening certainty, I knew the scars had come from the teeth of those dogs.

I withdrew my hand again, before I saw more. No need to overdose on mystery, right?

"The other explanation," I said, managing to keep my teeth from chattering, "is that we're a dumping ground for every planet to get rid of its mental defectives. That actually sounds a whole lot more plausible."

"I've heard that one, too." Stanzer's crooked grin looked more genuine than mine felt.

Right then, I decided to leave his mystery alone. It was enough to know he was on our side.

I gave him what information I had: hotel contact info, the dates my folks arrived on the island, the credit card bills for their expenses so far (I was on their bank account, to take care of all the bills) the plane tickets, what they had told us about their trip and people they had talked to during their first few check-in calls. Mum and Pop had even given me the first rough outline for a proposed book they had dreamed up on the plane trip, so I could write it up and have the foundation laid and reduce the work that needed to be done, when they returned.

They hadn't told us anything about their search for energy bursts that tied into the Lost Kids, or the big blank spot marked out by the spikes of power. Why hadn't they trusted us with that insight into the truth behind their research project?

Maybe they hadn't told us because they knew someone was listening? Maybe they dreamed up the new book, and lied about the research trip, to distract someone who was getting too close to the truth?

# Chapter Seven

I flashed to those glimpses through the years of the dark van and the dark car and the mysterious people who had sporadically visited Neighborlee—and the boy and the girl who had vanished from Neighborlee Children's Home at the same times those people had been spotted. What were their names again? Kurt would know. Or we could ask Mrs. Silvestri. If the Grandstones might be involved in Lost Kids vanishing, and turning other Lost Kids bad and essentially destroying all their potential for good, was it possible they were part of the danger that made my folks vanish?

If Sylvia Grandstone was in town, and I wasn't just hallucinating from stress, should she be worried that I might just turn her into a living bowling pin next time I saw her, and go supersonic with my wheelchair? Or maybe give myself a stroke, snatching her up with all my telekinetic power and slamming her into the nearest brick wall? And that was just for starters.

I didn't have any sense of impending doom, but that wasn't as much comfort as it should have been. Maybe my rising sense of frustration and of being left out of things kept that particular emotion down.

Bottom line: our folks were missing and might not make it home for Christmas. From an emotional point of view, it was the end of the world.

~~~~~

I got to relax a little during Sunday school the next day. It wasn't my week to be the teacher. Brian Welks had the lead teacher job that week, and augmented the lesson plan with the VeggieTales video, *Where is God When I'm Scared?* Not that the kids didn't love it and sit enraptured through the whole performance. They had probably seen the episode several dozen times already, between the church's daycare program and most of them owning every video and DVD.

The song, *God is Bigger Than the Boogie-Man*, kept running through my head for the rest of the day and made it hard to draw on my inner snark to work on my next installment of the *Terry*
~~~~~

column for the Evil Conglomerate. So I didn't work on it.

Harry had cooking duty for lunch after church, so he took Pete and me to a restaurant just over the border in Hadley. Nice place, with ramps to different levels of the building that used to be a warehouse/factory, lots of video games, and carnival games I was never tempted to use my telekinetic ability to win. The food was good, not too much grease, and the aisles were wide, so I never had to worry about navigating around people's chairs.

Gordon and his girlfriend, Mandy, came in just after we ordered. Mandy's real name was Hortense, thanks to family tradition, but a girl tall enough to be Gordon's girlfriend and not shatter when he hugged her was more appropriate to be named Brunhilda. I liked her too much to suggest such a thing. They were nearing their one-year anniversary of dating, and I wondered if she was hoping to get a ring for Christmas. Gordon smiled a lot more than I was used to seeing, and that might have been a warning sign right there.

They left the restaurant about the same time the boys and I did, and the five of us hung around in the slushy parking lot, enjoying the sunny weather and illusion of warmth for about twenty minutes. Most of our conversation revolved around plans for our Star Trek club's Christmas party. Since I was Commodore and both of them were officers and we only had three weeks left until the party, at Mandy's house, it would have been odd if we *hadn't* talked about it. We really didn't get much of anything accomplished, other than cutting a few items off the do-list, and griping about the grief our former communications officer was still wreaking on the club after going batso-wacko. After a while Gordon had to get to work on the afternoon shift.

Later, I decided that chance meeting and lingering in the parking lot wasn't by chance or coincidence. Looking back, I was pretty sure it was just another small example of God looking out for me.

Less than an hour after we got home, and while I still worked up the gumption to read the next idiotic request for advice from *Terry*, Gordon called. Someone had called the police station while we were in the parking lot at the restaurant and reported that I had just tried to run over a bunch of kids playing in the snow fort that extended into the street near my house. Fortunately, the dispatcher who took the call was my neighbor, Makenzie. She knew the kids who built the snow fort and called them, to get their side of the story. Gunther, the older boy, was a car freak and knew my Jeep well. When Makenzie asked if my Jeep had run over their melting snow fort, Gunther just laughed. Then he got mad, because being the smart thirteen-year-old that he was, he realized what someone tried to do to me.

Yes, according to him, a dark green Jeep had hit the snow fort, but it was four years newer than mine and didn't have the "My other car is a TARDIS" sticker halfway scraped off the bumper. Gunther had been outside scraping an inch of slushy ice from the driveway and saw the whole thing. The other kids who claimed ownership of the snow fort had been indoors at the time of the "accident," so no one was hurt.

Gordon provided my alibi, if no one believed a thirteen-year-old's testimony. The problem was, either someone who knew my ride well enough had jumped to conclusions when the green Jeep hit the snow fort, or someone had gone to some effort to frame me for something nasty. Someone who didn't know my Jeep down to the nth detail, who didn't know my schedule or where I should be on Sundays, maybe? Someone who knew I wasn't home, and thought they'd catch me during a time I couldn't alibi?

Scary, to say the least.

The same guy who slashed my tires? Maybe the same guy who tried to get into the house, and had set off Felicity's dogs?

For a while after Col. Hayward's visit, I had thought maybe my enemy was just a local loony trying to track down Mum and Pop. Maybe someone who was ticked that they didn't want to investigate something he found fascinating, and trying the "irritate them until they see my version of logic" routine. Trying to frame me for wanton destruction turned things a little more serious.

I knew all the kids on our street, so the assault on their snow fort made me angry. What if the idiot hadn't been paying attention when he drove through the fort, and someone *had* been inside one of the tunnels or hiding behind a slightly melted ice wall? Someone could have been badly hurt, and someone else had tried to place the blame on me.

Gordon and Makenzie both promised to spread the word to look for the other dark green Jeep around town, and told me not to worry. They would put a good word in with the chief for me. Not that I worried about Chief Tanner. He was more likely to laugh at such a claim, and then get angry on my behalf.

All that gave me a good excuse for not working on my *Terry* column that evening. Too distracted, right? Not that Daniel Sheridan would take that kind of an excuse. I got to work anyway.

*Dear Terry:*

*What do I get my girlfriend for Christmas? She's impossible to shop for. On her birthday, she said she wanted to go see "Cats" at Playhouse Square. That's the dumbest idea, so I knew she really didn't want it. That show has been to Cleveland five times already. Time to get a new script, you know? I got her a deluxe carwash kit, with the hard wax and the tar remover and bucket. She nearly hit me with it.*

*For Valentine's Day last year, she said she wanted a gift certificate to a bookstore, because there was a new book she wanted to read. I knew she was making it up, because she'd rather be with me than read. So I got her a gift card to Frederick's of Hollywood. She wouldn't talk to me for a week. Then she got made when I bought us tickets to the WWE exhibition. She said she got that book anyway, and she wanted to read it. Why would she want to read a stupid romance when she could go to the wrestling matches with me?*

*What is wrong with her? She wants to go see "The Nutcracker." Ballet is stupid and nobody in their right mind likes it. I told her so. She told me to go for a long walk off a short pier for Christmas, and never call her ever again.*

*I know she's just joking around, because she's crazy in love with me. Should I get her the Dirt Devil portable so she can help me clean my car, or a subscription to Sports Illustrated? I figure, the swimsuit issue will inspire her, you know? Finally wear a bikini for me. She's kind of dumb, really slow figuring out how to make me happy. But I figure, I should cut her some slack, because she loves me.*

*You're a woman, right? So tell me what she really wants. I'm ready to go nuts, trying to figure her out. How can I get her a great present if she won't tell me the truth?*

*Confused and Abused in Medina*

*~~*

*Dear Confused:*

*You're not the one being abused!*

*Read my lips: Women know what they want. Women don't say one thing when they mean another. (Unless they're politicians.) Except when you're being stupid and selfish. If she says she wants a book, that does not mean, "Buy me a gift card to a smut store to make YOU happy." When she's furious or bursts into tears, you ask, "What's wrong?" and she says, "Nothing," that's the only time she's not telling the truth.*

*The truth would scare you: you're nothing to her now. You ignore her, and then claim she won't tell you what she wants.*

*Here's the scoop: Asking a woman what gift she wants scores you points. It implies you want to make her happy. Points because you're asking for help. Points because you know you need to get her something.*

*But when you toss out what she told you she wanted and you get her something YOU want, that turns all your points negative. You're trying to change her to please you, when you refuse to do anything to please her.*

*The best gift you can give her now is silence. Vanish. Stay out of her life. You've insulted her multiple times by mocking her choices. When she told you to take a long walk off a short pier, she wasn't talking about some place in Florida, baby. She wants you taking a permanent swim in Lake Erie. NOW.*

*If your EX girlfriend is reading this: Honey, get out of town. Treat yourself to a couple days at a spa. Sit in front of the fire and read. Relax! You're at the breaking point, and I don't want you to go to jail for murder.*

*Dump the loser before he turns you into a loser. If you keep giving him another chance, he'll just drag you down to his level. Ignore the moronic lesson from "Grease." You should never remake yourself to please some guy. No guy is worth lowering your I.Q. and your standards.*

*Guys, if a woman tells you what she wants for Christmas, get it for her! No questions or exchanges. If your idea of a great gift is vastly different from hers, maybe you shouldn't be together in the first place. True love means listening.*

*Terry*

"Umm..." Pete sat back and put the printout of my column

down on my desk. "So, Lanie, what do you want for Christmas?"

"Besides Mum and Pop back home, with great tans and weird stories?" I fought not to grin, because there was real fear in his eyes. That was what he got for coming home from school early and asking how my column had turned out.

"No, really." He jumped when the phone rang.

"That'll be the Evil Overlord." I made no move to answer the phone. I checked my watch. "Man, he reads fast."

"You think he read your column already?"

"It was due at 3, and it's 3:20. He chose that jerk's question for this week's column, so I know he's interested in seeing me verbally flay Mr. Confused and Abused. Honestly, do the morons choose those labels, or does the main office assign them to protect the clueless and guilty?"

The answering machine clicked.

"Lanie, another great column." Sheridan's voice sounded suspiciously like he was fighting not to laugh.

"That's another five bucks Felicity owes me. I showed her the bozo's letter before she left with Jake. She was sure that what I had planned would get me fired," I muttered.

The Evil Overlord continued, saying something about letters from readers and the avalanche of positive reactions to my last two slightly scathing columns.

"You *want* to get fired?" Pete grinned now, obviously over his fright.

"I just want to be free of these idiots who don't even have the sense to realize they're mortally embarrassing themselves in public." I had to laugh, though. "Remember my first column, about the girl with the boyfriend who didn't spend any time with her?"

"He had a sweet deal going, but he messed it up." Snickering, he skipped back out of my reach. I did a mind-yank and a book did a backflip off the shelf next to the door and bopped him across the back of his head. Pete just grinned and bent to pick up the book.

"I heard she told everybody at her job about my response to her letter, all upset that I wasn't on her side. Then the boyfriend heard about it and told her in front of witnesses that she wasn't his girlfriend. He comes over because he likes her brothers' video game console. *Then* he was stupid enough to ask what she was making for him for dinner that night. In front of those same witnesses." I finished shutting down my computer.

"I bet all he got was a knuckle sandwich."

"And worse. From her brothers. They didn't realize the guy was leading her on until they read it in the paper. They're oblivious morons, but they do care about their sister."

"Not as much as I care about my big sister." Pete dropped to one knee and spread his arms like some melodrama hero.

"Uh huh." I held onto my skeptical look for about five seconds. Then we both burst out laughing.

"I still need to know what you want for Christmas."

~~~~~

Tuesday was a full day, meeting deadlines for the *Tattler* and then going straight from work to the high school for Pete's wrestling tournament. It promised to be a very late night, and I seriously contemplated not going into the office the next morning.

Neighborlee High had a chance of placing in the Lake Erie League this year. Even though I wasn't on the sports beat anymore, I wouldn't have missed the match for anything. I sat in my usual spot at the foot of the bleachers, behind the home team's bench, and heckled the wrestlers, like usual. Ricky Leone was the coach and taught science at the high school. We were friends, and had come pretty close to dating a few times during my first year as a teacher. Nothing like being heavily involved in school activities to crush any chance at a love life.

This would be my first sporting event that I could watch as a spectator, rather than as a reporter. I could cheer for someone and not worry that some snarky sports parent (worse than stage parents, from what I'd heard) would accuse me of favoritism, focusing on one player over their darling little star athlete.

I didn't know the lone reporter assigned by the Evil Conglomerate, who had the unenviable task of reporting the stats for all eight schools at the tournament. He looked frazzled, especially when at least three coaches showed a tendency to walk away or get involved in other conversations every time the poor guy approached. I wondered what was up, because no one had ever done that to me. My theory was that they didn't know he was the new reporter, and they were waiting for me to wheel on around the perimeter of the gym to get my data. That theory went up like the H-bomb when Coach Winslow, from Darbyville, sauntered over to
~~~~~

shake Ricky's hand after Pete pinned Winslow's man, and he stayed to talk to me.

"We don't like it at all," Winslow said in his trademarked molasses-and-gravel voice. "Just ain't fair, taking away what you're good at." Then he grinned, displaying those three gold teeth I had never gotten up the courage to ask about. "We figure, dig in our heels enough, they'll give you back to us."

It made me feel good to realize the coaches were angry on my behalf. And a few seconds later, the guilt and stringent code of ethics Mum and my Sunday school teachers had drilled into me took over, wiping away that greedy little bit of pride. It wasn't that reporter's fault he got assigned my beat. It wasn't right that the coaches made his job hard. He was probably a very good sports reporter, back at whatever paper had been his home base, and he probably wished he was back there.

"It's not his fault he's here," I told Coach Winslow. "Cut the guy some slack, okay?"

It was hard saying those words, even though they were true. I wanted someone to be unhappy doing my job, so maybe I could get it back. At the same time, I knew that wasn't about to happen.

Funny thing was, I actually grumbled, silently, as I wheeled around the perimeter, going to the various teams' benches, gathering up the stats and other media kit data from the coaches. Didn't I come tonight to watch and cheer for my brother and just relax? How come my plans kept getting turned inside out all the time? I couldn't just sit there and enjoy the tournament while the new guy on my beat struggled to do his job. I wasn't made that way. Besides, I wanted the story to be good, because Neighborlee had a better-than-usual chance of dominating at this match.

Come to think of it, my overwhelming sense of responsibility was what got me into this wheelchair in the first place.

Still, it was nice catching up with old friends. Traveling from bench to bench gave me an excuse to do it. And of course, my wheelchair was a passport that got me through "enemy territory" without challenge. I kind of enjoyed the feeling of having Moses' power to part the waters, because who wanted their shins rammed with footrests, or to look like an insensitive jerk for getting in the poor crippled girl's way? At least, that was the way it went until I got to one coach who had always been a pain to work with. He maintained women didn't have the genetics to understand the "ultimate, manly sport of wrestling," much less write about it. He was happy to have the new guy covering my beat. There's no pleasing everybody, is there?

"You are saving my life," Frank, the reporter said, when I handed him the paperwork he hadn't been able to track down yet. He was a little surprised, and confused, until I explained who I was. "I guess there's a lot of loyalty around here, huh? Hope I earn it before I get transferred to a new beat."

"Well, this is my hometown, that might be part of it," I offered.

"Hey, can I buy you a coffee? Do you need a ride home?" He took a step back and looked over my wheelchair. "Does that thing fold up?"

"Yes, it folds up, and I drove myself, but thanks." I had to swallow hard to keep from laughing at his surprise. Another person who just assumed that people in wheelchairs were totally helpless.

It was going to take generations to educate the Able-Bodied World. And by that time, gimps would have taken over completely, so that would be a lot of effort wasted.

It was a good night. Pete smeared his man, the Neighborlee High Pikes came in second and moved higher in the standings in the Lake Erie League, and I made a new friend who laughed when my tongue slipped and I referred to Sheridan's company as the Evil Conglomerate. Frank promised not to say anything to his co-workers or the higher-ups in the company, and suggested a mutual support pact among all the displaced and rearranged reporters. That suited me just fine.

I felt pretty good. Until I got home and found three messages on my answering machine from my credit card companies. People were trying to make major purchases on my accounts and they wanted to verify that I wasn't in foreign cities I'd never heard of, spending Euros like they were water. I knew the phone calls were scams. The callers said, "your credit card," and didn't identify which card. Plus I only had two credit cards, not three. Instead of calling the phone numbers left by the callers, I dug out my paperwork and called the customer service departments.

Unfortunately, I was right and wrong. Two calls were scams, but the third was legitimate. Somebody in Jamaica was trying to enjoy a vacation on my credit card, prepaying for a luxury suite, boat rental, scuba rental, and a party for about one hundred people. I put a stop to that in a hurry.

Listening to my gut instinct, I got online and did some work on my credit card accounts, making sure nothing weird was going on. One credit card was used strictly for online purchases, and I contacted customer service to notify them of what was happening with my other card. I made good use of the "contact us" blank email field, to list the companies I usually did business with online, and ask them to question any purchases from companies not on that list.

Before I shut down my computer for the night, a message popped into my mailbox from customer service, acknowledging my email. They informed me someone had contacted them, claiming to be me, wanting to change every detail of my account, including passwords and mailing address. There was no response to the security questions sent per protocol, and they assured me no changes would be made without the proper passwords and security questions.

Somebody was out to get me. Why? Maybe our whole family was the target? The Grandstones had a long-standing grudge against us, starting with my folks buying the farm they wanted. Somehow it was our fault that the original owners wouldn't lower their asking price by more than $50,000 to convenience Grandstone Orchards' plans to expand their holdings. Also, Mum and Pop had been involved in foiling a number of attempts by Grandstones over the years to falsely claim various buildings and properties in Neighborlee had been illegally taken from them.

It was too easy to try to blame the Grandstones for most of our problems. I needed to stop automatically doing that. Even if evidence was mounting that yes, the Grandstones *were* out to get everyone in our town.

I rolled down the hall to Harry's bedroom to tell him to get busy checking his credit and bank accounts. Then I saw his empty bed and remembered he was out of town on an overnight haul. Sighing, I got out my cell phone to call him. Better that he be awakened now to protect himself, than to check out of his hotel in the morning and find out he couldn't pay for it because his credit card was frozen or reported as stolen.

It was after 1am before I could get to bed. I was so riled up over things, my mind spinning over implications and theories, I forgot to say my bedtime prayers.

Not a smart thing to do.

~~~~~

Friday night after my comedy gig, Felicity, Kurt and I came home to find all the lights off in the house and the yard frighteningly quiet. The dogs were nowhere to be seen. A sure sign of trouble? The newest invention from Kurt's demented brain was supposed to turn *on* all the lights in the house if someone tried to break in while we were gone. Those two anomalies happening at the same time made me wish I could get out of my chair and run around, to work off my sudden burst of nervous energy.

We didn't have much choice in what we did next. Felicity would work herself into a major electromagnetic burst that could kill all the computers and flat-screen TVs on the street if we didn't find those dogs, and fast. Pete and Harry came home from a basketball game while Felicity and Kurt helped me slide from the Jeep to my chair. They teamed up, going around the house from one side while we went in through the gate and started around the house from the other side. Thanks to the snow that had been falling since that afternoon, any intruder footprints were wiped out. I suspected the snowfall and knowing his tracks would be covered up had given the intruder the courage to strike.

Felicity found her dogs before we had gone more than ten feet into the side yard. They lay curled up together in a snowdrift in the gap between the house and the garage apartment, half-covered with snow where their combined body heat didn't melt it. They were asleep. I knew they were asleep when I was five feet away, because those dogs snored. Kurt laughed just about the same moment I realized the dogs were snorting and wheezing and rumbling in almost perfect rhythm and harmony. We traded muffled grins while Felicity went to her knees, poking and shaking and muttering the dogs' names.

Those mutts didn't move, no matter how she shook them. Then Pete and Harry showed up with the big spotlight flashlight and we understood. Their bellies were round and tight. They had just eaten their biggest meal since Felicity killed the range two Thanksgivings ago, an hour into making dinner for twenty people. She was justified. Her boyfriend brought his *fiancée* to dinner.
~~~~~

"The only way somebody could get into the yard." Pete tapped Sheba's drum-tight stomach. I swore I heard a solid thud. "Bribery."

"Yeah, they're not dumb dogs, but their stomachs override common sense every time," Harry said. "Somebody came here prepared."

"Probably something in the food to make them sleep," Kurt added.

"That's something to be grateful for, I guess." Felicity struggled to her feet and wrapped her arms around herself.

"Grateful?" Pete said.

"That someone didn't poison her dogs, just put them to sleep for a while," I said.

There were times I didn't need to touch someone to tap into their thoughts, to know what they were thinking. I could see the fear and relief, and growing fury, in Felicity's eyes.

The next step was to go inside the house. Cautiously, of course. The lack of lights could mean we had an intruder, and the circuit breakers had all gone out when Kurt's burglar detector went into effect. Or all the circuit breakers had died for some other reason. Combine the drugging of Felicity's dogs with the fact she had spent the evening with me and couldn't have blown something in the house, and that left the intruder gambit.

Pete expected the computers to be gone. Harry worried about his business papers, especially the bank passbook and the little notebook with all his passwords and routes and contacts. I still felt too mellow from the combination of a really great evening at the comedy club and exhaustion to get beyond the irritated certainty we would find a gigantic mess strewn through the house.

Why did burglars have to make a mess all the time? Was it a way to leave their signature? Kind of like the Wet Bandits in *Home Alone*? My brand of logic said if they just took what they wanted and left things pretty much as the owners had them, a lot of robberies wouldn't be discovered until days later, thereby making it easier to sell whatever they had stolen before the police got a report circulated.

Then again, who ever said thieves used any sort of logic?

Or that my logic was anything like other people's logic?

# Chapter Eight

The door panel around the lock had scratch marks. Kurt examined the lock, probing a little with his gift for gizmos. No damage that he could detect, and everything was locked up as secure as I had left it four hours ago.

I handed him my keys. Felicity rested her hands on the handlebars of my chair, braced to yank backward and get me out of there if something went wrong. She had used that tactic too many times in truly dangerous situations, when we were on patrol, for me not to understand what she intended.

But honestly. Danger, in *my* house? What could she do, anyway, besides pull me away from whatever leaped out at us? *If* something was there, waiting to leap out at us. My sense for danger didn't wake up, so at the very least, I was assured of no bloodshed or broken bones in the near future.

Small comfort. There were a lot of ways to cause harm without physical assault. Thanks to the slowly dying defenses around Neighborlee, we had experience with nasty weirdness. Far too many negatively creative things that people coming in from other towns could do for revenge or curiosity or just plain thoughtlessness. It wasn't just on Senior Prank Night that people turned stupid and destructive. Some of the worst cruelty from outsiders came at Halloween, when college kids and high schoolers invaded, hunting down little kids with full bags of trick-or-treat goodies. We always had at least one incident every year, where a big football-player sized guy punched a little kid who could barely look him in the kneecap, because she wouldn't hand over her bag of candy. Or at Christmas, idiots would take bats to some of the 50,000 megawatt Christmas lights displays, and then claim it was their right to free speech, to express their disdain for the commercialism or whatever they had decided to protest about the holidays. So far, fortunately, no judge ever bought such a defense.

Kurt got the door open and shoved it aside while staying out on the doorstep. It banged softly against the coat tree/bench next to the door. Nothing creaked inside the house, no footsteps or echoes of something falling, and no skittering sounds of creepy-crawly, clawed things evading the light that spilled in from the spotlight over the door.

"Heck with this," Harry muttered, and nudged Kurt aside so he could go into the house. He walked out of the stream of light, into the darkness, and I heard him thump across the kitchen and around the corner to the utility room. I had the washer, dryer, furnace, water heater, and the control panel for Kurt's security system in that room.

"He's got a point," Kurt said.

We settled in the kitchen and shut the door. It had hung open too long, letting icy air into the house, and the furnace roared protest as it struggled to bring the indoor climate back to toasty.

"This is your house. It's kind of self-defeating to creep around, waiting for something to jump out at you."

The lights came on. I sucked in my breath as a new chill raced up my back.

The house was clean. Or at least as clean as I had left it. I could see down the hall to my office. The door hung open and my computer and all the rest of my equipment was still there on my desk in sloppy organization, just as I had left it. Nothing had been pulled from the kitchen cupboards, no messes on the floor, no broken dishes, no boxes and bags of food torn open and scattered around. In the dining room, the hutch with Mum's heirloom china and silver looked untouched. Someone else's heirlooms, granted, but she treasured them and refused to leave them in the farmhouse when they rented it out. A closer look showed no one had walked on the carpet since I vacuumed that afternoon. Unless the intruder vacuumed to hide his footprints?

Scary thought. Who wanted to be burgled by Felix Unger or the Happy Homemaker? Honestly, Betty White in all her incarnations scared me.

Pete got up and went to the family room. I didn't hear any exclamations, no banging, nothing falling. He came back a few seconds later, meeting Harry in the hall coming from the utility room.

"Nothing's gone. So what did the guy want?" he said.

"What makes you think it was a guy?" Felicity said. "Could have been a girl."

"Cat burglar who knows what she wants, gets in, gets it, gets out," Kurt said, nodding. "Maybe the lights going out scared them off before they could do anything?"

"I don't think so." Harry set the portable DVD screen/player combo down on the table. Kurt's security system included micro-miniature cameras all over the house, set to automatically activate when we left, with motion, heat, and smoke sensors. If the heat level changed drastically, or someone who didn't know the security code or carry the remote signal the size of a flash drive entered the house, the cameras automatically came on and caught everything that happened. There was even an infrared program that kicked in, with special filters on the cameras to catch what happened if the lights went out. Kurt must have expected a problem with the power system, to include that little detail. Plus his security system had its own power totally independent of the house. Just in case.

It took a few seconds to get the DVD player going. Felicity retreated to the door, where she could watch but her EM field wouldn't interfere with the machine if anything upset her. She was getting better at controlling her emotions, especially when she had warning, but better safe than sorry.

The camera showed Pete's bedroom window. From the light reflected off the snow, shadows were visible through the sheer curtains. His room actually looked livable, draped in shadows. A human shape crouched down in front of his window, outside. The rectangular silhouette was the old window opening outward. The curtains rippled, indicating heat flowing out and outside wind coming in. A few seconds later, a single dark figure dressed in camouflage gear, including ski mask and gloves, slid through the window, stepped onto the desk, then the chair, and to the floor. He looked back, and a second human shape handed a dark duffle bag to him through the window.

"How'd he get the window open without breaking it? Those old windows are pretty stiff, and they have those lever locks," Harry said, frowning at the screen.

"Umm…" Pete scooted his chair back a few inches and gave me that I-think-I-did-something-stupid, hope-I'm-too-cute-to-pound expression he had perfected in third grade. "I like to sleep with my window open. Maybe I didn't close it all the way when I left for school this morning."

"Enough of a gap to be noticeable, and to let the intruder get something in and wedge it open," Kurt said, nodding. He pressed the pause button on the player. "Go look."

Pete skidded down the hall. I heard his door creak open, and a thread of chilly air raced into the kitchen. That answered that question.

"The window's only about halfway closed. Nothing's broken. It's probably too stiff for them to close all the way, once they forced it," he reported when he came back, shoulders slumped. The sheepish look on his face made a real sheep look like a Phi Beta Kappa. "With the door closed, the thermostat didn't react."

"We have a smart cat burglar." I wanted to throttle Pete, but I really didn't have any right to be angry. I liked to have some fresh air when I went to bed, too. I usually opened my window to air out my room half an hour before I went to bed, but the window was always locked up tight again before I went to sleep. Pete liked to have chilly air on his face all night, while sleeping under a foot thickness of covers.

"So what did he want?" Harry said, as he reached to turn on the DVD player again.

The different cameras flickered into life, in infrared once the lights died in the main rooms of the house. They followed the intruder through our house. Sitting there in the lit, warm kitchen, I got a creepy, chilled, threatened feeling. Someone we didn't know (or worse, someone we *did*, who hid evil under a friendly face) had gone through my house without permission. Someone with a nasty enough agenda to drug Felicity's dogs. I didn't feel like a superhero in that moment. The only time I had felt less like someone with special God-given talents to help the helpless was when I woke up with my back shattered into a jigsaw puzzle.

I felt helpless and exposed, and unjustly targeted for attack. And since I didn't like feeling helpless, I got angry. And duh, through all that, I prayed. Not a nice prayer. Mostly along the lines of, *Please, God, help us find this crook so we can slap him around a little and stop him from doing this to other people.*

I paused for a big blob of satisfaction in the thought of slapping around the intruder.

Even superheroes had their flaws. One of mine happened to be a hunger for vigilante justice before I let the guys with the badges and training get their hands on the bad guys. That was why I enjoyed TV shows like *Stingray* or the *Lone Ranger* or *The A-Team*, where tough guys working outside the law made sure the real criminals got caught and victims got justice before the legal system stepped in and worked a little too hard for equal treatment on both sides. Making sure criminals got a decent defense just seemed like victimizing the victims a second time, and with taxpayer money.

"There." Kurt tapped the controls, freezing the blurry, off-color negative image of the burglar sliding something under the TV cabinet.

"What?" Felicity said, stepping out of her safe distance zone.

"Stop!" He glared at her, but with a flicker of laughter in his eyes. She made a face at him, then retreated to her safe spot again.

Kurt made the image move in slow motion, which didn't do much for the quality of the picture. We had to strain our eyes, but we could see every move our unwanted visitor made. Even with the slo-mo, the guy had the moves, smooth and sure. I felt a little more chilled, knowing this was someone with experience. Using it against me and my family.

What if this was someone looking for something my folks might have left behind? What if someone had kidnapped Mum and Pop to find out something they knew, and when my folks wouldn't tell them, expected the information to be in our house? Maybe they had watched the military search the farmhouse, and knew that whatever they wanted wasn't locked away in the hidden office in the basement. What was really frustrating was that Pete and Harry and I still couldn't remember anything unusual that might give us a clue. Mum and Pop weren't mysterious and secretive, by any means. It was more a tendency to forget to tell people important things, because they were caught up in whatever fascinated them, to the point of distraction. To the point of forgetting the everyday details, and not-so-everyday things. Like picking Pete up at the airport after a summer missions trip. Or getting distracted by a great idea on the way to the grocery store, and bringing home a trunk full of paving tiles for the patio instead of my birthday cake. Little things like that.

Speculations weren't helping the situation. I had to make a mental effort to put my theories and growing anger aside until we had something concrete to work on. I couldn't afford to get distracted and miss something vital right now, anyway.

On the DVD screen, we watched the intruder slide something into the dark recesses under the TV cabinet, where unused video games and broken VCR tapes had a habit of migrating and staying, now that my brothers were in the house. Why did guys have an allergic reaction to throwing something away when it broke? Yes, eventually they threw it away, but only after it sat for weeks, until someone tripped or ran over it, and broke it into smaller pieces.

The guy in the ski mask and camo could have been a guest in our house, judging from the ease with which he found the remote controls, the electrical outlets, and other items in the family room. He did something with two of the four remotes. With the image recorded in infrared, I couldn't tell if it was the DVD remote, the TV remote, the stereo system remote, or the gizmo Kurt had rigged for the main switch box. It tied everything together, so we didn't have to keep pushing switches or pulling plugs when we wanted to play on any of the four different ages and brands of video game consoles. Not that I played video games. The guys had brought all that junk with them when they moved in with me. Connecting it to my existing, simple system had wreaked unholy havoc with everything until Kurt came to the rescue.

"Okay, so he wants us to trigger whatever it is ourselves," Harry said, after we watched the sequence of the intruder's actions three times. From Pete's bedroom window to the family room, then out again through Pete's bedroom. No detours. Whoever it was didn't even try to take anything on his way out, which just made his actions a little scarier. This was no taking-advantage-of-an-empty-house burglar. "We know where it is, but what does it do?"

"Do we want to really know?" Felicity said. "Just kill it and then try to figure it out afterwards."

"She's got a point." Kurt grinned, got up from the table, and bowed, gesturing for Felicity to go ahead of him.

The rest of us were right behind them. As far as we could tell, the intruder hadn't installed any spy-eyes of his own, to watch the results of his dirty work. For all we knew, the box he put under the TV and linked to the remotes was there to watch us. Why? What did he want to learn about us? Did we have any enemies who wanted to get inside information on us before they struck? And just what vital information could they learn, watching from under the

TV? Wouldn't they get more info from my office?

Which of us was the intruder after? Why the TV, and not some more strategic spot in the house? I couldn't imagine the guy in camo wanted Pete's inside secrets to winning antique video games. Who would be expected to spend most of their free time in front of the TV at our house? Our camouflaged enemy didn't know any of us very well, to expect us to be couch potatoes. If anyone was expected to vegetate in our house…

One of my lamest jokes echoed through my head: *My friends call me Cauliflower. I'm their favorite white vegetable.*

How often did I complain about people who assumed since my legs didn't work, my brain had turned to mush?

Did someone expect to find something out about me, in particular, by setting up a spy-eye under the TV? Did they think watching the screen was all I could do, when I was at home? What could they hope to find?

I must have made a noise when the next nauseating thought hit me, because Felicity turned around, eyes wide, and the old-style floor-to-ceiling light pole next to the door flickered. Kurt was already on his knees in front of the TV. He looked back over his shoulder, his gaze locked with mine, and his expression hardened.

"What?" he demanded, and leaped to his feet and to my side in only two steps.

"The ones who took the other kids," I said. "What if they're onto us, and they want to watch us for a while before they act?"

Kurt thought for about five seconds, his jaw working, the muscles in his throat clenching like he might be sick or let loose a stream of utterly impressive profanity. He could do it, too, with enough power to have physical effects on the object of his disgust. We could never figure out if that was a trick he had accidentally borrowed from me, or it was one of his inborn gifts, because he had only telekinetically knocked that one drug-hopped child molester off the terrified trick-or-treater, and never did it again.

"Mistress Felicity," he growled, and bowed so deep his fingers touched the floor. "Have at it."

Felicity stuck her tongue out at him, and sparks flew from her eyes. Real sparks. Orange and green. She had caught his fury, so that her usual irritation with his teasing got swallowed up like a drop of dirty water in a dam break. Felicity didn't take any chances.

She did that gorgeous, sliding-dropping motion like a ballet dancer that I had always envied, went down on her stomach in front of the TV cabinet, and stuck both hands into the dark space underneath. A loud *crack-snap* and a flash of poisonous green light meant success. There was a momentary smell like hair caught in the coils of a hairdryer as she slid back, getting up onto her knees, pulling a box the size of a two-slice toaster out from under the TV.

*Why are nasty gizmos always the size of a toaster, anyway?*

She yanked hard, and there was a *snap-thud* as something unplugged from the wall. The creep had dared to plug his gizmo into *my* wall, using *my* electricity against me!

Kurt worked on dismantling the surprise package in the kitchen and made sure there were no surprises in the remotes the intruder messed with. Pete and I inspected the rest of the house, making sure there were no other surprises. The intruder could have tossed something into open doorways on his walk from Pete's bedroom to the family room and back, and we might have missed it. Infrared wasn't that generous when it came to recording details. Just because the intruder hadn't gone into the rest of the house, hadn't wasted time on vandalism or petty thievery, we still needed to reassure ourselves that our home was safe and undefiled.

Felicity went outside to check on her dogs, and Harry helped her move them inside her place, so they would be warm and have reassuring scents and sights when they woke up. I bit my tongue against suggesting that maybe the mutts would be disgustingly sick when they woke up. All that drugged meat in their stomachs had to have a nasty side effect. It was her choice, her dogs, and she had tile floors, an indoor hose bib, and a penned off area with a drain to keep the mutts confined for a reason. Anything fragile, she kept in the loft part of the garage apartment, what used to be the attic, and trained her dogs not to climb the winding stairs.

Harry came back and got to work on cooking. He worked around Kurt and offered suggestions the whole time. I knew I was useless in dissecting gizmos, and I was wound too tight to be much help just sitting and watching. Honestly, I was geared up for snark. So when the house inspection was done, I fired up my computer and got to work on my next *Terry* column. Pete settled in the kitchen, getting Kurt whatever tools or anything else he needed, and helping Harry cook. Did I have great, smart brothers, or what?

The evening went even further downhill, once I got online and checked on the batch of questions the Evil Overlord wanted me to try to answer. Funny thing: I didn't get as much satisfaction from snarking at people now that I knew Sheridan actually *wanted* me to point out their illogical mindsets. The questions themselves weren't the trapdoor-ready-to-break-open part of the evening. There were three possibilities of fun, off-on-a-tangent snark that I could see, right off the bat.

The first letter I put aside for later consideration was from *Desperate in Dayton*. He was in a Cyrano de Bergerac situation, with another guy trying to take the credit for his anonymous admirer work. I kind of liked the guy, which was a nice change from the oblivious morons who made me want to legislate for genetic screening, to keep them from procreating.

The second one was from *Passionate in Parma*, who was in love with her boss. She was sure they were soul mates, but from the things she said about her boss, odds were ten to one that *Passionate's* boss knew exactly how she felt about him, and he was using her to make his work life a whole lot sweeter. Chances were good that while she was a hard worker and a gem at the office, she was either a social klutz, snorted when she laughed, dressed like a colorblind golfer, chewed with her mouth open, or had a figure like a pagan fertility goddess rather than a nymph. Poor girl. She probably would make his personal life a whole lot smoother, but she would shrivel up and blow away on the wind with a husband who married her for convenience rather than love and companionship.

The third was signed *Legal Beagle*, and I liked the guy immediately. He was ready to sacrifice himself for the girl he loved and the cause she believed in, and it was making him miserable.

I felt close to heaving the moment I got the awful suspicion I was starting to enjoy the *Talk to Terry* column. No way in a million years would I ever admit it to the Evil Overlord, of course. I made a few notes for how to answer *Beagle*, then I opened up the next piece of email from the office.

My shriek brought Felicity running. She skidded to a stop in the doorway, grabbing onto the doorframe to stop herself from going any further. Just in time, too, because my computer and office lights flickered.

"They want me to do public appearances as Terry!" I snarled, when she demanded to know what was wrong.

Felicity slid to the floor, laughing so hard she had tears running down her cheeks. I considered running her over.

"Who does?" she said, when she got her breath back.

"Sheridan says he's had requests from a romance writers group—"

"What?" Now it was her turn to shriek. My monitor started rolling, so she took three steps backwards into the hall.

"A romance writers group. They must think I know what real romance is, I guess." My sour mood slipped sideways at the irony of that idea. That tight band of tension that had wrapped around my chest loosened enough to let me laugh. "And a high school journalism class wants me to talk to them about the new trend in newspaper writing."

"What new trend?"

"Heck if I know." I scanned the Evil Overlord's email once more. No explanation. He wanted me to come to his office in Independence for a meeting next Wednesday. Supposedly I would get the full explanation, or the entire request letter, at the meeting. Not something I looked forward to. I could imagine a dozen other unpleasant bombs he could drop on me at that time. Maybe I could claim a doctor's appointment? He had to know my schedule, and that I was free half the day, so I couldn't claim work to keep me away. Besides, he was the boss, and work couldn't keep me away from the meeting if the meeting itself was work-related.

Did I mention how much I hated the inhibited, responsibility-minded upbringing my parents drilled into me? Much as I complained and made snarky comments, I couldn't outright lie and say I was busy. While I did want to get fired, I really didn't want to get *fired*, fired. Not from the newspaper. Just from being *Terry*. I didn't want to have to consider finding some new income, and while I had loved being a teacher, I just couldn't make myself face all the paperwork and recertification and other requirements to go back to being a teacher. So telling my main source of income I didn't want to talk to him face-to-face wasn't a smart move.

Besides, what kind of attitude was that for a superhero? Even a damaged superhero? *God, why did You make me a superhero? What did I ever do to You?* I guess Kurt's Marvel School of Superhero Training idealism had infected me, too. Spider-man was a wisecracking kind of guy, but I couldn't recall him ever saying, "Hey, world, fix yourself for a change." And then there was Wolverine, with his oft-quoted and misquoted, "Once again, a good beer takes a back seat to saving the world." He griped, but he went ahead and did his duty. Even when it was a great big doody.

How could I betray such illustrious examples?

"You aren't doing it, are you?" Felicity tentatively stepped back into my office. She had calmed down, so there were no flickers of the lights or my monitor. She didn't look so amused, either.

"Of course not. The minute people know what *Terry* looks like, I won't have a minute's peace. Because face it, how many chicks in chairs are there around here? The Evil Overlord has to know I can't keep my snarky honesty going without being anonymous."

"Evil Overlord?" She snorted but didn't laugh again. Probably just as worried by the personal appearance request as I was.

"It's open," Kurt called from the kitchen.

Felicity and I exchanged eye-rolls and she led the way out to the kitchen to see the results of the surgery. It was impressive. I didn't know much about gadgets and gizmos, but from the miniaturized electronic gear and the tiny batteries and computer circuit bars spread across the table, our camouflaged intruder was high-tech. Kurt waited to give his little presentation until all five of us were around the table, with the aroma of Harry's homemade chili filling the air to help us relax a little.

"This is filled with something." He held up a black, rubbery-looking bag slightly smaller than his fist. It didn't slosh, and he put it down with extreme caution that made me jumpy. "I'm guessing gas. It feels like it has ribs, either for support or maybe internal compartments. Maybe there are separate components to whatever is supposed to be released by a really complex control mechanism, hooked up to motion and heat sensors and a limited fish-eye lens. Someone wanted control, which is why it didn't go off when Felicity killed it. I'm thinking whatever is being held separate inside is supposed to mix on contact with the air and do something nasty."

"Like explode?" Pete's upper lip curled and he slid his chair back from the table about half a foot. Yeah, like that would make any difference?

"So the question is, what do we do with it? I don't have the resources to analyze whatever is inside. We need to know what was left for you, what it was intended to do, so we have some clue to just how nasty and how connected your prowler is." Kurt picked up a long, narrow circuit board and twirled it between his fingers while he talked, like another man would twirl a pencil.

"Would we be able to track down his identity through the supplies he bought?" Harry frowned at the bag as he got up to stir the chili. He had his priorities in place. Burned chili wouldn't be much fun. Especially since we were going to need to do some major chowing down to work off the tension curling around the room.

"That's a possibility. Depends on who we call in to help." He looked at me for a long moment. There were a lot of messages, questions, warnings in his eyes, and I could only consciously grab onto a few of them. The same possibilities and worries ran through my mind. "Do we turn to someone with a lot of power, or someone who might not find out everything, but he'll at least keep us in the loop?"

"Stanzer or the military," I said, nodding. Well, that was part of what Kurt had silently communicated to me. "You think this might be tied into our folks vanishing? Probably."

"The Colonel will get the analysis done, but he won't tell us everything. Maybe not anything. We won't even know if they catch the guy," Pete said, disgust thick in his voice.

I wanted to laugh. Of course my little brother would be more interested in answers than punishment. I agreed with him. We were Charlie and Rainbow Zephyr's children, after all, and they had raised us to want answers, not platitudes, or to be patted on the head and sent to bed with milk and cookies.

"You think Stanzer has the connections to get our little surprise package analyzed?" I pointed at the bag. "I'd rather go to him, myself. The Colonel is our friend, but I'll bet there are a dozen other people over him, or at least equal with him, who would take it out of his hands, no matter how careful he is. And no matter how much he wants to help us, there's a point where he can't risk his career for us. He needs to be where he can have warning, if powerful people wake up and realize what's going on here." Just thinking about the political games Hayward had to play, for the sake of defending our home, made me tired. He was a superhero in his own way.

And that decided it for me. Yes, I knew that was exactly the wrong choice to make. I thoroughly hated books and movies where the hero and heroine became Too Stupid to Live, and decided against all logic to handle the problem themselves, instead of going to the proper authorities. Going to a private investigator for help instead of the military, who had more resources and the power to protect us, was equal to the dumb movie heroine going into the spooky woods wearing a tight skirt and high heels, or making out in an abandoned summer camp on a remote lake. And we didn't even have the spooky music to warn us when the psycho killer got close.

At the same time, we weren't handling this alone. We would include Angela and Ford Longfellow, our senior guardians, in what was going on. Being in Neighborlee, with our history of handling weirdness, and the protective field, however unreliable it had become, gave us advantages the idiots in those horror flicks didn't have. We were on home turf. We had superhero gifts, however half-baked they were. We could depend on a church full of really hard-praying friends, who wouldn't ask hard-to-answer questions if we said the problem was confidential. And most important, we *needed* to handle this ourselves. There was too much at stake to risk the wrong people finding out about the weirdness embedded in the air and soil of Neighborlee. Especially if our enemy turned out to be the mysterious people who made other Lost Kids vanish. Double especially if it turned out we had been betrayed all these years by someone who should have been one of our own. How nauseating, to think that the original Grandstone had been a Lost Kid.

We had agreed a long time ago, the less attention Neighborlee got from people with a lot of resources and power and big laboratories, the better for everyone. What if we really were aliens, and not some escaped genetic experiment? Look what happened to *E.T.* On the other hand, look what happened in other movies when the aliens invaded. We had made a vow back when we were in school, half-joking, that we considered ourselves Earthlings, not aliens, no matter what we eventually learned about ourselves. We would fight *for* our adopted planet.

I made a call to Stanzer, leaving a message on his answering machine. It felt like a bad spy movie to speak in euphemisms, asking him if we could meet Saturday about some new developments in the investigation he was conducting for us. Kurt had the responsibility to go to Ford Longfellow with what we had been doing and what we theorized. Felicity would report to Angela. If either of them felt we made the wrong choices, all they had to say was "stop," and we would.

That business taken care of, Felicity and Pete helped Kurt pack up the pieces of our surprise package to put into safe storage, while I helped Harry set the table and pull out bread and butter, shredded cheese, onions and sour cream, to go with that chili. We needed to eat.

# Chapter Nine

*Dear Terry:*

*I'm in love with my boss. Am I pathetic? At least he isn't married. I don't understand why, because he's just wonderful. His hair. His eyes. His laugh. His suits. His cologne.*

*How do I tell him I'm in love with him? We make a great team at work. Why not in the rest of our lives? Whatever he needs, he always comes to me. A presentation put together at the last minute? Me. A luncheon for fifty, with only two days' notice? Me. Staying at work until nearly midnight, to track down missing data for an important report? Me. Who fetches his lunch three days a week, and takes his extra suit to the drycleaner for a rush job? Me.*

*I know he appreciates all my hard work. At least once a week, he holds my hand and looks into my eyes and tells me how he just couldn't get along without me. But I want more than big bonus checks and lovely tokens of appreciation like expensive perfume.*

*Please help me find my bliss. Our hearts were made to dance down the path of life together, but he just doesn't seem to realize I can fill his coffee cup outside the office, too.*

*Passionate in Parma*

~~

*Dear Passionate:*

*If this were a romance novel, I'd tell you to go for it. I'd also tell you to get a serious makeover. Hair, nails, wardrobe. Elocution lessons. Whatever it takes to be Cinderella.*

*Reality check: This is no romance novel. Honey, Cinderella was a long time ago. There are no faerie godmothers to wave their wands and fulfill your dreams.*

*I have to be cruel to be kind: Your boss is a total bozo, a use-'em-and-lose-'em creep. It sounds like the office is the only place where he needs and notices you. What do you know about his personal life? Nothing, it sounds like. Which means he's keeping you squarely isolated in his office life. Why?*

*You sound like the soul of efficiency, incredibly talented*

109

*and smart – except you're letting this jerk walk all over you. Why should you get his laundry, for pete's sake? Why should you do all that last-minute work, when he should have thought of it and delegated someone else to do it a week ago?*

*He knows you're there to serve his every need. He's using you. He's giving you just enough attention to keep you coming back. He's not worthy of your adoration.*

*Be careful that when you're down there kissing his feet, he doesn't kick you in the teeth.*

*Wake up and smell the copy machine toner, Toots. This ain't no faerie tale, and this ain't no romance novel. Focus your passion on someone who will appreciate the person inside the Gal Friday persona.*

*Telling it like it is,*

*Terry*

"Ouch," Conrad said, after he had read through my column. Twice. "Rough audience at the club last night?"

"Rough everywhere *but* the club," I said, and bit my tongue. The list of things I could complain about started with remembering I had left my calendar notebook at the office. I came in Saturday morning to retrieve it, only to find Conrad working in the silent, shadowy building. Talk about dedication, working on a Saturday. Or maybe it wasn't dedication, but a need to avoid the shopping rush insanity dominating the world. Even in quiet, chain-store-free Neighborlee.

I kept quiet and let him think what he wanted. Everything that had happened after we got home the night before had made me too keyed up to go to sleep. I couldn't blame the chili, despite the mountain of spices Harry liked to use. If anything, the chili soothed me and helped me relax. I thought I had been rather mellow with my latest *Terry* column. Conrad had been reading it when I wheeled in, and he waved me over to his corner of the big, open editorial room. How could I refuse? I couldn't pretend I didn't see him.

"Something got you going." He finally put down the printout. Why he couldn't just read it off the screen, I could never figure out, especially since Conrad was always harping on how we needed to be green-minded and eco-friendly. "Your inner snark is louder than ever. This whole new set-up really has you going, doesn't it?"

"I miss my winter sports, Connie," I wailed, only half-joking. There was no way I could tell him what was happening at our house. Better for him to think I wanted to leave tread marks on Sheridan's face.

"Why? All the traveling in bad weather. The smelly gyms. The noise. The bad food. The idiots who threaten to put you back into the hospital, because a woman in a wheelchair can't know anything about sports."

"I live for that kind of stress."

"Yeah. Right." He nodded slowly, meeting my gaze for about three seconds. Then he grinned wide enough to split his saggy-baggy face in half, and we both laughed. "Okay. The boss-man already gave his approval—"

"What, he has an alert on his computer, to tell him when I turn in my column?"

*That* thought gave me the creeps. I did my column two days ahead of time, just because I had so much energy and needed to take my bad mood out on someone.

"I think the guy mainlines liquid caffeine. Doesn't know what sleep is, except something that happens to other people." He shuddered, joking. "Okay, you've done your part for making the world a sadder but wiser place. What's on the agenda for the rest of the day?"

"Christmas shopping." I didn't have to pretend to nausea. "And no, don't ask me what to get Clarice for Christmas. I don't know what to get her from *me*, let alone from you."

Conrad's wife had been my roommate in college. Even after five years of marriage, she continued to say she owed me for introducing her to him. Half the time, it was a good thing. The other half of the time, she threatened me with dire consequences. There were times when Conrad was a pal, and other times I really wished he hadn't held a job open for me while I was in the hospital—and wished I hadn't taken him up on it. Writing the *Terry* column was one of those times. I could have gone back to teaching at the high school. The school board would have given me my job back, even without pressure from the teachers' union. For some reason I could never quite remember, I chose newspaper work, full-time, instead of going back to teaching.

Just as he tried to do every year since he had the good taste to fall for Clarice, Conrad expected me to help him find something wonderful for her. Sure, she had been my buddy in college, but she had quit our Star Trek club shortly after marrying Conrad. Did I really know her that well now? After all, she had chosen to marry *him*, for reasons I could never quite grasp.

"There's always hope you'll have a flash of brilliance." Conrad got up to move a couple chairs and the industrial-sized recycling bin, so I could maneuver my chair around to exit. I could have backed straight out without needing a rearview mirror, but why bother when I could get my boss to make it easier on me? Neither of us belonged in the office on a beautiful, clear, un-snowy December Saturday. There was a reason we had chosen to work at a twice-weekly newspaper, rather than a daily. We weren't fools.

All too soon, I was out on the street, my tires crunching on the little drifts of salt and sand that remained after last night's snow melted in the current warm snap. I didn't have to go into the street, now that the sidewalks were visible. It was a relatively nice day for December. The wind didn't rip through the alleys between the buildings like a tidal surge, threatening to lift me out of my chair.

I decided to wheel down through the shopping district instead of getting into my Jeep, driving a block and hoping to find a handicapped parking spot closer to Stanzer's office. I wasn't in the mood to put up with the idiots who thought the yellow diagonal stripes on either side of a handicapped parking spot meant: "Try to squeeze your car in here, please." Half the time, it wasn't the closeness to buildings that made handicapped spots so valuable, but the extra space so those of us with wheelchairs could open our car doors wide enough to haul our second set of wheels out of the back seat.

I paused when I went past the Spindelmutter building, but no vision flashed across my inner eyes. Too bad. I really needed the promise of a spa. I could use a massage, at least every other week, and a facial, and maybe I'd indulge in a pedicure. Just because I didn't use my legs for anything except to make my pants look good didn't mean I should neglect my feet, right?

Besides, spa gift certificates would be easy gifts for Pete and Harry to get me. There was a point where their hints grew irritating and their increasing panic stopped being funny.

My mood plummeted when it occurred to me that Mum would

love the spa, whenever it moved into town. Would I ever be able to share it with her?

I took the opportunity to visit my favorite haunts. Sylvia's Stationery, full of books and office supplies, cards, and nifty novelties that I would never buy but still liked to look at. And Old-Tyme, made to look like an old-fashioned drugstore, squeezed in between two larger stores. At thirty feet back from the front door and the narrow face it presented to the world, Old-Tyme expanded to take up the spaces behind both of its neighbor stores, and stocked videos, hardware, a grocery store, and the best deli outside the East Side of Cleveland. I didn't come up with any ideas for Christmas gifts in either spot, and decided I would have to give in to Felicity and go on an all-day shopping expedition to the outlet malls. That was, of course, only if I failed to dredge up inspiration for more Internet shopping.

When I left Old-Tyme, I still had half an hour until my appointment with Stanzer. The padded, reinforced box Kurt had given me, holding the bag we wanted analyzed, was safely tucked into the saddlebag hanging off the back of my chair. I didn't have enough time to go to Divine's and then go back to Stanzer's office, so I decided to indulge in a hot chai at the Sipping Post, and get a mocha almond decaf to take to him. I knew Stanzer only drank his coffee black, thick enough for the spoon to stand up straight, but I reasoned that he needed to learn to appreciate the finer things.

When I reached the corner where Stanzer's building stood, he was coming down the sidewalk from the opposite direction. From the corner of my eye, I saw a red pickup truck come to a stop on the cross-street, meaning my light was about to change. I coasted to a stop and waved. Hard stops were not wise with two steaming paper cups in a cardboard tray on my lap.

He waved back.

My light turned green and the walk signal came on.

Signals didn't mean padiddly when some psycho wanted to flatten me under his dirty red pickup truck.

The sequence of events burned themselves into my brain. The walk signal came on, and I had a flash of inspiration for a new comedy bit about demanding that handicapped accessible curbs meant the "walk" and "don't walk" signals should show wheelchairs as well as physically able people. "Roll" and "don't roll"? I mentally filed that idea and shoved myself down the shallow ramp into the street.

Sparkles of pink and green swirled past my eyes. Looking back, I still can't decide whether to take the winkies' sudden appearance as warning or distraction.

The pickup truck had the red light. I know he saw it, because he'd come to a dead stop before I started to cross. My mama didn't raise no fool, after all. Better to make sure oncoming traffic obeyed the law before insisting on my right-of-way.

The engine roared. Tires squealed, the stink of burned rubber filled the air, and that truck leaped across the street from a dead stop. There was no way the driver ever could have claimed he hadn't seen the red light. For half a second, I saw teeth gaping wide in the grillwork of that truck.

"Lanie!" Stanzer shouted.

I gave my wheelchair a nice hard shove with my brain. Enough effort to stab spikes of painful white lightning into the backs of my eyeballs. The winkies settled down, through the shoulders of my coat, into my skin. I swear a burst of energy shot through my veins. In that same split second, I prayed one of those panicked, no-need-for-words-because-God-knows-our-hearts prayers. Mainly, *God, help!* My wheelchair shot across the street, out of the way, faster than my nicely defined upper torso muscles could do.

*Something* big and black and sizzling with electric blue sparks stopped my wheelchair for about a quarter of a second when I was halfway across the street. I grabbed my chair with one hand to keep from being thrown out into the street and under the wheels of the truck. With the other hand, I grabbed those sealed cups of coffee, because I didn't want to have to change my pants. Amazing, the things that fill your brain when your life is about to be squashed under enormous, muddy black wheels.

Then that big black and sparkling blue *something* yanked me up and twisted me around. I saw big, sharp teeth, heard something growl, and felt hot breath on the back of my neck. My wheelchair hit the sidewalk in front of Stanzer's office with a thud that nearly gave me whiplash. Stanzer grabbed me and kept me from falling. I lost my grip on the cardboard coffee tray but—*Thank You, Lord*—kept a grip on my bladder.

For half a second, I saw a big, black dog, almost as tall as

Stanzer. Its eyes swirled with electric blue and silver sparks. Enormous, glistening white, sharp teeth parted, revealing a mouth big enough to swallow him whole. But that giant dog licked the side of Stanzer's face and…faded into thin air. The red pickup truck screeched past us. I glimpsed a quick impression of a pale face inside a black hood, and dark sunglasses. Then the truck vanished around the next corner.

Stanzer and I held still for about five seconds, remembering how to breathe. We grinned at each other, weird contrast to the terror still making my heart race. Terror equally strong burned bright in his eyes. Then Stanzer tipped me back into my chair and reached up to wipe his face where that big black dog licked him. He glanced around. Maybe he expected it to still be there, ready for round two? When he turned back to me, his terrified expression mutated into wariness. I nearly laughed aloud when it occurred to me that Stanzer was worried that I had seen it. Whatever *it* was.

"You have pretty strange friends, but they come in handy, don't they?" I said, with a little more wobble in my voice than I liked to hear.

"The Hounds." His voice cracked like an adolescent's. "Umm… Are you okay?"

"Considering the truck missed me and those hot drinks missed my clothes, yeah, fine. When you carry stuff on your lap, you have a tendency for things to splash in really inconvenient, kind of embarrassing spots, y'know?"

He snorted, half of that a gasp for breath, bent and picked up the empty cups and lids and the soggy tray from the sidewalk. With a jerk of his head, he beckoned for me to follow him into his office.

I was grateful that he didn't ask if I needed a push, even though a little assistance wouldn't have been unwelcome. My arms felt as rubbery as my legs usually felt. Then I realized something. Stanzer's office door was a good ten yards down the sidewalk from the corner where I crossed the street, but I didn't remember traveling from the spot in the middle of the crosswalk to where I landed.

"Teleportation?" I said, once we were in his office with the door closed and blessed heat soaking into my sweaty shirt.

The problem with being a semi-pseudo-superhero (tired of hearing this by now?) wasn't the inconvenience of powers manifesting at the most embarrassing times and attracting the wrong kind of attention, but that being invincible wasn't one of them. As a result of that lack of invincibility, when my physical well-being faced a threat, I sweated like a horse.

"Teleport—Oh, that." Stanzer tossed the trash into the nearest wastebasket and dropped down into his chair without taking his coat off. He rested his face in his hands for a few seconds, then rubbed his eyes and continued the motion up, to rake his fingers through his hair. "You shouldn't be able to see the Hounds. I know you're not one of us. So how can you see them?"

"Tell me about the Hounds." It kind of comforted me to know Stanzer was as rattled as I still felt.

"Inter-dimensional beings. Guardian angels, if you want the simplified explanation. The Hounds of Hamin serve and guard and guide the Hunt. That's us." He jabbed a thumb into his chest. "To save us from… Well, that's a long story. The short version is that to save the lives of quite a few innocent children, we were dedicated to Hamin's service—essentially, Hamin is my home dimension's face of Creator God—and we were given into the care of the Hounds."

"How many of you are there?"

"It's been so long. I was just a kid … So far, I haven't been able to find anyone else. For all I know, they never got this far." He slumped a little, and I almost could have cried at the flicker of homesickness and loneliness in his big, dark eyes. Stanzer shook his head, took a deep breath, and sat up straight again. "So, that still doesn't answer the question of how you saw a Hound."

"I know you reported to Angela as soon as you moved to town, and she gave her approval of you. So I'm guessing you sense or maybe can even see some of the otherness at Divine's."

"Oh yeah. When I was looking for a place to settle down, a Hound came close to dragging me here, then straight to Divine's. She can see the Hounds, but she didn't indicate anyone else could. Why do I have the feeling she didn't tell you about me?"

"She didn't. But a lot of times, Angela works on a need-to-know basis. She trusts us to do our job without checking in with her every hour." I shrugged. This conversation felt so odd, and yet so right, so normal, in some ways. I could only pray the conversations would run like this whenever we managed to track down other

Lost Kids with semi-pseudo-superhero powers. "Essentially, we work with her. We're the guardians of all the magical, wonderful, and weird in Neighborlee."

"Uh huh. That explains …" He grinned. "Some of it."

To answer the challenge in his eyes, I focused on the paper clip dispenser on his desk. I mentally lifted it about six inches, turned it end over end three times, and then put it down on the desk. That was about all I could manage, after expending so much telekinetic energy on trying to get across the street before the Hound rescued me. A low-grade throbbing settled into my temples, but I could live with that. Mostly because I was just grateful to be alive, period.

"Uh huh. Neighborlee does have that effect on people, doesn't it?" Stanzer stared at the paper clip dispenser, a grin slowly growing across his face. "How many of you are there?"

"Guardians, Ford Longfellow, and his granddaughters are sort of in training. Me and Felicity and Kurt. Everyone who is a guardian is a Lost Kid, or their children or grandchildren. We know there are others, but they all got adopted away as soon as their talents manifested. We kept ours hidden, so no one took us."

"You know, I suspected something about Kurt, but Felicity? What does she do?"

"Hide all your sensitive electronics if you ever get her mad." I couldn't resist that little-boy-in-mischief sparkle in his eyes, and a few seconds later, we were both laughing.

The laughter didn't last long, and even the memory of it vanished when I took out the reinforced box from the back of my chair and gave it to Stanzer, explaining what had happened Friday night. He handled it with all the caution I expected from someone with his brains and common sense. He admitted to knowing a few people who should be able to analyze the contents, discretely, and promised he'd get to work on it.

~~~~~

I had a comedy gig that night at a Christmas party for a shipping company. They asked me to do my "he's so boring/she's so dumb/he's so evil" material. Since I was in a major growling mood, thanks to the break-in and attempt to run me over, I was happy to oblige. It was somewhat of an experiment for me, to see how many snarky comments in a row people could listen to before their eyes glazed over and they stopped listening to me.
~~~~~

Then again, wasn't that what happened every four years during the presidential elections, one nasty comment after another? People still listened, and cheered, so chances were good I'd still have people laughing at the end of my twenty minutes.

"Hey, gang, I'm Lanie Zephyr, and this is what happens if you don't tip your waitress." I pivoted back on my main wheels and waggled the guide wheels. "Let that be a warning."

A hoot came from the back of the darkened room, where I had seen the waitresses, including two friends, hanging out. Was that amusement, or agreement? Chances were good they were used to being stiffed by big crowds. I hoped the owner of this party center believed in building the gratuity into the bill. Being a waitress wasn't easy. I had done enough service work to know the drill.

The laughter from the fifty-plus people at the cluster of round tables sounded cheerful enough, if weak. I didn't catch any alcohol fumes, so their brains were still engaged and unclouded, for the most part. Once again, the magical effect of showing up in a wheelchair created a barrier. Either that, or someone had been given a lecture on political correctness recently, and they were afraid to laugh at the "poor little crippled girl."

Boy, were they in for a rough night.

"Hey, is anybody out there? Are you in your after-dinner nap?"

They did want me to heckle them, after all. I had it in writing, from the Human Resources director who hired me. After the events of the last twenty-four hours, I was loaded for bear.

I snarked at them, I snarked about politicians and the stupidity of criminals who butchered their spam emails with bad grammar so no one would ever believe they were writing from the target victim's bank or insurance agency or a nice old lady who wanted to get her husband's fortune out of mainland China before the government confiscated it. I especially snarked about stupid bosses with entitlement attitudes. Then I rounded out the evening by pointing out the silliness of classic horror movies, and how the monsters like the Mummy and Wolfman had lost their zing, thanks to the horrors of modern society.

"This gang is so tough, the Mummy walked through their neighborhood and they rolled houses with him." Shrieks and giggles. Okay, that surprised them. "When the Terminator walked through their neighborhood, he ended up in a chop-shop. Did you hear about the werewolf that was terrorizing the Flats for a few weekends? You didn't? Well, this gang's girlfriends decided they wanted fur coats. If ya know what I mean. When Frankenstein's monster came into their neighborhood, they sold him to a medical school. I tell you, people just don't have any respect for the handicapped anymore." I did another wheelie, waggling my footrests at them. "Let that be a warning to ya, folks!"

A few people stood up when I gave them my little salute-bow and wheeled backwards down the ramp at the back of the temporary platform. I scooted around the side of the room as the lights came up, to the back where the waitresses had been sitting. Two were friends, and I wanted to get their feedback.

A tall, square-shouldered figure in a very loud, psychedelic rainbow sweater got up from the table I was passing at the very back of the room. I skidded to a stop and almost blew out a wheel when the man stepped into the light — Daniel Sheridan.

"You weren't expecting me," he said, after we looked at each other for about five seconds.

"Well, duh." *If I was expecting you, would I have snarked so long about stupid bosses?*

That got a grin. Oh, why did he have to look so gorgeous when he smiled like that? Like a real person, with some awareness of how he messed up other people's lives? Someone with a conscience, even? I was pretty sure by then that a lot of my ire was over the fact that he had the most gorgeous head of blue-black curls, light olive complexion, and shoulders a gymnast would envy. He should have been blond. Blonds had always done me wrong, for most of my life, starting with Sylvia and including the pedophile who romanced me to get at my students. It was easier accepting unthinking cruelty from someone I could give a Nazi salute to, behind his back.

"Did you know I was going to be here?" I had to ask.

"If you think I'm following you around, think again." Sheridan smiled as he said that.

Good for me.

Or maybe not so good. I wanted to lose the *Talk to Terry* column, didn't I? Of course, he knew I wanted to lose it, so if I provoked him enough, he might just stick me with even worse assignments. Maybe even leak my secret identity to the world. Might help my comedy routines. Might set me up as a revenge target for all the spineless and neurotic and brainless creatures who wrote to a complete stranger, thinking their request for advice could somehow stay anonymous despite appearing in print. They needed some common sense, at so very many different levels.

"So, you're good friends with the owner?" I asked.

"He coached my Little League team."

"Aren't you a little old for Little League?" I turned my chair to try to edge around him, and he kindly took the hint and moved out of my path.

"Har har." Sheridan followed me.

I didn't like the itchy feeling that generated in my neck, and wished for half a second I had a wheelchair with a higher back. I preferred my low-slung racing wheelchair, an older model I retired from playing basketball. It was easy to tip over, but it let me maneuver better than the more solid chairs. Unfortunately, it exposed my neck and a good portion of my back. I wondered if the Evil Overlord had a tendency to kick people in the butt.

Something told me that after the show I had just done, I wouldn't get the usual amount of sympathy for being the "poor little crippled girl" if he did give me something back for my smart mouth. I had proved I wasn't emotionally fragile and in need of defending.

Of course, the jury was still out on my emotional and mental *damage*.

"You know," I felt compelled to point out, "you can pretend you don't know me. Neither of us is at work. We aren't friends. We don't even have to talk at work because we aren't in the same office."

"You really loathe me, don't you?" He sounded a little amused, but not outright laughing. At least he didn't whine or sound confused.

"You took away my sports. You stuck me with the freaking whiney lovelorn column!"

"But you're having fun with it, aren't you?"

Now he sounded confused.

# Chapter Ten

"Conrad already explained the economics to me. Are you telling me you gave me the column like tossing someone a bone?" A horrid thought hit me, and I wheeled up close enough to ram his shinbones with my footrests. He backed up, and that made me angrier. I wanted to run him over, knock him down and leave tread marks on that horrific sweater. "You gave me that column so I wouldn't get mad and send the gimp Mafia after you, is that it?"

"I wanted you for that column long before I bought the *Tattler*." He stepped forward and leaned down, reaching out as if he would rest his hands on the table between us. One problem: no table between us. Did he think he would put his hands on my armrests?

*Think again, Evil Overlord.* No armrests on that model of wheelchair. The horrified realization widened his eyes. He froze in that position, reaching for something that wasn't there, for about five seconds. Then suddenly we were both laughing.

The equally horrified realization that I might just grow to like the Evil Overlord flashed through my head. I laughed anyway.

He backed up and finally found a place to put his hands. His back pockets. That gesture made him seem a little less powerful, more down-home. Likable. Which should have made me angry. I didn't want to like the guy. I had a lot more material about the Evil Overlord to come up with, and I couldn't do that if I liked him.

Then what he had said flashed to the forefront of my brain. The realization must have showed on my face. He immediately looked worried, pulled up a chair, and sat down so we were nearly knee-to-knee.

"What?"

"How many of my shows have you seen?"

He shrugged. "Lost count."

"Oh, man…a stalker." But I grinned, to let him know I didn't completely think that.

"Don't go getting it into your head that I bought the *Tattler* just to force you to work for me."

"Thought never crossed my mind. Thanks for the idea. You

might just be giving me some inspiration."

"Like I haven't already?"

"Ah... Look—"

"I've decided to be flattered."

"You okay?" Harry had finally decided to come into the banquet room. He stepped up next to my chair, rested a hand on the handlebar in that proprietary, don't-mess-with-my-sister way he had, all soft smile and hard eyes, and looked Sheridan up and down.

"Daniel Sheridan, my brother, Harry Zephyr."

"This is…your new boss, huh?" Harry shrugged, as if he hadn't been about to say, "the Evil Overlord." They shook hands, then Sheridan excused himself and I wheeled over to where Tabitha and Grace waited with the other waitresses.

It felt like hours later when we finally got out to Harry's truck and he took care of the chair. Part of me wished I had taken my Jeep and drove myself. It was so much easier maneuvering myself around, getting my chair in and out. Heaving my folded chair into the back of his truck was more trouble than it was worth.

The plain truth was that after that break-in and sabotage, and while we waited to find out what exactly was in that bag Kurt took out of the gizmo, I was a little leery of going out alone to unfamiliar places. Maybe that was wimpy, since I could protect myself with my lungpower, my fists, and my minor telekinetic ability. When Harry had decided he would drive me, I didn't believe for a minute his claim that it would let him talk to the VIPs of this company, to try to get some trucking contract worked out. He was watching out for his big sister.

"Kind of a hectic day, huh?" he said, once we had left the parking lot.

"Tell me about it."

"You don't have any new powers showing up under stress, do you?"

"What?" My voice didn't quite ring around the cab of the truck, but it came close.

"You know, like mental influence. Making the Evil Overlord your friend. He sure looked chummy there, for someone who's ruined a lot of careers."

"Actually…" I thought over what Sheridan had told me before

I repeated it back to Harry. "Sounds like he thinks about the people he's moving around on his chessboard."

"Definitely a stalker." He held that fake little frown for about two seconds, until I reached across the cab and swatted him.

We were still grinning, and Harry was still coming up with teasing remarks, threatening me with curfews if I accepted a date with Sheridan, when we got home. I had to admit, I was a bad influence on him. After watching me work on my comedy routines, he knew how it worked, how to put things together. Sometimes I felt like I had fashioned the weapon that skewered me.

"Pete, get your butt out here," Harry shouted. It wasn't too late in the evening for him to be so loud. The music coming from three doors down and the movie playing four houses away on the other side—one of the Terminator movies, from the sound effects—were almost louder than him. "He didn't scrape up the slush on the ramp like you told him," Harry explained, as he brought my chair around to the passenger door.

"What's up?" Pete flung the kitchen door open. "Hey, where are the dogs?"

"Indoors, like anything with half a brain on a cold night like this," Harry said.

"Felicity had to go out, something came up at Eden, and she let the dogs out when she left. She said Sheba keeps trying to eat the sofa when she's not around."

"Then where are they?" I said, as several unpleasant ideas crossed my mind.

"Not again." Pete shot out of the house, no coat, wearing ratty moccasins instead of the boots he should have put on.

The ramp banged and shook with his first two steps. That prickly feeling of warning raced up my spine and I opened my mouth to shout at him to get back inside. I saw the ramp collapse under him. Two seconds *before* it actually did. It was like getting an involuntary instant replay of the pipes and wooden panels collapsing as if all the cotter pins and bolts had been taken out. Rattling and thudding like a Lincoln Logs cabin bowled over by a toddler on a tricycle.

Pete slid sideways, grappling for the railing, missing, hitting on his hip and tumbling so he went face-first into the melting snow that had piled up next to the ramp. He let out a yelp, but got his mouth closed before he hit the slush.

That was meant for me. I knew it, without any help from my unreliable gift of foresight.

~~~~~

"Okay, I'm getting really tired of this," Pete said as he rejoined us in the kitchen. "Dogs?" He threw his wet and dirty clothes into the doorway of the laundry room. From the slide-scrape sound, he had hit the laundry basket dead on. Too bad he wasn't allowed to play with the Ezekiel's Wheels.

"Sleeping and stuffed," Harry reported. "Just like last time. I even found them in the same place."

He had also checked out my ramp and found that indeed, all the bolts and cotter pins holding the support pipes together and all the boards tightly in place had been removed. Tape had held the pieces in place, waiting until the first hard breath of wind or someone stepping on the ramp made everything fall apart.

"Does this guy want me dead, or just irritated?" That sounded just as egotistical as I feared, the moment the words left my lips.

Making the ramp fall apart under me, in my chair, wouldn't have caused much damage. The ramp only had to get me up the height of three steps to the back door. It wasn't even a high enough fall to scare me, just make me angry. Granted, twice as angry because the bozo had hurt my little brother.

"If it's Toby, I hope it's just irritated," Harry said after a moment of thought.

"Still don't want to believe it's him," Pete said.

"All that high-tech stuff." Harry slouched so the back of his head rested on the chair and his feet nearly poked out from under the other side of the table. "What did he specialize in, when he was in the Marines?"

I got that sick, dropping sensation in my stomach. That horrified, oh-heck-I'm-falling feeling that had never bothered me until my back shattered and I lost the ability to fly. I had never been afraid of heights or falling, until then. I had loved roller coasters, until then. Toby Malone had just thrown me onto a roller coaster where I couldn't see the tracks.

"No." I listened to my gut instinct. "Toby might be involved. His coming back to town might be a trigger or a signal or whatever for what's happening, but I can't believe he'd be trying to hurt or
~~~~~

kill me. Or any of us."

"Whatever was in the bag, whoever is after you has some way of knowing the bomb he put under the TV didn't go off," Harry said. "Too bad we didn't get the bag to Stanzer until today."

"We only found the gizmo last night," I protested.

"We need more data," Pete said with a shrug. Then he winced. He must have fallen on that shoulder pretty hard.

To say Felicity was upset when she came back would have been like saying that Pompeii had a minor volcanic ash problem. I was watching when she came home, about an hour later. Mostly because I couldn't sleep. I knew the moment she found the note Harry put on her door. The light over her door strobed as fast as a heartbeat. In that quiet like before a snowstorm hit, I heard her door open and the slap of her boots on the tile. Every light in her cottage flashed on, then off again, and I knew she had found her dogs, most likely groggy and trying to get to their feet by this time.

I was sitting in my office, trying to work on my next column. My monitor started to scroll, touched by her emotional EM field even that far away. A definite gauge of just how irate she felt. I picked up the phone and called her, to let her know she could come talk, someone was awake to help if she needed it. Plus I wanted to interrupt her hissy-fit and save the work of more than an hour, when it felt like every word was printed with blood drawn from under my nails.

"Why does he have to pick on my dogs?" she wailed as she answered the phone.

"It's not your dogs. He's after me, and your dogs happen to be in the way." I held my breath, but no fireworks erupted from her house and my monitor stopped rolling and flickering. Something to think about helped to settle her emotions. "I think maybe we should get your dogs away from here altogether."

"Then he'll just have easier access to your house," Felicity said after a few seconds. I could almost hear the sizzle of her thinking, weighing different considerations. She sighed, and I heard the creak of the thick, old-fashioned springs in her couch. "What'd he do to you tonight?"

"Sabotaged the ramp."

"Lanie—"

"Pete got dumped into the snow, not me. The thing is, Pete was here the whole time, and he didn't hear or see anything. He swears he was studying, not playing video games, so this guy is good at the stealth."

"And my mutts like him enough not to make a peep when he shows up. Shows how dumb they are, they don't associate being so sick with the food he gave them."

"Well," I offered, "you can't have beauty *and* brains." That got her to laugh.

"What are you going to do?"

"We'll figure something out, but I was serious when I said we should get your dogs out of the line of fire."

~~~~~

We ended up sending Felicity and her canine circus to Kurt's place. He had a fenced-in backyard, for security when he had big, potentially hazardous projects that he worked on outside. Since his garage had been turned into a super-clean workshop years ago, he had a carport with walls on three sides for his truck and motorcycle. That would serve as shelter for all the dogs, so they wouldn't have to go inside the house. Felicity had to promise to only use the kitchen, the back bedroom, and the downstairs bath, and not go into the rest of the house. The slightest loss of her control could kill a dozen mechanical projects and experiments Kurt was working on.

Kurt moved into Felicity's place, to better monitor what went on around the house, and because he didn't want to be around those dogs. He wasn't allergic, and he liked dogs, but he preferred them one at a time, not a half dozen in one loud, slobbery, shedding lump.

Sunday morning, while the guys and I went to church, Kurt made the first few steps in setting up a prototype security system that, until about a week ago, had been nothing but a twinkle in his eye. Or maybe more accurately, a brainstorm ready to erupt. All of it was the product of several very weird dreams he admitted he hadn't wanted to confide to me and Felicity. Considering that Kurt, Felicity and I regularly shared all our dreams, just on the chance we got ideas or clues or memories from when we were abandoned outside town, that was an indication of just how weird those dreams were. I hoped he wouldn't make too much noise, or generate fireworks, and let the neighbors know somebody was hanging around the house. Although, if someone was home and
~~~~~

acting outside the normal routine, maybe that would encourage our enemy to stay away.

I had charge of my rug-rat Sunday school class that morning. Ordinarily, that would have been fine, *if* I had been given enough warning to prepare the lesson. I worked with three other teachers, teaching four and five-year-olds. The numbers of our prisoners — err, students — ranged anywhere from eight to twenty. It depended on a number of factors, including which parent had custody that weekend, which grandparents were watching them while their parents worked, if it was summer and time to go out on the boat on Lake Erie, and other assorted excuses for not being in church. Yeah, that was a pretty cynical viewpoint, but my fellow teachers and I were grateful the kids came at all.

That Sunday, with the various weird things going on at my house, I wasn't in the best of moods when I rolled down the hall to the classroom at twenty minutes before class started. I found six of my students performing gymnastics on the coat racks outside the closed door. Bridget usually got the room open and started setting up the snack a good half hour before class started. We operated on the principle that the kids would be more eager to get to class with a food lure. Sure, it was only an hour or so since breakfast for most of them, but sugar always worked wonders as bait. Chocolate chip cookies bought by the barrel, and the cheapest, reddest, sweetest powdered fruit punch mix, guaranteed to stain mouths, fingers and clothes for eternity, were staples of church nurseries and Sunday schools around the world. And helped to calm the nerves of countless generations of Sunday school teachers.

If Bridget hadn't opened up the classroom, odds were good the Rapture had occurred while I was on my way to church, and I got left behind by some clerical error.

"Hey, gang."

Tonya Parker — no relation to Jay, of the Senior Prank Night fiasco — grinned at me and flipped around on the coat rack to hang by her knees. Fortunately, she still wore her snow pants, so we didn't get treated to a display of whatever cartoon hero underwear she wore that day. The other five ignored me, giggling and pushing and trying to take their boots and coats off without unzipping or unbuttoning.

Panic shot adrenaline through me. Fortunately, I was an

adrenaline junkie, and it helped me think clearly. Well, as clearly as I could think under any circumstances.

"All right, crewmen. Red alert! Snap to it. Roll call. Take the position!"

It just shows what a bad influence I was on these kids, that they immediately stood up or dropped down and got into line, arms at their sides, eyes facing forward and mouths closed. For the most part, anyway. We played "spaceship" quite a few times during minor emergencies in class. Emergencies usually involved someone puking at the front of the room, necessitating my distracting the other children before they followed suit, while the other teachers cleaned up and took the sick child/children to find parents. There were some advantages in being stuck in a wheelchair, starting with it being rather hard to clean the floor while sitting two feet above it.

I was the spaceship captain, and the kids were my crew. We built our spaceship out of the two long, knee-high tables turned on their sides, with their little chairs lined up inside like a school bus. The regular attendees of my class had their ranks and jobs, with the irregulars (don't tell them I called them that, and especially don't tell their parents) filling in different duties, depending on what adventure we decided to take.

"First Officer, open the hatch." I hooked my thumb at the door. Gina Pastori gave me the Vulcan salute. She was First Officer because she was the only one besides me who could manage that finger position. Then she broke the mood by grinning wide enough to show two missing teeth. She hurried to open the door and waited while everyone else filed inside.

"Everyone aboard, Captain," she chirped, and saluted again.

What could I say? I was a recovering Trekker and had passed the disease to these unsuspecting children.

I zipped through the door, positive if I left my "crew" alone for more than ten seconds, they would dismantle the room. No one had turned the lights on, so I slapped the switches next to the door as I came through, and pivoted around, looking in vain for a note or some indication why I was alone with the kiddies. That wasn't supposed to happen. I was an *assistant* teacher, good for crowd control, for listening to memory verses, and threatening to make sure the mini juvenile delinquents ended up on milk cartons.

Funny thing was, the kids had no idea what the reference to missing children appearing on milk cartons meant. Probably because their parents bought milk by the gallon, in plastic jugs. They still laughed at my threat.

No notes from Bridget or Sherry. No signs of the snack being ready. What was going on? God wouldn't take everyone but me if the Rapture really had occurred, would He? I hadn't been so bad I'd been left behind with my rug-rats to face the Anti-Christ, had I?

*Come to think of it, maybe I should feel sorry for the Anti-Christ...*

"Lanie?" DeNita, who had duty in the church office during the services, stuck her head into the classroom. The coward, that was all she ever put into any classroom with students under the age of eighteen. I know she feared being coerced into helping teach.

She was right to be afraid. That was how I ended up as a Sunday school teacher. I wheeled inside this very classroom about two years before, to investigate the pandemonium. Four kids immediately latched onto my chair, asking questions and demanding rides. I made up stories, like I always did, and the next thing I knew, the class hour was halfway over. The teachers put me on a major guilt-trip to get me to come back and help out from then on.

"What's up, Dee?" I didn't need telepathy to read her thoughts. Someone had bailed and I was only now getting the message. *Thanks a lot, Bridge and Sher!*

"Bridget's at the hospital. Her sister is in labor, and she's the Lamaze coach," DeNita hurried to add, when all six little faces turned to her in wide-eyed panic and all six kids gasped loudly enough to create a sonic boom. "She called and left a message here when they headed for the hospital. Unfortunately, right after her message, Sherry left one saying she had to drive up to Bowling Green. Her daughter got sick and the campus nurse wants to transfer her to a hospital. They're thinking appendicitis."

"And I bet each one left a message on the other's cell phone, and neither one has checked their messages yet, because someone should have called—" I groaned as my cell phone chose that moment to go off. My six crewmen giggled, because it was a church rule that all cell phones and pagers were supposed to be turned off as soon as we walked—or rolled—through the front door. I opened up my phone and quelled the masses with a glare while I answered.

DeNita had the courtesy to stay in the doorway and keep an eye on the kids until I took care of my phone call. It was Sherry, who had just arrived at her daughter's college, realized her cell phone had been on buzzer during the entire trip, in her purse, in the back seat, and only now found Bridget's message. Then DeNita beat a retreat for the office, leaving me alone with the kids. Eight more had arrived in the two minutes it took to assure Sherry that everything would be all right.

All right, let me say right here that I *did* prepare for class. I had read the lesson. I knew the story. I wished that I had thought to bring a VeggieTales DVD to fill up some time. Brian had let us know last week that he wouldn't be in class today, so I couldn't call on him for help, either.

"All right, crew, we're officially stranded on a desert planet with just the..." I did a quick count, because more had come in while I quietly panicked and took inventory of my resources and options. "The eighteen of us. A galactic storm is gathering on the horizon. We need to hunker down and brace for some rough times."

"Can I have some juice?" Trevor Winslow said, waving his hand with the same panicky speed he usually reserved for a trip to the bathroom.

He had nothing on my level of panic in that moment.

Juice meant activating little bladders. I had gone into the boys' bathroom a grand total of three times in all my years at church. Once on a dare, once by accident, when I was half-blinded with cheap mascara that I never used again, and once to help the church janitor clean. The smell was disgusting. And that was just the air sanitizer. I would rather have my fingernails pulled out by pliers than make a fourth visit. Especially when it meant I had to help wriggly little boys with zippers and snaps and buttons, and a talent for the most embarrassing questions in the world while I struggled to help them and simultaneously preserve my sense of modesty.

All right, I admit it—I have been a prude since I realized the difference between boys and girls. So, sue me.

Helping one little lawn lizard at a time was fine. I had done it before and survived. But the problem with little kids in Sunday school was that when one wanted to go, four or five more decided to go, too. Power of suggestion. I would be relieved when boys got old enough to decide to buck the rule of "safety in numbers" when it came to potty breaks.

"No juice. Our supplies have been contaminated. We have to ration all water." I took pity on them and gestured at the closet where Sherry kept the industrial-sized plastic bins of chocolate chip cookies. Those bulk store cookies were pretty good, I had to admit. "To avoid wasting supplies, I'm doubling all other rations. Doctor Penny, you and your orderlies take charge of distributing rations."

Penny, Lisa and Chuckie got to be my medical crew because they were the tallest and most obedient, and I could depend on them to retrieve supplies off high shelves without making messes. They grinned and raced each other across the room, and nearly pushed the sliding door of the supply closet right out of the tracks.

I turned off the lights and built a storm shelter, with the tables and chairs to indicate the walls. The children sat on the foam floor mat/puzzle pieces the daycare center used during the week in this same room. Setting the stage and getting the cookies distributed had taken up nearly twenty-five minutes. That took me ten minutes into the class hour. Fifty minutes left to fill. I had Penny pull my bag off my chair, and took out my copy of the lesson book. I had read through everything, I was prepared, but that was when I was only going to drill the children on their memory verse for next week and watch over them while they colored pictures of David and Goliath.

"Okay, crew, how many of you know the story of David and Goliath?"

"Don't you mean *Dave and the Giant Pickle*?" Trevor said. The confusion on his square little face made me want to laugh. Sometimes I had to wonder just how much of the Bible the really little kids understood, thanks to VeggieTales, and how much had to be straightened out when they got older and had to separate Big Idea's version from reality.

"That's one version of the story. The real David wasn't an asparagus. And Goliath was a giant, not a giant pickle." I looked around my group, sitting on the floor and all watching me with big eyes and only a few whispers among them.

God was merciful. For some reason, I had their attention. I knew how to work an audience and keep their attention.

At least, I was pretty sure I did. I knew I couldn't use my brand of humor on them, mostly because they didn't have the cultural references to understand even a tenth of the things I said.

Simply reading the story took up twenty-five of the fifty minutes I had to fill. Every few sentences, someone piped up with a question. That was fine with me. The more questions they asked, the less I had to add to the lesson. We didn't have the pictures to color because Sherry was the one who stopped at the office to get copies run off before class. I needed to fill as much time as possible, or risk losing control.

"Miss Lanie?" Gregory got up on his knees and rested his elbows on the chrome bar of my left wheel. "How come God didn't just smash the finkerstones?"

I bit my lip to keep from correcting him with "Philistines." Let his parents spend some time figuring out what he was saying. I could still remember the fun we had over Sunday lunch when I was a kid, straightening out the misunderstandings from Sunday school lessons.

"David had to learn to trust God to help him, and to learn that sometimes God wants us to do the work ourselves. If we don't exercise, we'll get weak. God makes us do things the hard way sometimes to make us stronger. He doesn't fix our problems, so we can use our brains to fix things, and get smarter."

"Why didn't God fix your legs?" He patted the rubber treads of my wheel and looked up at me with that wide-eyed, deeply thinking and astonished look of his.

The kid had a future in politics, because who could resist him when he used that look? Who could be upset at questions that would be considered thoughtless and rude in someone just five years older?

"Doesn't God want you to exercise?"

"My arms are a lot stronger. As you very well know." Before he could react, I grabbed him under his armpits and lifted him over my head, then swung him over so he landed on my other side. The other children laughed, and immediately demanded that I swing them up over my chair, too.

That probably hadn't been a smart illustration, but on the plus side, the demonstration of my arm strength did take up another ten minutes of class time.

After that, I let the children ask whatever questions they wanted, and talk about whatever crossed their incredible, alien brains. A lot of them wanted to know what it was like, living in my wheelchair. As usual, someone wanted to know if my legs felt anything, and someone else wanted to know how I went to the bathroom. Did I use a tube and a vacuum like the astronauts? They talked about blind people and Seeing Eye dogs, and the people in our church with hearing aids.

"How come God doesn't fix everybody at our church?" Amy asked. She was one of my quiet ones, a deep thinker who seemed to have the weight of the world on her delicate little shoulders at age five. "Jesus fixed everybody who asked Him to. Why doesn't He fix you?"

"Because…"

Oh, how I hated times like these. I usually loved talking with little kids, mostly because they hadn't learned the social inhibitions and courtesies, false faces and innuendo-laden nastiness of so-called civilized conversation. I usually loved their honesty and curiosity and the weird tangents their minds took. But that meant they asked the really hard questions, and they didn't have enough experience to understand the answers. Of course, that might have said something about the honesty and validity of the answers adults made up to answer the hard questions. What was wrong with saying, "I don't know"?

Thank You, Lord, inspiration struck in that moment.

"Because God wants people to see that being a Christian isn't easy. He wants people to follow Him because they love Him, because it's the right thing to do—not because they'll get all their problems fixed. If everybody was your friend because you gave them candy, would you think they were *really* your friends?"

"I'd be friends if they gave me candy," Gina said with a giggle. Her little friends giggled with her.

"Would you stay friends if somebody *stopped* giving you candy?"

Her giggles stopped.

"God wants people to give their hearts to Him because they know He loves them, and they love Him, not because they want Him to give them things." I patted my wheels. "God leaves me in my wheelchair to show people that being a Christian isn't always fun and easy."

"Why not?" Casey's lower lip stuck out. She was my crier. I had to constantly resist the temptation to look for a switch in the back of her head, to turn off the waterworks.

"You mean, why doesn't God make it always fun and easy to be a Christian?" I sighed and sent up another prayer, my thousandth for the hour. "Because...the world is broken. Things don't work right, even for good people. Things won't be fixed all the way until Jesus comes back."

The big problem for Sunday school teachers, when students ask questions like that, is the temptation to say, "Ask your parents." Maybe a generation or two ago, we could get away with telling our rug-rats to ask their parents the hard questions, because chances were good their parents had the answers. Nowadays, the parents didn't know much more about the Bible and righteous living than the children did. Sometimes I suspected the children knew more, but they lost that knowledge and got warped and stained by everyday living in our increasingly dangerous, dirty, mutated society.

*Cynical? Moi?*

Fortunately, class was nearly over and I could get away with breaking up the discussion by ordering my crew to dismantle our shelter and prepare to be evacuated from the planet. I had a lot to think about, and hoped I wouldn't get curious, maybe even upset phone calls from the parents, asking just what the h-e-hockey sticks I was teaching their children.

I only heard about half of Pastor Rocky's sermon that morning. The discussion with the class had gotten me started on a slightly depressing turn of thought. What was God teaching me, leaving me in my wheelchair and through the present troubles hitting me? Would my problems stop when I had learned whatever He wanted? Or (this was the depressing part) would the lessons just get harder as time went on?

Considering how much renovation God had to do with my mind and heart, it was going to take into the next millennium before I got to the place where I was good enough for Heaven. That might not be depressing for those who wanted to live forever. As for me, the sooner I got my new body and could escape my wheelchair and the constant numb-tingle conflict in my legs, the happier I would be.

~~~~~
~~~~~

Kurt spent the entire day setting up a new security system around my house. One that allowed him to indulge his every paranoid fancy. Felicity wouldn't be anywhere near the house, so there was no chance of her blowing delicate circuits and burning out sensors. Pete helped him lay hair-fine wires and install micro-miniaturized sound/heat/light/motion detectors and the micro-digital video cameras to catch everything in high-definition detail. The two of them had a lot of fun, which would have been irritating if I had been trying to work on my next column. Instead I kept track as different parts of the house, inside and outside, came alive on the multi-frame monitor Kurt had me watching.

"You didn't make all this stuff, did you?" Pete asked, when they came in from what was hopefully their last trip outside. Dusk had crept in and they shook big, fluffy-dry snowflakes off their hats and shoulders when they came indoors.

"Nope. Bought a lot of it at Muldoon's." Kurt grinned and shrugged. "I get a bulk discount. I swear, the guy must be a survivalist or he retired from working for the CIA. He always has the latest, sweetest gadgets. Everything you need to make sure no one can sneak up on you from a hundred miles away, while civilization crumbles around you."

"You know, if he was a friend, it'd be really easy to make sure nobody can trace the stuff back to you." Pete froze when he saw both of us staring at him. "But that's not going to happen. Muldoon is a geek and his son is the biggest jerk in the…"

"What?" I wanted to reach across the table and yank on his collar, so I could shake him and get his mouth in gear. Or at the very least wipe that look of dawning horror off his face.

"Muldoon. Steve. He's a jerk. Always blaming someone else when he's the one who messed up."

"Everybody in town knows that," Kurt said. "What about it?"

"He went into the Marines, just like Toby did." Pete paused, nodding, visibly waiting for us to catch on. He sighed and dropped like a basket of rocks into the chair when we didn't say anything. "Muldoon was there at the quarries. And when they got caught and thrown in jail, he blamed you guys. He said if you hadn't shown up, nobody ever would have known who stole the equipment. He said it was just a stupid prank, and it's your fault they almost lost their diplomas and he had to go into the military."

"How long did he last in the Marines?" Kurt asked on a near-whisper.

"The last I heard, he was still in the Marines."

"But I saw him at the store." He sank down at the table next to Pete. "We were close, anyway."

"Muldoon is after me, using his father's equipment?" I shuddered. "You think Stanzer is home right now? You think we can trace all that equipment the housebreaker left back to Muldoon's shop?" I asked Kurt, when Pete jumped up and went to the phone to make the call.

"Unless he knows how to hide records. When we track the serial numbers back to the store, if we can, it could all be recorded as sold to Toby." Kurt thumped the table and gestured for Pete to hold up, before he even picked up the phone. "What if they're working together? We saw two people on that video. I don't think we'll find anything, because I've only found a few serial numbers on that equipment, and no answers yet."

Rather than making a phone call, we decided to put everything in writing. There was just a little too much to think through and digest, and it was too late in the day to get Stanzer worked up on a new tangent in the investigation. We made notes on what had happened and our theories, and I sent it as an email to him, along with some digital photos Harry had shot of the broken ramp and the area around it. The blood tests Kurt got a friend to do on the dogs the first time they had been fed and drugged asleep hadn't yielded anything, so we hadn't even tried this last time. All we could do was sit and wait and hope Stanzer had better connections and ideas. And pray, of course.

How come we always waited until things got to the strangulation point of weird and frustrating before we thought to pray?

# Chapter Eleven

Kurt left to settle into his temporary quarters at Felicity's house. Pete filled the house up with the stink of the sports rub he used on the aches and bruises still making him stiff. I went into my office to finish my next advice column. It didn't matter that it was nearly midnight. My brain had too many twisting thoughts to let me settle down to sleep.

*Dear Terry:*

*Secret admirers are romantic, right? I've been in love with this girl since 2nd grade. She was always a pudge, but that didn't matter to me, because I just thought she was the greatest. She helped me with my homework and when I broke my glasses, she led me home from school, and she got her brothers to protect me when the bullies picked on me. We took piano lessons together and she was so relieved when we had duets for recitals, so she didn't have to share the piano bench with the kid who picked his nose. When she had birthday parties, I always fought my mom to get Mary a gift she wanted, instead of the useful stuff moms like.*

*We've been best pals all our lives. Our senior year of high school, she lost weight, and got rid of her braces, and got contacts. Suddenly all the guys noticed her. I panicked. I finally figured out that it was great that she was a girl and I was a boy. Only she never realized that I was a guy.*

*I'm a coward. I got her candy for Valentine's Day and roses on Sweetest Day, and I could never get up the courage to just give them to her. I always left everything at her dorm door, or in her school mailbox, with really corny notes, telling her how much I love her. It's easy to say on paper, when you're not looking into her beautiful green eyes. I'd just die if she laughed at me, or got scared, or sick.*

*She told her friends about her secret admirer. Now the kid who used to pick his nose at piano lessons is a big football hero and he drives a Corvette. He's claiming that he's been her secret admirer all along.*

*How do I keep her from falling for this jerk? She's mine!*

*Desperate in Dayton*

~~

*Dear Desperate:*

*There's this new-fangled concept: communication. Talk! She knows you, right? She trusts you? She might not believe you right away, when you tell her you're her secret admirer, but if she's really your pal, she'll believe even without evidence. So tell her to her face.*

*And what I just said: evidence. Even if she told her friends about her secret admirer, I doubt she told them everything. You wrote her love notes, right? I'll bet, being a girl myself, she's kept some things to herself. So this lying nose-picker can't know everything you've written to her. Get the sequence of events right. What was the first gift you gave her? Where did you leave it for her? The little details will convince her.*

*I guarantee, she'll feel embarrassed. She might even be angry with you, for not trusting her enough to speak up sooner. It's going to be difficult to transition from pals to sweethearts. She might be flustered enough to reject you and encourage the lying football player. He does have a Corvette. She might be angry enough to forget this jerk has been lying, claiming credit for things he hasn't done. But be persistent. Be honest. Communicate. Either she'll come around or there will be permanent damage to your relationship.*

*But do you really want to go for the rest of your life, kicking yourself for not speaking up, eating your heart out over her? Seeing her end up with the lying football player? In the long run, a Corvette doesn't make up for knowing this guy picked his nose before he played the piano. Yes, you run the risk of losing this close friendship. Once you make the big reveal, your relationship will change. You'll lose the closeness, if she isn't open to being sweethearts. Romance does bring in a new dynamic.*

*Think about the time Cyrano and Roxanne wasted, when they could have been together. Don't waste any more time. Eventually, the truth will come out. Wouldn't you rather have it happen now, so you can either move into the new phase of your friendship or move on and find someone who really loves you? Or do you want to look back on years of longing and let regrets poison what happiness you do find? You both deserve to be happy. Cyrano confessed his love to Roxanne and then died in her arms. That was a lousy trick to play on her. Yes, love can hurt, but there's no reason for needless suffering, is there?*

*Choose: years of agonizing over "what if" and "if only I had," or risk losing her now through rejection. The time for masks and the Cyrano de Bergerac routine is over. Face her in the daylight.*

*Good luck.*

*Terry*

Okay, that wasn't the snarkiest of my responses, but I kind of liked the guy. I felt a little jealous, actually. It would be nice to have a secret admirer.

Come to think of it, I was suffering the polar opposite. A secret loather? I wanted this bozo to come out into the open and reveal his identity and his reasons for harassing me.

~~~~~

That Wednesday, I had my meeting with Sheridan, at his office in Independence. I honestly thought writing a nice, helpful, non-snarky column would get me fired, since the Evil Overlord liked my advice to have fangs. So to speak.

"Your best column yet," he said, almost before I got settled into his office.

Then he laughed when I could only stare at him for a good five-count. Part of my reaction could be blamed on the setting for this grudging little meeting. He didn't have the plush office suite I expected, with the oak desk big enough to park a Cessna inside it, and thick carpet that could snag my wheels. Sheridan had an office just a little bit bigger than the others I passed on the way to the back of the big, open room full of shoulder-high cubicle walls. I counted six doors, all evenly spaced apart, hanging open, showing the typical desk and filing cabinet arrangements. His office was bigger only because he had more furniture—a long table, presumably for meetings, eight chairs around it, an ordinary-sized desk and three times as many filing cabinets as I saw in the other offices. There was barely room for my chair to get between the meeting table and the filing cabinets, to sit in front of his desk. He had to pull aside the two ordinary padded office chairs for me to park facing him. Not a bit of mahogany or leather or brocade anywhere in the office. He had shelves up to the ceiling and the walls were painted plain,
~~~~~

institutional beige. No showy works of classical art or the weirdness of modern art. What happened to all the perks that the head of a big conglomerate ordinarily latched onto?

I really hated it when people didn't act or look like I thought they should.

"Okay." I took a deep breath. "Maybe I don't need to be snarky all the time." That was a big admission for me, especially when I kept hoping I'd go over the line and he'd be forced to cut me loose.

"I like variety." He settled back in his chair, interlaced his fingers, and rested his hands on the desk. Doggone it, but he looked ready to relax and have a long, cozy talk.

Not my idea of a pleasant afternoon.

"Can't I find anything to do that you won't like?"

"Why do you want to lose the column?"

"*Losing* implies you tried to hold onto it."

The Evil Overlord just leaned back a little further in his chair and laughed. "You admitted you were having fun, Saturday."

"I did not!" I played with the idea of levitating myself just long enough to leap over the desk and slap my hands over his mouth. Anything to hide that grin and stop that laughter.

The sound was contagious. It overrode my common sense. Somehow, I don't know how, my mouth twisted so I felt a grin pushing up on my cheeks. Dang, but that feeling kind of hurt when I fought it.

Since I had never been a fan of pain, I stopped fighting the smile. I let myself relax a little. Then I took a few deep breaths, trying to exhale all the tension I had let build up on the drive over to Independence. If I had to be honest (not that I'd ever say it out loud) I *was* having a little fun with the dratted column.

"You do know I'm a fan, don't you?"

"Stop scaring me."

"I sure hope one of these days, we can be friends." Sheridan sat forward again, resting his elbows on his desk. From the rumpled state of his shirt, he had put in a full day at work already. What had happened to the high-power executive who played chess with people's jobs and never broke a sweat?

Not that I'd ever admit it, but I was starting to like the guy. Just a little.

"That's fraternizing with the enemy," I offered. It felt kind of good when he just grinned wider.

Kind of scary, that he understood me.

"I'm in something of an awkward situation here. I know the area, but I've been gone long enough to feel like a stranger. Everything's changed so much. My family is from the Cincinnati area, and I've been handling the New Mexico holdings for the last ten years or so. When we decided to venture into publishing, I moved up north again to head up our acquisitions." He tipped his head to one side, pausing just long enough it made me wonder if he expected me to say something. "I remember trips up to Neighborlee when I was a kid. My grandfather is from there. We even stayed in town one summer. Divine's Emporium always stayed in my mind. There's something special about Neighborlee."

"So you took over our paper, like a souvenir?"

"My way of setting down roots, I guess. I'm assembling a council of representatives from all the papers. I want you on it."

"You must like ulcers."

"Maybe. And I figure I can trust what you say more than a dozen people who want to be my best friends."

"So if I become your best buddy, you won't think I'm honest anymore and you'll set me free?" I bared my teeth in a cheesy grin.

"I'm thinking of having a party in a loge at the Cavs game next Saturday, for all the council reps. Can you be there?"

"Sorry, I already have plans."

"That grimace makes me think you prefer some other basketball team. I know you like sports. Don't you play basketball?"

"Playing is one thing. I can't stand watching someone else play basketball because I spend the whole game thinking of what I would do differently. Actually, as far as I'm concerned, there are no professional sports in Cleveland until spring training starts. But that has nothing to do with it." I shrugged and fought not to show all the relief I felt that I honestly had an easy out. "I have plans."

"Fun plans?"

"Possibly."

"I think you're blushing."

"I am not!" For half a second, I thought about backing out of there, but I was in unfamiliar territory and the tight squeeze made it hard to maneuver.

"What are you doing, then?"

"A…club I belong to is having our Christmas party."

"Can't be much of a club if you won't even admit what it is."

"Star Trek, okay?" As soon as the words left my lips, I realized I had been neatly maneuvered by a master. I thought I was the one with the license to play games with people's brains. What happened?

"I love Trek! Are you strictly Classic Trek, or do you play in the Next Gen universe?"

"Uh… You know, you really do scare me."

"I was communications officer on my ship. Lieutenant J.G. What rank do you hold?"

"This is just a bad dream, right?"

"Lanie." He leaned forward, halfway across his desk, and lowered his voice. "Just consider the fact that you now have blackmail material to use against me. Mutual protection society."

I sighed. He had a point. The problem was that I felt like another safe part of my life had been invaded. Not only did he know about my comedy career, and owned more than one CD of my routine, but now he was a Trekker.

"Commodore."

Okay, I know I said I was a recovering Trekker, but it's one thing to stop looking at life through Trek-shaped glasses, and another to stop socializing with people who know how to have a good time without getting drunk or doing drugs or turning into amateur terrorists.

"I think I just struck gold. You would not believe how much I've been missing my crew."

"Didn't you write to Starfleet to find the local club?"

"I did. My application letter came back undeliverable — no forwarding address — and the email address they gave me bounced, too."

"Oh. Sorry."

"Sorry?" His voice cracked, making me laugh.

"Our last communications officer was… Well, to put it nicely, he was a whack job. We had to forcefully eject him, put him under permanent non-communication status. He was trying to get enough money together to build a life-size model of the *Enterprise-D*, and intimidated the wrong kid to hand over mega-bucks. The kid's father was a big-time lawyer. We had to excommunicate Riley to keep the rest of the club from being prosecuted. What saved us was that none of us had given him money. There was documentation in emails and on our Facebook page that a lot of members had tried to talk sense into him and discourage the whole stupid project."

"Ouch."

"Double ouch. Riley sabotaged our records with Starfleet. Since he had all the contact information, it's been taking months to get everything straightened out."

"So…" Sheridan leaned back in his chair again and gave me one of those slow grins that meant I was in trouble, but I might just enjoy it. "I'm guessing you need a new communications officer."

"Maybe."

~~~~~

I drove home in something of a daze. The universe had to be poised on the brink of imploding. Not only was I making nice with the Evil Overlord, but he wanted to play Star Trek with a bunch of lunatics he had never met.

Being that distracted, I didn't see the red pickup truck until it zipped past me, so close I heard something scrape. I swear it left flakes of paint on my driver's side door handle. I stared at the rear end where the license plate belonged, wondering if this was the same one that had tried to run me over just a few days ago. The truck was muddy where it wasn't white with salt. If there was a license plate under all that grime, it was invisible.

I turned right down Riverside Turnpike to cut through the Metroparks, heading for Neighborlee, and came to an immediate stop. Between the tow truck blocking both lanes, Gordon in his truck, and the two cars sitting in opposite ditches, there was no way I was going to get down that road any time soon.

Gordon saw me and strolled over from his truck to confirm what I could already see. We chatted for a few minutes, watching the truck's driver and his assistant hook up the first car to pull it out of the ditch. The drivers of the two cars stood well out of the way, watching and exchanging pieces of paper that I assumed had their insurance information on it. The big patch of shiny ice covering a low spot, where the blacktop had worn away to gravel road, spelled out the whole story. One car started to slide, the other swerved to avoid it, the first car overreacted, and they both ended up in the
~~~~~

ditches. From where I sat, it didn't look like they collided, which was a good thing.

"Guess I'll check out Spike's for a Christmas tree, since I'll be detouring anyway," I said to Gordon as I prepared to back up and do a three-point turn.

"Good idea. Think I should pick up a little tree for Mandy after work?"

"Sounds romantic to me."

"I should be off shift already. Maybe I'll see you over there after I finish up here." He waved me off. Just before I finished my turn, I saw him square his shoulders and walk over to where the two drivers watched the tow truck work on the second car.

Less than five minutes later, maybe half a mile after I crossed the line into Darbyville territory, I got pulled over by one of those hideous black cop cars. Why did Darbyville think it had to pursue the Nazi look, with black uniforms and black cars? It wasn't like they were invisible on dark nights.

"Out of the car," the hatchet-faced patrolman snapped, as soon as he got up to my open window. He had *D. Hartman* on the little strip over his pocket.

"Umm, what did I do?"

"Out." He leaned close and inhaled loudly. Then he leaned back, looking distinctly upset. Maybe he didn't like the cherry air freshener hanging from my rearview mirror?

"I'm going to need—" I started to gesture toward my chair in my back seat.

"I'm not going to tell you a second time. Just give me a reason to cite you. I can get another cruiser over here in ten minutes to drive you in to the station and impound your car." He stepped back and gestured at my door.

For about half a second, I considered asking him to open the back door for me, to get my chair out. I had the strength and control in my legs to hold myself upright long enough to swing my chair in or out of the Jeep. If he was in a hurry—I had no idea why—then it would be in his best interests to help me.

Looking at the scowl on his wind-burned face, I decided to keep my mouth shut, and opened the door. My legs twinged bad enough to get a few spasms in my feet, as I swung my legs around and slid down to the blacktop. My knees folded halfway before I could fight the spasms and pull myself upright again.

That little difficulty got a *hmph* that sounded awfully satisfied, but I was too busy avoiding falling onto that snowy, gritty blacktop road to see his face. What was this guy's problem?

"Just like I thought," he muttered, and took another step back.

"What did I do?" I asked, and reached for the door to hold myself up while I adjusted my feet so I could get the other door open and swing out my chair. Even on my worst days, I could stand up, but not for long. Today was a bad day, with all the stress of that anticipated meeting with Sheridan. Any attempt to hold myself upright for longer than thirty seconds resulted in a lot of pain.

What I wouldn't have given for Wolverine's rapid healing ability.

"You've got a lot of gall, pretending to be innocent." He gestured at the solid yellow divider line, barely visible under the crust of ice and snow. "Walk that line. Heel to toe, turn without going off the line, and go back."

I didn't have to be a genius to know that telling him he wasn't following proper procedure for the sobriety field tests wouldn't score any points for me. Why had he decided to pull me over for drunk driving anyway, at just three in the afternoon? Discretion said to keep my mouth shut and hope the sight of the wheelchair in my back seat would shake his common sense awake. This was one of those times where I didn't feel any guilt playing the sympathy card.

The problem was, my rough afternoon caught up with me and I couldn't resist the smart remark that spilled from my brain to my tongue with lighting speed.

"I would if I could. Believe me."

Fury widened his eyes. He grabbed my arm and yanked me off balance. I snatched at the door handle, but another spasm made my left knee fold. I couldn't hold myself up on one leg, and went down, catching myself with my hands before my face hit the pavement. Thank You, Lord, I had my thick leather driving gloves on.

Hartman yanked handcuffs from the loop on his belt and bared his teeth in a "just make my day" grin as he approached. He grabbed my right hand. Fortunately not the one I leaned on to try to get myself sitting upright. That would have sent me face-first into the ice and gravel. He was going to slap cuffs on me.

For what?

I wanted to use my telekinetic powers to send him flying, but I didn't need the headache with all the stress I was going through. I had enough common sense to know tossing a cop would only make things worse, even if he couldn't prove I had done it. If he had one of those in-dash cameras going, I would have all the proof I needed that I didn't touch him. However, I had heard enough rumors of tricks Darbyville cops played, I couldn't rely on that video evidence. After what Doni Halliday went through last March with a Darbyville cop, I didn't have high hopes for fair treatment. Obviously, this neo-Nazi facing me hadn't learned anything from his overzealous friend.

Then, through the pounding of my heart in my ears, I heard a car drive up, skid to a stop, and a heavy door slam open. I felt the first brush of the handcuff against the bare skin of my wrist. Gordon shouted my name, the handcuffs hit the ground, and half a second later he yanked me to my feet.

"What do you think you're doing?" Hartman growled. He at least had the sense not to interfere as Gordon settled me back in my driver's seat. Respect for another uniform or just plain intimidation from my friend's size, it didn't matter. "You're interfering in a DUI stop, officer. And you're outside your jurisdiction."

"DUI? Lanie?" Gordon shook his head. "Since when is manhandling a suspect part of the field test?"

"She wasn't cooperating."

"Sergeant Slaughter didn't give me a chance," I offered, when Gordon turned to me, one eyebrow raised in question. Why did I feel like a kid who just got called to the principal's office? I was the victim here, wasn't I?

"She can't even stand on her own feet. That's proof enough for me," the other cop sneered.

"Gee, I never noticed you had that problem, Lanie." Gordon sidestepped out of the way and opened my back door. "Take a look and think for five seconds."

# Chapter Twelve

It took all my self-control not to snort when the Darbyville cop's mouth dropped open at the sight of my wheelchair. He closed his mouth, swallowed hard, and I saw that surprise turn back to anger. Probably fueled with embarrassment now, instead of whatever self-righteousness he had been running on before.

"Handicapped woman doesn't have any business—"

"If the DMV says she's capable of driving, you don't have the right to argue."

"Probably her medication making her a hazard."

"You on any medication, Lanie?" Gordon said, and punctuated his words with a hard slam of the back door.

"Only if you count dark chocolate. What makes you think I was a hazard?" I had to ask.

"The guy who came through a few minutes before you gave me your license plate number and said you were swerving all over the road. Claimed you tried to force him into a ditch. There's red paint on your door, for proof."

"I thought that scumbag got too close." I shook my head, feeling a little dizzy. "That takes some fancy driving, to scrape paint without sending both of us into a ditch. I knew it was him. That's proof. Too bad I couldn't see his license plate this time, either."

"Who, Lanie?" Gordon asked. "What do you mean, 'this time'?"

"I don't know. Some guy with a beef against me."

Gordon and the Darbyville cop made me back up and tell them my side of the story. Finally! Then Gordon asked the kind of questions I couldn't avoid answering without feeling like the guilty party. In less than ten minutes, he had the story of the attempted run-down by Stanzer's office on Saturday, and the drugging of Felicity's dogs Friday night.

I didn't tell him about the gizmo the housebreaker left under my TV. That was a little too much hush-hush for Gordon to forgive, even if I was his commanding officer. When it came to police work, Star Trek had nothing to do with reality. But about halfway through the story, it occurred to me that the lab report would come up sooner or later, and the local cops would need to know what we were doing and what had been going on. Especially if we had to approach the suspects. Keeping things secret had become a mixture of survival technique and bad habit, for Felicity and Kurt and me. It actually hurt to force out the words, when I admitted we had found the suspicious black bag the housebreaker had left behind, and sent it away for testing. It didn't take much thinking for Gordon to tie everything else to the ruckus at our house the Friday after Thanksgiving, and the false report of me running over those kids last week.

"How come you didn't report any of this?" he demanded, leaning one hand on the roof of my Jeep and towering over me as only Gordon could do.

"Umm..."

"No. Wait a minute. Stanzer did. Anonymous reports, no names of the victims. Professional courtesy on a case he's investigating. Doggone it, Lanie, how are we supposed to protect folks in our town if they won't cooperate?" He thumped the roof hard enough to make my Jeep rock a little.

That was not the time to bring up the fact that I was protecting the town, too. Kind of hard to prove I was a superhero when I couldn't fly or bend metal or catch bullets with my teeth. Besides, Officer Hartman didn't look entirely convinced that I wasn't drunk. No need to make him think I really was on medication, or some illegal substances. Or delusional.

"We didn't think it was that serious. Until Saturday," I hurried to add. "We've got Stanzer working on it."

"Shouldn't go outside regular channels," Hartman offered. He flinched and offered a dopey smile when Gordon glared at him.

"When are you going to stop trying to be the hero all the time?" Gordon said with a sigh.

I nearly choked on that one. If he only knew.

"This isn't a game, Lanie. Didn't you learn anything when you broke your back? This isn't Senior Prank Night anymore, this is serious stuff. Next time, you could go over the cliff instead of jumping off in time."

Hartman waved his hands, flagging down Gordon while he was still warming up. I was almost grateful. Until his request for information resulted in Gordon identifying me as the town hero, for pulling Toby off the truck. Well, at least he looked at my wheelchair and my spazzy legs in a different light now.

It occurred to me that we were still dealing with the fallout from that Senior Prank Night disaster. Those three boys were still involved in something dangerous and stupid and maybe …

I broke out in a cold sweat and prayed Gordon and Hartman didn't notice. I hoped I wasn't as pale as I felt, when the possibility slammed into my brain.

What if that Senior Prank Night had gone so bad because our interdimensional enemy had interfered and manipulated things just as we had theorized four years ago?

And what if those three boys were somehow under the snake's control or influence back then, and *still* under its influence now?

That threw the events of the last week or two in an entirely different light. Especially since it certainly looked like I was the chosen target. Four years ago, I could believe that the boys and I were just random victims. We were convenient, we were within reach to take the brunt of the snake's viciousness. Now, though, there was purpose and choice behind all the odd and increasingly dangerous events.

I needed to talk with Angela ASAP. I needed to get all the guardians together. I needed to get away from these two cops who thought I was being an idiot trying to deal with things way over my head.

If only they knew.

So as usual, I figured out the smart strategy a little late.

I was praying hard as they finished lecturing me and getting details nailed down. I should have been turning all of this over to God a lot sooner. That was the proper order of things when evil struck at us. First, we should run to God. Then, depending on the level of weirdness and danger, we could either go to the police, or to Angela. When it came to Neighborlee weirdness, more often it was Angela and never the police.

I drove away about ten minutes later, after Hartman apologized a couple more times. I didn't make him beg me not to press charges. After all, I had to drive down the Darbyville section of this road to get to a lot of places. Besides, it wasn't really his fault. The guy in the red truck had really worked him up over the supposed danger I presented. Gordon would let him know just how lucky he was to get off that lightly.

Gordon expressing disappointment in a fellow officer, and the guilt he could inspire, was a far worse punishment than anything that might show up as a blip on Hartman's service record. From the look in Gordon's eye, he wasn't going to get to the Green family's Christmas tree farm any time soon. He would probably give his fellow officer a friendly lecture on proper procedure for handling DUI stops. Such as making sure there was evidence. Hartman hadn't smelled any alcohol on me (that explained the big inhale) so he assumed I was on something else. Okay, that was logical, but treating me like an escaped criminal still wearing a detention center orange jumpsuit went over the line.

The whole problem was one more strike against the guy in the red truck. Steve Muldoon? Toby Malone? Or someone else? I really did pray it wasn't Toby, because I liked the big stupid kid. Or whatever remained of the big, stupid kid under the sullen, slightly vacant expression he wore the last time I had seen him. Why was Steve Muldoon home, when he should have still been in the military? I had to admit, the circumstances were highly suspicious; both he and Toby home when no one really expected them. And why had Toby avoided coming to see me, after telling his father he had? Could the snake reach that far from Neighborlee to make all this happen? Or was someone else involved? With my luck, the mysterious old men in the dark van were probably part of this.

Unless "going to see Lanie" equated to trying to break into my house and drugging Felicity's dogs?

"Please, God, we don't need all this on top of Mum and Pop vanishing," I whispered, as I made the opposite turn from the one I should have taken, if I was going to Spike's parents' Christmas tree farm. Thanks to the DUI stop, I wasn't in the mood for shopping.

I was on autopilot, trying to force a few coherent prayers through the swirling of thoughts and suspicions in my head. Before I knew it, I was pulling up in front of Divine's. Angela came out the door before I had put my Jeep in park. She had her peacock shawl wrapped around her shoulders, not a coat. I knew she had felt me coming. She gestured for me to stay in my Jeep. I leaned over to unlock the door as she came through the gate, and she climbed in the passenger seat.

"Ford has had some odd dreams, and only last night saw you

in them."

"Then I'm not nutso." I tried to give her a cheeky smile, but my mouth kind of trembled. "The snake was involved, moving the boys that night at the quarries. At least two of them are back in town, and they're after me. Why am I the target?"

I really, really wanted Angela to scold me about being on an ego trip, but she just sighed and reached across to hug me. It took very little time to relate what had happened. Kurt had kept her updated on the other attacks, while consulting with Ford about the security system and the suspected bomb. At least I didn't get a scolding from her about not keeping her in the loop.

"I have learned over the years that pieces are put into place long before they are needed in the … well, it's not a game, certainly, but a massive, eons-old contest of strategies. Our enemy senses when changes are about to commence and new duties are given to us, or new members of our team join us. I sensed that Doni would be joining us as a guardian, when she came to town. That attack through Athena's computer program was a result of the snake sensing her presence and reacting. I suspect that a new phase in the contest is about to commence, and our enemy senses power centering on you. Or senses changes about to take place." Angela shrugged delicately. "I know that isn't much comfort."

"Well, at least we have some warning," I offered.

"At least our enemy has a pattern of over-reacting. He or it or they strike, trying to catch us unprepared, without adequate energy reserves. They shackle themselves because their premature actions mean they are not ready for battle, either."

"Should we be talking like this? What if the snake is listening and actually wises up and learns something?"

Yeah, my sense of humor was a defense mechanism, even if it could be really lame and badly timed. But look at me—I was permanently lame.

Fortunately, that got a smile from Angela. She hugged me, and as she slid out of the Jeep, she reminded me to pray, and suggested that the prayer chain at church get involved. Just to pray for the welfare of our town. They didn't need any details beyond that to call down the defenses and power reserves of heaven. I promised I would call the church office when I got home. Angela stayed standing on the sidewalk, one hand on the wrought iron gate of

Divine's, watching me as I drove away.

~~~~~

Neither one of my brothers was home when I got there, and that was good. It gave me time to think and calm down more and figure out how I would tell them about this latest attack from the camouflage guys. I didn't want to inflame them to the point of pulling a stupid stunt, after all.

Of course, that was assuming a camouflage guy was the driver of the red truck. It couldn't be two separate enemies, could it? Why would they booby-trap my house, possibly with poison or nerve gas or something in that black bag, and then turn around and pull nasty tricks that wouldn't do anything except waste time, frustrate, or embarrass me? Getting me stopped on a false DUI was in the nasty trick category, rather than trying to do physical damage. Nothing was consistent.

Kurt came over to check the security system soon after I got home, and to invite himself to dinner. I told him what happened, and we were still tossing theories back and forth when the boys got home. It felt good to see how angry they got over the DUI stop. They were sure Steve Muldoon was the guilty party, rather than Toby, because it was more like what Muldoon had done in school.

Oh, that was a comforting rationalization. Did that mean that if Toby was involved, he was the one trying to kill me, rather than humiliate me?

The really ironic, depressing part in all this was that I kept letting myself get distracted, and didn't call the church right away to ask for prayers.

~~~~~

I should have paid more attention to what Pete and Harry said after my run-in with the guy in the red truck and the Darbyville cop. I should have tried to find out more about Steve Muldoon, for one thing. If I had, I might have had an inkling, even a vision, of what waited for me. Part of the problem was that neither Steve Muldoon, nor the third member of the trio, Jay Parker, had been in any of my classes when I taught at Neighborlee High. I didn't know what they looked like, outside the yearbooks. I had never made contact with the Muldoons, never reacted to the nasty things Steve said about me after my back was shattered. Maybe my lack of any reaction at that time inspired him to hate me, and carry a grudge.

Which made him an open, accessible vessel and tool for the snake. If our enemy from below and beyond was behind all this trouble.

Then again, something that happened to him in boot camp or during his service in the Marines might have knocked his brain off track, too. It rather bothered me that Stanzer's initial investigation stated that Steve Muldoon was still in the service, even though both Kurt and my brothers had seen him at his father's electronics store. Some very skillful blocking kept Stanzer's contacts from getting much more information than that. Words like "classified" and "security clearance required" stamped across the files or flashing on the computer screen, denying access. The very quietness of the denials for further information made Stanzer suspicious, and I agreed with him.

So, we had one vengeful Marine sneaking around town, either using Toby Malone as a cover for his activities, or working with him, and using his father's merchandise to spy on and booby-trap my house. Reason enough to take some actions.

My live-in heroes, Pete and Harry, decided to take the law into their own hands. They decided they were justified in what they did next. We had semi-reliable proof that the equipment we found under the TV, with some of the serial numbers filed away and the others subtly altered with a scary level of skill and intent, had to have come from Muldoon's store.

Friday afternoon, I had a visit at work from our friendly neighborhood police officer. Gordon looked peeved, which was kind of shocking to see, because his face was made for slow and easygoing expressions.

"Got a complaint from Shaun Muldoon about your brothers," Gordon said, as he settled down on the edge of my desk at the *Neighborlee Tattler's* office.

He had the tact to wait until the office was nearly deserted, everyone either out on stories or gone for the day, before he came to visit me. Working in a newspaper sort of came with a built-in handicap of nosey people who knew how to get information no matter how hard you tried to hide it.

"What'd they do?" I tried to imagine either of the boys breaking windows or harassing someone inside the store.

What was the worst they could do? Stand outside and tell people going inside for Christmas shopping not to buy from

Muldoon's? My brothers, even at their angriest, just weren't the type to settle things with their fists or vandalism or outright threats.

On top of that, I had a hard time imagining Harry getting into mischief of any kind. Not just because he was nearly as easygoing as Gordon, but because he was so busy nowadays, making deliveries. Christmas didn't put just merchants into the black for the accounting year. Someone had to bring them their merchandise and make deliveries, after all.

That left Pete to get into trouble. So why hadn't he gotten himself caught in the middle of mischief by himself?

"Shaun caught them skulking around the back of his store. He thought it was odd enough, but they're following Steve around. He says his son's pretty touchy, being home on unexpected leave, no explanation." Gordon's frown deepened. "Funny thing is, I didn't even know Steve was back in town. How long have your brothers been tailing him? And why?"

"You know the weird things at my house, and that fake DUI stop?" I didn't have to go any further. Gordon's brain always worked in extreme contrast to his outer appearance. He was on the verge of being promoted to detective, after all. He sat up straighter and his eyes widened a little less than two seconds after I spoke.

"Won't help your case, getting into trouble following him around. He can claim he's reacting to the boys hassling him. That Steve Muldoon wasn't the most forgiving guy, even in high school."

"You knew him then?" I glanced around, praying nobody else was close enough to overhear what we were talking about. God listened, even before I prayed, because in the minute or two since Gordon sat down on my desk, the office had emptied.

"Too well. Our first run-in, I caught him doctoring some other guy's tailpipe with a potato. Fighting over a girl, of course." He nudged my wheel with the toe of his boot. "I started wondering what your brothers would want, tailing an arrogant jerk like Steve. Then I remembered the last time your family tangled with his."

"Tangled?" I had to laugh.

"You were pretty out of it, but sentiment around Neighborlee wasn't too friendly toward any of those three boys. Common thought was that Muldoon was the ringleader of that trio of idiots. Toby got all the press, since he stole his dad's keys, and saving his neck landed you here. Muldoon, though, he got nasty when talk put some blame on him. His dad's a good guy, a little heavy with his fists, but with a rock-head like Steve in the house, he probably has to be." Gordon shook his head and studied the toe of his slowly swinging boot. "Steve said some nasty things about you, how if you hadn't gotten in the way and messed things up, nobody would have been hurt."

"Except Toby would be dead. That truck would still have gone right over the edge into the quarry and taken him along with it."

I choked for a second, as a new thought came to me. Based on my new suspicions. What if Kurt, Felicity and I hadn't been at the quarries that night? Would everything have gone as Toby and his friends planned? Would they have just parked the two stolen city trucks at the quarries and walked home in the rain? Had our presence prompted the snake to blind Toby in the storm, send him driving through the barricades and down the cliff road? If I hadn't come swooping down to check on him, would he have been able to jump free of the truck, instead of his coat getting caught?

Was everything somehow my fault? Well, not my fault as in I had caused the problems, but my fault because the snake was out to get me, and used Toby.

"Yeah, well, the guys who are in the wrong usually end up making the most noise and the nastiest threats. Anyway, what I'm saying is, if your brothers heard he was in town and decided to take some late revenge... Well, I know they're not. But Steve Muldoon was a liar and a bully before. He's had some training, learned some nasty tricks. And he's had four years to nurse his grudges."

"So knock their heads together and get them to lay off before Steve Muldoon decides everybody's picking on poor pitiful him." I nodded, and felt like a hundred-pound weight had landed on my shoulders with all the subtlety of a dynamited building.

"People like him try to erase the proof or evidence against them by making others look bad. They never admit they're wrong," Gordon added.

Harry and Pete looked suitably repentant when I got home that evening and found them just coming out of the garage apartment, after visiting Kurt. I suspected Gordon had given them a more direct version of the warning visit he had given me, and they had gone to Kurt for advice. Which was nice, and convenient that Kurt was there, but it irked me.

"We're laying off," Harry said. "The guy's slime. He acts like he expects to be followed. Always looking over his shoulder, moving in the shadows. He's guilty, as far as I'm concerned."

"Yeah, well, the courts aren't going to listen to your gut instinct. They'll want proof, and all they'll have is a police report filed by Muldoon against you two," I had to say.

I wanted to hug them, for coming to my defense. I was in charge of them while Mum and Pop were away, after all, so I had to be the adult. I was kind of sick of having to be mature.

A tap on the kitchen door and Kurt walking in a second later kept Pete from retorting. From the fire in his eyes and the hardness of his mouth when he took that deep breath before speaking, it was probably something angry. Nice to know my brothers were protective of me.

"Any more info from Stanzer and his contacts?" Kurt asked. From the looks he exchanged with Pete and Harry, I had the feeling he had come in to either shut them up or mitigate the lecture I was about to give them.

Only I wasn't about to lecture. I was too tired. I figured they had been lectured enough. Besides, the snarky part of me wanted Steve Muldoon to know he wasn't going to get away with his nasty tricks, we suspected him, and we were on the alert.

"How about Chinese tonight?" I said instead. "And nope, not a word from Stanzer. He emailed me that he hoped for an answer by tomorrow, but nothing beyond that. And don't call him. The guy has to spend some time on his other clients," I added, when Pete looked at the phone. "Call Manchu's, will you?"

~~~~~

*Dear Terry:*

*I think I'm stuck. Help? I'm in law school because my girlfriend needs me to be a lawyer. I don't want to be a lawyer. I want to be a housepainter and design video games with my buddy and start our own business. But my girlfriend is a social worker and she needs a lawyer who can fight for all these kids who are just breaking her heart.*

*But I hate law school. I'm good at it, but I hate arguing and the whole suit-and-tie routine. Why can't I fix the kids' problems by being their pal and letting them live with me?*

*My girlfriend is the greatest girl in the whole world, and she*
~~~~~

*wants to make a difference, and I want to help her. What am I going to do? One semester has just about killed me. I can't imagine spending the rest of my life in courtrooms, and buried under paperwork. Besides, all this studying is interfering with this really killer game program me and my buddy are this close to finishing. We could be millionaires. But I have to use my computer for studying, not programming.*

*What am I going to do? How do I tell her?*

*Legal Beagle*

~~

*Dear Beagle:*
*Did your girlfriend ask you to become a lawyer? Or did you decide that was what you had to do, because she cares so much?*

*You seem to like kids. Here's an idea: help a few, hands-on. Instead of working on changes that could take years, why not do what can be done now?*

*How about becoming a Big Brother? If you're at least 30, how about a foster parent? If this girl means so much to you that you'd kill yourself to make her happy and be her hero, have you considered marrying her and being foster parents together?*

*Working one-on-one with one kid could make all the difference in the world. One kid at a time. Why give yourself a lifetime of ulcers doing something you hate, when you could make just as much impact for good by doing something you enjoy?*

*Become a millionaire with that video game, so you can help a dozen kids. That makes more sense than a life sentence in a three-piece suit and buried under mountains of paperwork.*

*Go get 'em, superhero.*

*Terry*

Felicity called just as I finished sending my column piece and was thinking about shutting down my computer for the night. She was Downtown, calling on Jake's cell phone. She didn't have a phone of her own, other than the landline in her apartment. Too expensive and too troublesome to protect all those sensitive electronics. And after a while, she got sick and tired of trying to explain to the guys at the stores why the phones kept dying. She got a reputation, and they refused to sell her phones unless she waived the warranty. I knew she had already warned Jake about her "high bio-electrical current" that zapped electronics, so it was a sign of true love that he let her use his phone.

And that meant it was also an emergency for her to call me.

"That Malone kid is out here, looking pretty suspicious," she said, before I could do more than say hello.

"What do you mean by suspicious? Who's he with?" Right there, I sent up a fast, desperate prayer that Toby was alone, not with Steve Muldoon.

"Nobody. That's the weird thing. He's just been driving or walking around. Jake is mellow enough right now, he's willing to drive me around, or sit and wait. We're in the parking lot under the Rapid tracks, up behind Tower City, just watching him. He sits and just listens to his cell phone. Which is kind of creepy. For all we know, he's getting instructions from his evil master. Or he has a girlfriend who's giving him what-for," she added with a snicker.

"What has he done besides drive around and park?"

"Nothing. No going into stores. No meeting people. No dropping things off. I've gone up to him twice, just testing, you know? He looks right at me, and then through me, like I'm in the way of the view and I'm not even important enough for him to ask me to get out of the way."

"I think you guys should get out of there. We're up against two guys who've had military training. I haven't had any impressions warning me of anything, but that doesn't make me feel any better."

"Lanie--"

"We haven't heard from Stanzer yet. He admitted that it has to be something pretty high-tech or nasty, if his connections haven't given him an answer. It means they aren't able to, yet. I think —"

"Can't talk now. He's heading this way."

Felicity hung up the phone. I hit the redial, and went right to voicemail. That meant she knew I would try calling her back, and she had turned off the phone. Usually she left her phone off the hook, when we were arguing or teasing each other. Smart, Felicity was. And just cocky enough to not want to listen when I was in Mother Hen mode. Granted, she was with Jake, a security expert, but if the snake was using Toby, and he was working with Muldoon, they might be in over their heads.

I wasn't surprised when I got the call nearly two hours later, to come to the hospital.

Felicity and Jake had followed Toby to a picnic shelter in the

Metroparks in North Olmsted. Jake took pictures of Toby taking a brown duffel bag from the otherwise empty shelter and putting it in his car. Then he drove back to Neighborlee, where he parked in the empty lot kitty-corner behind my house, sheltered by the big pine trees and shadows, and unpacked the bag, using his trunk as a worktable. Felicity and Jake set up in the yard next door. Mrs. McTavish was our second-grade teacher and had us over every other month for junk food and action movies, so Felicity was semi-legal when she camped out there.

The problem came when Toby unpacked a twin to the little black bag we had found in the surprise package the intruder had left under the TV. Felicity was using Jake's binoculars with night vision lenses, and she knew what she was looking at. She crept up to the fence and didn't pay attention when she got tense and grabbed the chain links. That plastic coating on the fence didn't provide much insulation when she got upset. She overloaded. The steel of the fence magnified the electro-magnetic pulse. A fireworks display went off in Toby's car. It triggered the mechanism of the gizmo he was working on, and released a gas from the little black bag. For two seconds, it seemed to sparkle, swirling around Toby like it was trying to stick to him. Then it faded to a phosphorescent green-gray and wisped away in the cold night breeze.

Toby collapsed. Felicity leaped over the fence and got a whiff of gas before Jake shouted for her to cover her mouth and nose.

Jake had riot gear in his trunk. Scary? That meant he was ready to race to a problem spot even when he was off duty. He grabbed his gas mask before he went after them. Felicity was fine, not even dizzy, by the time I showed up at the hospital. I never noticed the commotion in the yards behind us, because there *wasn't* much commotion. The fireworks only lasted for about five seconds. Jake and Felicity got Toby into Jake's car and drove to the hospital, where they called the police about the car in the empty lot.

Fortunately, Jake had the smarts and experience to get the black bag sealed up in an evidence bag from his emergency kit. His first thought was to try to figure out an antidote to whatever took Toby down. His training helped in the investigation and saved us from a lot of skepticism and delays, because that was all the evidence we had. When the police showed up to examine the car, it was gone. Along with the rest of the gizmo Toby had been assembling. Nothing left but tire tracks and several sets of footprints in the snow to prove the incident hadn't been a delusion. Not good. It meant whoever Toby was working with knew what happened, and took care of damage control quickly.

"The kid is acting weird," Felicity told me, when Kurt and I joined them in the emergency room. "And it's not the gas, because I got some of it and I'm not loopy."

"That's a matter of opinion." Jake grinned and wrapped his arm around her waist. Felicity just grinned back at him.

Must have been nice to be in love enough to joke with a guy. Not that I would know from personal experience.

Tom Malone showed up then. That just showed how much more efficient superheroes are than hospital administrators, when it came to calling the parents of patients admitted to the ER. Dr. Trane stepped out of the examination room a few seconds later, so Felicity let him take over explaining. He had been the on-call doctor at the orphanage when we were kids, so he had a lot of experience in dealing with weirdness. Rumors said that when anyone was brought in for treatment for something that happened within the borders of Neighborlee, he was always called. Even before the doctor on duty started the examination.

"The police will have to analyze what remains in the container that released the gas, but my first guess is some kind of nerve gas, or at the very least a new kind of tranquilizer." Dr. Trane included us, even though we only had sketchy reasons to be there at all. "Toby isn't coming out of it as fast as I'd like. Felicity here is just fine, and she wasn't when she came in twenty minutes ago."

"What was he doing?" Tom demanded with a mournful, confused look and tone. I breathed a silent sigh of relief that he wasn't blaming us already.

In a way, it *was* our fault. If Felicity hadn't followed Toby and zapped his car, none of us would be there right that moment.

"I think it's time we laid all our cards on the table," Kurt said. He nudged my wheelchair around to face the two-seater sofa where Tom and Dr. Trane sat, then pulled up a chair for himself. Felicity and Jake joined us, pulling up chairs to form a circle. I had a mental image of a wagon train bracing for an Indian attack and someone shouting, "Circle the wagons!"

Then Kurt went through a list of everything weird that had

happened since we knew Toby came back to town, in chronological order. He didn't say specifically the vandalism and intrusions had started with Toby's return. From the widening of Tom's eyes and the creeping loss of color in his face, he picked up the implications.

"Why would he want to hurt you?" Tom said, almost pleading. The look in his eyes made me feel like I was the guilty party, yet he didn't blame me at all.

I have always hated that kind of situation. Those uncomfortable, squeezed moments gave me some insight into why some superheroes became super-villains. It has always been a lot easier to lash out at everyone who crossed their eyes at you, rather than try to make peace and communicate, and help the people who considered you a freak or dangerous or both.

"I don't know. Unless," I had to admit, prompted by that thick streak of guilt Mum had instilled in me, "he blames me for having to go into the military."

"You saved his life. He would have gone into the quarry with that truck if you hadn't pulled him off." Tom leaped to his feet.

I understood the crackling tension that demanded he move or explode. What I wouldn't have given to be able to pace, right that moment.

"Like I've been saying too many times lately," Kurt offered, "a lot of times, the ones with the most guilt are the loudest and nastiest and most eager to lay blame on someone else. A drunk tears through a neighborhood at three in the morning, sideswipes someone's car, totals it, and then tries to sue the owner of the car for the dent in his fender, claiming that car shouldn't have been parked in the street. That's the way the world is."

"That's not the way I raised my boy." His expression switched from hurting to determined and angry.

I grabbed my wheels and rolled after him when he turned and walked down the short hall to Toby's room. I kept up with him so close, I almost jabbed his ankles with my footrests before I saw he had stopped.

Toby was awake, frowning at some spot in the air over his bed. Not a good sign. He turned his head toward the door, moving slowly like someone else was running the controls inside his head and didn't quite have the moves down.

"How're you feeling, boy?" Tom said.

Toby just looked at him like he didn't recognize him. Or maybe that blank look of disinterest just meant he barely registered that his father stood about four steps into the room.

I turned my chair to get a better angle to see. Big mistake.

Toby caught the movement and his eyes widened. Color washed his face and his lips pulled back from his teeth in a snarl. "You're dead," he growled.

For about a heartbeat, I could have sworn someone else's voice came out of his mouth.

"What're you talking about?" Tom said.

"You are so dead. We're gonna make like you never existed!" Toby sat up—or rather, tried to. Someone had used those restraining straps on him that I usually saw on TV shows and never believed were real.

Thank goodness they were real, because Toby tried to yank his arms free and reach for me. His fingernails were dirty and broken. I had a sudden image of him clawing me and infecting me with some disgusting disease that would rot my flesh before I died.

"Why?" I managed to demand in a reasonably calm voice. Forget trying to sound authoritative and powerful, and scare the truth out of him. I couldn't manage it when I taught high school, so why try that trick now? "What have I done?"

"Freaks!" His voice rose into a howl, strong enough to rattle the acoustic tiles in the ceiling. Two octaves higher, he might have had the strength to shatter glass. "Gotta kill the freaks! It's all your fault!"

Dr. Trane, as I mentioned, had experience dealing with Neighborlee-related weirdness. Toby must have been putting on this show earlier, because the doctor and a male nurse raced into the room just about the time Toby said, "Kill." They jabbed a needle into his arm by the time he said, "fault." Toby let out a howl and threw himself back into his pillow, as if that would free him of the needle. He thrashed against the restraints and foamed at the mouth. Interesting. I had never seen that happen on a human before.

The question was whether Toby was still human.

# Chapter Thirteen

Felicity grabbed my chair and Kurt yanked on Tom's arm and got both of us out of there. Tom just shook his head and stumbled a little before we were all back in our circle, minus Dr. Trane. No more sounds came from Toby's room.

"That's not my boy," Tom said. "Whatever he inhaled did that to him. Doc said nerve gas, right?"

"Right," Kurt said.

~~~~~

"The thing about drugs is that a lot of times, they release what's already in the mind and soul," Harry said.

Pete and Harry joined Felicity, Kurt and me in my kitchen for some serious talking and a junk food binge. Jake had to go in for a midnight shift security detail.

"Drugs don't put any new thoughts inside your head. They just knock down the barriers you put up to keep you from acting on your homicidal daydreams."

"Unless someone brainwashed Toby and put those ideas in his head." Felicity cringed a little, like she felt guilty for making the suggestion.

Well, it needed to be said.

"So, did somebody do the same thing to Muldoon," Pete said, "or is he the ringleader?"

"That's the next question." Kurt slouched so deeply in that stiff kitchen chair that his head rested on the top rail and he was in serious danger of sliding under the table. "So, we're pretty much agreed Toby isn't to blame?"

"Except for putting himself where someone had access to him to program him," I said. "Dang! I wish I hadn't watched all those dumb TV shows about government conspiracies and super-spies and brainwashing and all that." The attempt at humor fell flat almost before it left my mouth.

"Yeah, but you wouldn't give up *Stingray* to save your life, so just shut up," Felicity retorted with a half-hearted grin.

She was right. There was just something about the combination
~~~~~

of vintage Corvette, black leather jacket, and mysterious Italian male that always got to me. It was an addiction. So sue me.

Hey, something had to replace Star Trek in my obsessions.

"What scares me is that with the military connection between them … what if it isn't just the snake this time? What if it's the guys who have been taking Lost Kids? Suppose it's a government conspiracy, not some lunatic with a grudge against you," Kurt said.

"Maybe it's not Lanie, in particular?" Pete looked about as scared as a high school smart-alec could look, without admitting it. I wished he was little enough to sit on my lap again, so I could cuddle him. I needed some cuddling right about then, too. "And maybe it's not the snake at all."

"Meaning?" Harry said.

"What if it's just a test run? You know, Toby has something against Lanie. Whaddayacallit, some deep emotional bond like they've been talking about in psych class. They're creating robot soldiers, and they couldn't care less about Lanie, but she's an easy target."

"Sitting duck," I muttered. That got a few crooked smiles.

"I don't know what's worse," Kurt said. "Choosing her as a convenient target, or someone suspects about us and made Toby — maybe Muldoon, too — the weapons to go after us. Toby did scream something about killing freaks, didn't he?"

I really wished he hadn't brought that up. I wanted to forget that part.

~~~~~

Monday night, we just continued the conversation and theorizing. Kurt, Felicity and I went to Stanzer's office, to hear what he had learned in two intense days of scrambling and digging and harassing his sources.

Since Steve Muldoon seemed to be marginally involved, we decided it would be smart to investigate the third boy there that fateful Senior Prank Night at the quarry. Jay Parker, according to the suspiciously brief records, had a decent career as a chaplain's assistant, up until seventeen months ago, when he had a reunion with Toby and Steve, got transferred to a training facility in Arizona (can we say N.I.D., straight out of *Stargate*?) and then vanished.

"Speaking of vanished. Or rather, the opposite. As in, mysterious appearances." Stanzer paused for dramatic effect. "He's
~~~~~

one of you."

"One of—" Felicity sat up straight and gripped the front edge of his desk. "Another Lost Kid?"

"No such thing as coincidences," Kurt murmured.

"Okay, now I'm getting scared. What if he's after all of us?"

"They're depending on high-tech, so you're safe," I offered. She gave me a withering look, which was actually a good sign. If she could limit herself to sarcastic looks and snarky comments, then Felicity could still think clearly. She was in control and wouldn't wipe out all the electronics in Stanzer's building.

"The question is if Parker is the leader of the trio. Maybe he's locked in some mad scientist's laboratory somewhere, and the other two were sent to bring us in," Kurt said.

"Nobody saw you two doing anything except drive around that night," I pointed out. "All they know is that I got Toby off that truck in time to avoid a crash landing. They suspect me of being— or maybe having been—more than I appear to be. They might think I'm just pretending to be in a wheelchair, that my back healed against all logic—"

"It did." Felicity's expression shifted from ticked back to scared. "You should be on a ventilator and a catheter, not playing basketball and getting yourself around without any help."

"Yeah, but the doctors all say they misdiagnosed me. It's in my records that I wasn't as bad as everyone first thought." I mustered a brave smile, despite the ice trying to congeal through my lungs and guts. "Whoever is after me or watching me or whatever, they might just believe I have some more tricks left to me, even if I am stuck in this chair."

"Shades of comic book mutants," Stanzer muttered. "Doesn't it occur to them that if you had that kind of power, you could protect yourself? Maybe even sense enemies before they attack?"

"Yeah, but we're the good mutants, not the bad ones," Kurt pointed out.

"More important than that, we have to answer to Angela if we turn into bullies," I said with a long-suffering sigh.

At the back of my mind, I was very sure she would approve defending ourselves with whatever it took. Just as long as we had sufficient provocation and there was no other choice than to react with equivalent violence.

That lightened the atmosphere a little, but not for long. We had learned long ago that the rules for mutant battles in comic books didn't apply to real life. The fact remained that we had enemies out there, and no real proof to convince the authorities to arrest Toby and Steve. I could ask Col. Hayward to step in, but he already had a pretty nasty crick in his neck from looking the other way when it came to Neighborlee. We didn't dare take the law into our hands. Usually, to protect our town, we worked under cover of darkness. This time, to put our enemies off our trail and convince them we were harmless, we would have to work in broad daylight. We couldn't give any more clues that we were indeed more than mere mortals.

When we left Stanzer, he was already hard at work on his computer. He hinted he was owed favors by people who knew how to get information that had been hidden so deeply even the people who put it there had forgotten it existed. We had to wait until morning to pay a call on Mrs. Silvestri and see if she could remember Jay Parker, and if anything was weird about him. Weirder than the usual weirdness that populated Neighborlee, of course.

Too late, it occurred to me to ask Stanzer how the Christmas play went last Saturday. Well, chances were good I would see him quite often before this Saturday's two performances. I could ask him then.

If I wasn't in the hospital or gassed or some worse condition.

~~~~~

Mrs. Silvestri didn't have much of anything to tell us about Jay Parker when we went to visit her at the retirement village on Tuesday. He wasn't that different from the other boys in his age group at the orphanage. Nothing unusual happened when he was around.

"He did have a problem with anger, though," she said, after sitting and thinking, eyes narrowed and lips pursed, for about ten minutes.

The three of us waited patiently. We were used to Mrs. S. and her long thinking sessions. It was nice not to be on the receiving end of some of her creative punishments. She was never cruel, and we knew she loved us. The worst part of any punishment, for most residents of Neighborlee Children's Home, was knowing we had
~~~~~

disappointed her. I had to wonder if Jay was one of the few who didn't care about Mrs. S's feelings.

"Then again, what boy his age, in his circumstances, didn't have a problem with anger?" Mrs. S. sighed and sat back in her easy chair, nodding. "Looking back, I'm surprised he *didn't* get into trouble. Not one little bit."

"That's suspicious," Kurt muttered.

"The boys he ran around with, though…none of them were orphanage boys. There were no boys his age, so he didn't have any close friends among his housemates." She shook her head, eyes narrowing in thought again. "Those boys were constantly in trouble. Getting into fights, racing their bikes in the most dangerous parts of the quarries." She snorted. "How blind we are, when someone acts the way we want them to."

"What's that supposed to mean?" Felicity said, grinning.

"That means Parker was such a model inmate, she didn't think maybe he was the ringleader and got everyone else to do his dirty work," I guessed.

Mrs. Silvestri scowled and shook her head, making us all laugh.

"I thought he had straightened up when he took up with Toby Malone. Then that Steve Muldoon made them a trio and dragged them both down to his level. What's he gone and done?" she demanded, shaking her finger at us. "There are times you shouldn't keep your cards so close to your vest. After what happened to you the last time you tangled with that threesome, I should think at least you'd have the sense to leave this to the authorities, young lady. Then again…" One corner of her mouth quirked up. "You three have been a team since you were in diapers."

"Considering we're not all the same age, that puts weird images in my head." That earned me a friendly swat on my leg.

"It's time you three 'fess up what you're doing. What's so special about Jay Parker? Does it have anything to do with this hunt of yours? I didn't think he was like you and the ones who vanished, just because he didn't do anything unusual."

"Unusual." Kurt snorted and slouched in his chair until his tailbone balanced on the front edge and his legs stuck out across the tiny living room. I was pretty sure the only places he touched the ground or the chair were at his neck, his tailbone, and his heels.

We knew a long time ago not to keep secrets from her. She knew we could do things most kids our age couldn't, but pretended not to notice. She bandaged our wounds when we miscalculated our growing abilities, if Angela wasn't around when we got caught in the fallout. Like when Kurt fixed a compressor for the airbrush equipment a little too well, and blew up the art room at the high school, nearly blinding himself with debris. Or when I flew crooked, to rescue a little girl caught in a tree trying to rescue her cat, and hit the main trunk with my face. Mrs. S. was to us what Alfred was to Batman.

We had never spoken out loud the things we silently understood among the four of us.

With much editing, to protect Stanzer's secrets, we told her about the break-in and vandalism at my house. Felicity's dogs getting drugged. The false police reports and incidents. The nerve gas that had knocked Toby out, which Stanzer's connections hadn't identified yet. Saturday's incidents with the car that went haywire and then vanished, and Toby's mental fireworks. We finished up with what Stanzer had learned and hadn't been able to learn, and how we were pretty sure it all tied into that Senior Prank Night when I saved Toby's life.

"My, you three do have a talent for finding complications, don't you?" Mrs. S shook her head, giving us an ironic smile. "I will do some digging of my own and see what I can find. I do have all my old connections, even though I'm retired. And some connections my superiors never knew about. The less they knew, the better off my children were, I always figured."

She nodded for emphasis, and I knew Kurt and Felicity felt just as encouraged as I did. Mrs. S. had some superhero talents of her own, we were sure. What Stanzer couldn't dig up, maybe she could.

Then, because she had just confessed to more connections, and because we knew better than to withhold any information. we told her about the grim patterns and ties Kurt had put together and confirmed on his last trip. How the Grandstones had been involved in essentially ruining the lives of other Lost Kids, cancelling their potential, maybe even cutting short their lives. Only the Lost Kids who stayed free of Grandstone influence stayed in Neighborlee and made something of their lives. And they were the only Lost Kids, other than the few who married into the Grandstone family, who had children and grandchildren.

"I keep track of the descendants of my children," Mrs. Silvestri said, her voice soft, her gaze distant. "I must admit some dismay to realize that I never caught that particular pattern or trend or what have you. Yes, so very few of you have children, to pass on your talents and your duties. I have been paying particular attention to the Longfellow granddaughters, wondering just what this third generation will do, what they will become. Do something for me?"

She blinked and her gaze came back to the room, and there was a hint of something like tears in her eyes and voice.

"Anything," Kurt said. "Just name it."

Felicity and I nodded. We didn't have to raise our hands in pledge or sign a document in blood. We had just made a vow that would hold us stronger than the most stringent, iron-clad contract.

"Watch out for those girls. Even more than you three, the future of Neighborlee could depend on them." A tiny smile curved up the left corner of her mouth. "Until you start having children."

Felicity blushed hard enough there were little pink sparks off the ends of her curls. I certainly hoped Jake was planning on giving her a ring for Christmas.

~~~~~

Tom got Toby released from the hospital on Wednesday. There was nothing we could do to keep him locked up, anyway. All the tests showed he had recovered from the gas. He claimed he couldn't remember what happened from the time he got into his car Saturday afternoon. I believed him.

Just because we couldn't keep Toby where people with long needles and drugs and restraining straps could watch him didn't mean we were helpless or defeated. Tom was on our side. He wanted whatever was wrong with his son cured. Or if someone was controlling his mind, as we feared, he wanted that control severed and Toby set free. So he worked with us.

The entire Malone family went shopping on Friday, hitting the biggest malls in our part of Ohio. That left their house unoccupied for most of the day. Kurt and Harry spent the day rigging their house with sensors, and installing keypads on the locks. Without the codes, nobody was getting out of that house unless they could go up the chimney. Since the Malones had electric heat, the opening into the chimney was too small for Toby. Unless he developed a
~~~~~

sudden ability to turn into a guinea pig with suction cups on his prickly little feet.

Tom looked grim when he dropped by my house that evening to report on the shopping trip. We would have had to be stupidly optimistic to hope something weird *wouldn't* happen so soon after Toby got released. I knew it was bad news even before he reported that Toby went glassy-eyed four times and tried to walk away from his parents during the day. Each time they stopped him, he struggled a few seconds, then looked around like he had no idea what had just happened. By the third time it happened, Toby understood something was wrong. It scared him.

"All these years, I thought it was just bad jokes. Talking about Black Ops and mind control," Tom said, after he gave us his report on the day's excursion. He slumped on the edge of the couch, his hands hanging down between his knees, as exhausted as a man could be after a day of Christmas shopping. His eyes begged us for some good news and hope.

"It could just be hypnotism," Pete offered. "You know, like he's programmed to do things. Not that anyone is actually controlling him, right now."

I had seen a couple of TV shows where that kind of situation had been part of the plot. The uncomfortable part of Pete's theory was what happened if the people who were programmed to do something nasty (like try to kill me) were kept from acting. In that *Stargate SG-1* episode that I remembered far too clearly for comfort, the operatives went suicidal when they were prevented from carrying out their programmed mission. Not what I wanted to happen to Toby, even if I held a grudge against him for the shattering of my back. Which I didn't.

At least, I didn't think so.

"So what do we do?" Tom asked.

"We wait." I had some ideas I wasn't about to share with him. He had enough weight on his shoulders, feeling guilty all over again for what happened between me and his son. "Go on home and keep watch over Toby. Don't let him out of the house, whenever possible. If he has to go out, never let him go without at least two people to watch him."

"You have the injector pens handy, that the hospital gave you?" Kurt said.

For answer, Tom patted his jeans pocket.

Tranquilizers and security codes and locks on all doors and windows added up to the best we could do for Tom.

The next step was all mine.

What irked me in all this was that I had a week until Christmas and hadn't even begun producing all those boxes of cookies and homemade candy I gave away for Christmas. We really had to wrap up this problem so I could get to work on what really mattered.

Through all this, we never forgot that Mum and Pop were missing. Stanzer hadn't made any progress on finding out anything we didn't already know. Athena reported every four days with whatever her team had found. So far it looked like all the official local reports were honest, they hadn't been tampered with or edited. London and Sherwood were out of touch, tied up with a big project that was demanding all their focus and energy. They had told Athena that it involved defending Neighborlee. That had to be good enough for all of us. Sometimes it was hard to remember that they were essentially computer programs who had become self-aware. Sherwood wasn't even a year old, but who knew how that translated between the World Wide Web concept of time and age and Human years? The two of them were learning what they were and what they could do as they went along, and sometimes that meant they couldn't explain what they were up to because they were still figuring it out. Athena could only promise she would ask them for help next time they made contact.

It was a waiting game. There were times that praying and knowing the folks at church were praying for us wasn't that much comfort.

<div style="text-align: center">~~~~~</div>

Mandy, Gordon's girlfriend, was our ship's counselor, aka social director for the *USS H'lastra*. She had volunteered in a moment of weakness to host this year's Christmas party, the Saturday before Christmas. That suited me just fine. There used to be plenty of room at my house, before Pete and Harry moved in with me for the duration. Still, if I had been able to host at my place, everyone would have been broken up into small groups, scattered through the living room and family room and kitchen and my two (formerly) spare rooms. Mandy's place had the advantage of a walk-out basement, and the driveway curved down around behind the house, so it was easy for me to roll from my Jeep, through the sliding door. Unlike other places, I wouldn't have to depend on the dubious chivalry of some of the guys in our ship lowering my chair down the stairs.

In some respects, using my telekinetic powers in front of a bunch of Trekkers was almost as dangerous as performing in front of a bunch of military scientists. They would have believed without a moment's hesitation, but the uproar and demands that I either teach them how to do it or explain what planet I came from would have created everlasting headaches for me. Knowing how some people in our club talked, the wrong people would have found out what I could do within a week.

So I was stuck depending on the kindness of strangers, or strange friends, to get me up and down stairs, or else stay stuck on the first floor. That was why the only options for our club parties were expensive party rooms, the little community theater building where we had our monthly meetings — not available — my place, or Mandy's.

Kurt and Felicity didn't come to the party. They were club members. They enjoyed the irony of belonging to a group of people who wanted to believe superpowers, aliens and other civilizations were real. Kurt had an overnight job in Indiana to do, some major repairs on a surveillance system he had designed for a friend. Felicity and Jake had better things to do on a Saturday night than hang with a bunch of Trekkers of all ages and sizes.

Sheridan arrived about ten seconds after I pulled into the drive. I had the sneaking suspicion he had followed me and Pete most of the way. There was no way in the world I was going to let him ride with us, and I was grateful that he didn't ask if we could carpool. The last thing I needed was my nosey crewmates deciding that the Commodore — *moi* — had a boyfriend. There were at least eight people dying to throw a full-blown Star Trek-themed wedding, complete with uniforms, alien food, and music from the soundtracks of all the movies and TV series.

Did I mention my friends tended toward the lunatic fringe when it came to Star Trek and all things fandom?

Harmless, fun people, but certified lunatics.

# Chapter Fourteen

Have you ever seen a red-haired, six-foot-five Vulcan wearing red and green glittery tunic and leggings (she looked good) and antennae topped with mistletoe? That was Mandy. She was busy making last-minute adjustments to the feast spread around the room on four eight-by-four folding tables, and singing along with the *Partridge Family Christmas Album* at the top of her lungs, when Pete, Sheridan and I came through the door. When she saw us, she let out a shriek of delight (as if Pete and I hadn't seen her two days before at the grocery store?) and ran to hug us. She hugged Sheridan, too, smearing green glittery eyeshadow on his shoulder before she stepped back.

"Uh, Mandy—" I said, trying to make introductions before the Evil Overlord died of a heart attack. Mandy's hugs could be fatal, except for those who knew how to hold our breaths until she let go.

"How long has it been?" she demanded, taking hold of his hand and dragging him farther into the room. "That con in Springfield?"

"Houston." Sheridan grinned and shook his head. "If I'd known you were here in Neighborlee, I could have saved a lot of frustration."

"Oh, heck. The jerk's sabotage is still making it hard for people to find us?" She turned to me. "Do you guys know each other?"

"Lanie has the misfortune to work for one of the papers my company bought," he said, before I could answer. "I practically blackmailed her into letting me come, when I found out she belonged to a Trek club. Hi, I'm Daniel Sheridan," he added, holding out a hand to Pete, who had hung back from the moment he saw the Evil Overlord getting out of his truck.

Not a Lexus or BMW, but a nice, dark green, extended cab pickup. I was either going to have to admit I was wrong, or... well, I wasn't quite sure what I would do, but I suspected it was going to be uncomfortable. And I would have to stop calling him the Evil Overlord. Anyone Mandy liked had to be a decent guy. There were times I suspected she had some empathic talent, because about ninety-five percent of the time, she could read people with pinpoint accuracy, picking out the jerks and saboteurs who had fooled everyone else. Another reason why she was ship's counselor.

Pete and Sheridan shook hands. Before Mandy took me off to one side to talk about the next issue of our club fanzine, I heard Sheridan ask my little brother if he would consider doing caricatures for some of the other editorial columns the newspaper conglomerate carried. I could almost hear the thud of Pete jumping over to the "The Evil Overlord isn't such a Bad Guy" camp. When half a dozen other people came in at the same time, he was already introducing him as "Daniel," with no last name. Pete had the sense to say Mandy knew Daniel from out-of-state Trek cons.

Sheridan joined us when Mandy pulled out the galleys for the club's fanzine. We only had so much room in the 'zine for the Captain's Log adventures. Otherwise known as flash fiction disguised as "episodes" of the ship's adventures, which appeared in each newsletter. Mandy had ten stories she wanted to use, and only room for four more. It was my unenviable task to decide who stayed and who had to wait until the next issue of the 'zine. Sheridan glanced through them while we discussed the problems of continuity and appearing to favor one writer in our group over another. He let out quite a few of those warm, low chuckles as he read. I felt a little more of my resistance melting away. The guy not only enjoyed our harmless insanity, but he understood it. How could I loathe someone like that?

I couldn't yet call him Daniel, like Mandy did. That was a little too far a leap for me, in only a few days.

Gordon showed up next. It was almost funny to see the way he stopped in mid-stride and his face lost all expression, the moment he walked in and saw Sheridan sitting next to Mandy, laughing and talking with her. Mandy and Gordon were perfect for each other, and she told me she knew he was the one she had been waiting for, from the very first moment they laid eyes on each other. Mandy was also very smart, and she knew better than to give Gordon the slightest inkling that his fate had been sealed. She played it very calm and casual with him, with the result that Gordon never quite knew how secure their relationship was. Which meant he felt a little jealous every time he saw another guy having fun with Mandy.

I took notes every time I saw her plan to snare Gordon working with such perfection. Not that I ever thought I'd have reason to use the lessons Mandy demonstrated, but I figured it wouldn't hurt to be prepared.

"Ship's ambassador, not security?" Sheridan shook his head and tipped his head back to grin up at Gordon, after they had been introduced.

"Who'd argue with a face like that?" Mandy said, reaching up to squeeze Gordon's face between her hands, making his mouth pout out in that goldfish pucker that made the meanest face look silly. Only Mandy could get away with doing that to him.

True love, definitely.

"Mandy—" Gordon sighed, the sound muffled when she went up on her tiptoes and planted a noisy one right on those puckered up lips. He laughed. With Gordon, his laughter starts with a soft rumble, like an earthquake just warming up.

Sheridan took a step back and watched the by-play. I thought I saw a little bit of envy under that grin. Despite Mandy being an Amazon and Gordon a Grizzly, they were a cute couple.

"Besides," Gordon said, once Mandy stepped back, "he's Chief of Security." He hooked a thumb over his shoulder at the table where all the hot food was laid out.

Ben Wallace held his first full-to-overflowing plate of the evening balanced on his left hand, and grazed with the right hand. On the outside, he was a pimply tenth-grader with a gymnast's build and a few wisps of scraggly red beard hanging off his pointy chin. That exterior hid the sharpest military mind in existence, when it came to role-playing games. Ben scared me, quite frankly. I could only be grateful that he indeed knew the difference between reality and his fantasy world, and he refused to take his cold, cruel strategizing skills out of fantasy into the real world. The military would have a field day with him. Or any terrorist organization that could get their hands on him. Ben planned on hitting the next Olympic games, and leading the men's gymnastics team. Failing that, he wanted to be a dancer on Broadway.

The majority of our ship came for the party that night, arriving in clumps over the next half hour, until we had over forty people crammed into Mandy's basement. No one wore uniforms, but there were Vulcan ears, Tellarite snouts, and Andorian antennae. (And no, I did not dress up as Captain Pike for our yearly costume party at Halloween. Give me some credit for avoiding the obvious.) There were lots of shiny, sparkly clothes and Federation or Klingon jewelry people had picked up at conventions over the years.

Nearly to a person, everyone who heard Sheridan was not only a dedicated Trekker, but wanted to work as communications officer, welcomed him with open arms. I was profoundly relieved and grateful that I hadn't griped to anyone in the club about my trials and tribulations with the Evil Overlord, except for Felicity, Kurt, and Pete. My little brother had learned discretion a long time ago. Besides, he knew he would have to walk home from Mandy's if he breathed one word of the things I had said about no-please-call-me-Daniel Sheridan, aka the head of the Evil Conglomerate that had rearranged my journalistic career.

Athena took me aside for a brief report, when she and Doni and their uncle Jinx showed up. London was still tied up, but Sherwood had taken a brief break to report that they thought they had discovered a way to link with the defensive field surrounding Divine's Emporium. If they could do that, maybe they could monitor the energy protecting Neighborlee. The possibilities resulting from that, bridging from the computerized world to touch on the realm of the magical, made me feel dizzy for a few seconds. Good thing I was sitting down.

Then again, the very existence of London and Sherwood bridged the gap between tech and magic. I was ready to believe they had gained souls, somehow. Or, when Athena used that strange video camera to record Doni four years ago, she had somehow taken a tiny piece of Doni's soul, to clone or bud like with a plant clipping, to create London Holiday. Someday we might need to consult Pastor Rocky on all the theological and philosophical implications, but that wasn't my job and certainly not my concern. Not right now. Tonight was a Christmas party and we had earned the right to goof off and just have some good, clean, slightly wacky, geeky fun.

Penny Traciczuk arrived last, as always, her arms loaded with a five-gallon plastic barrel of her yearly attempt to create non-alcoholic Romulan ale. From the blue tint of her smile when she greeted us, I suspected she had hit paydirt. Finally. A few guys hurried to take the barrel from her arms and set it in the place of honor at the end of the beverage table. Penny took one look at Sheridan standing next to my chair, and I could see the speculations sparkling in her eyes. She shrugged out of her military-issue parka with her husband's name on the pocket. (Bruno was currently on duty overseas, and she wore something of his everywhere, every day, to remind herself and others to pray for our troops.) Then she sauntered over to join me and Sheridan. Her gold sequined dress glimmered in the candlelight filling Mandy's basement, and her fingers signed at lightning speed.

*Where'd you catch tall, dark and athletic? He's cute. You put your tag on him already, I hope?*

I prayed Sheridan couldn't read sign language, or I was going to have to arrange for him to die a swift and painful death. Maybe I could convince him to go flying with Kurt, Felicity and me, and then lose my grip over the quarries?

Penny didn't say or sign anything else about Sheridan. Excuse me: Daniel. I had to start calling him Daniel, or "Evil Overlord" would slip out somewhere at the worst possible moment. Besides, everyone else in the room called him Daniel, and it would look extremely suspicious if I didn't.

Now that the last member of the crew had arrived, Mandy started off the party with the traditional reading of the official Star Trek Christmas poem. It had been passed along through fandom from one person to another, photocopied until almost illegible, with different editors along the way making tweaks and revisions. Somewhere in its misty history, it sounded like "A Visit from St. Nicholas," and started aboard the *Enterprise*. Naturally. As each ship adopted it, the names of the ships and crewmembers were adjusted to personalize the poem. But Santa Claus's stand-in, and the oversized elf who reluctantly helped him distribute the gifts, were always the same, and the poem always ended the same:

> And I heard him exclaim,
> As he beamed out of sight,
> "I'm a Doc, not a Santa,
> Hope I got it all right!"

Applause rang through the basement as Mandy finished and bowed as gracefully as only a Vulcan Amazon in glitter could do. I swore I heard Sheridan—sorry, Daniel—quoting the refrain with her and about a dozen other members of the club. Strange as it seemed, I had a nice warm spot inside at the realization that he felt comfortable among my lunatic fringe friends.

After that, the real eating began. Penny's Romulan blue was exceedingly blue, with blue cream soda and blueberry juice as the base ingredients, and a strong dose of blue raspberry Sno-Cone syrup to give it body. I swore my teeth started rotting with the first sip, just from all that concentrated sugar. Everyone agreed, this year she had finally found the right recipe. Who needed alcohol to get a buzz? The volume and the speed of conversation went up about four notches after everyone had drunk at least one cup.

The party slid into that comfortable, rowdy zone about fifteen minutes into our traditional game of "Quote Me That Quote." It was played something along the lines of *Jeopardy*, with the quote given, and the contestant required to identify who said it, to whom, in what series, and the episode title. The game was, admittedly, much easier when all we had to draw on was Classic Trek. Points were given for speed in answering and for the shortness and difficulty of the quote. I was still the record holder with "Forget," coming from Classic Trek, Spock to Kirk, and the episode *Requiem for Methuselah*, answered in just under four seconds.

Of course, that was before becoming a high school teacher totally rewired my brain, and I went over to the Dark Side of maturity and responsibility and being a good role model.

The arrival of Sergeant Slaughter, aka Dirk Hartman of the Darbyville PD, ruined our groove.

What really irritated me was that Gordon *told* him where to find me and didn't warn me he was coming. The first thing I knew about it was when the motion sensors flicked on Mandy's patio lights, and a dark shape stepped up to knock on the sliding door. Light sparkled on snow and the badge that shone to an advantage on that black leather jacket. Four of the younger guys in the crew immediately dove for the beverage table. A sure sign someone had tried to slip something alcoholic among the bottles and cans contributed to the feast. Gordon hooked a thumb toward the furnace room at the far end of the basement and the guys fled to sanctuary while he went to open the door.

"Hey, Dirk. You made good time." He stepped aside so Hartman could step inside. I couldn't get past the weirdness of Gordon calling the other officer by name, as if they were friends. I thought he had chewed out the Darbyville cop for how he manhandled me during that fake DUI stop. How could they be friends?

Then they were both looking at me. Gordon's relaxed look faded into his shoulders-back, chin-out, I'm-on-duty-ma'am stance that always made him look like such an intimidating figure, even to those who knew he was a Teddy bear.

The only place for us to talk privately, without going outside or struggling up Mandy's narrow, steep basement stairs, was into the furnace room. Any other time, I would have had a struggle not to laugh at the panic on the faces of Jamal, Tony, Aaron, and Cooper, as Gordon led the way to the furnace room. A quick glance around showed nothing visible. I hoped they hadn't stashed their beer or wine coolers or whatever close to the furnace.

"We found the red pickup truck," Hartman said, before Gordon or I could even ask what brought him there. "Someone did a good job trying to burn it beyond recognition, but we got enough of the VIN plate to identify it." He glanced at Gordon, and something in the look they exchanged let me know they had done more than make friends after I left the scene on Wednesday. They were obviously teaming up to protect the poor, persecuted crippled girl. "It was stolen two months ago."

"Sounds like whoever is after you, they've been planning this for a while now." Gordon's voice had changed, going sort of gravelly and somber. I really hated that sound, because it meant big-time serious trouble.

Well, duh, as if I hadn't figured that out already.

"What has your P.I. found out lately?" Hartman asked.

The only way to know was to pull out my cell phone and ask. I didn't know if I wanted Stanzer to be busy with the play, his phone turned off and left in the dressing room, or if I wanted him to be in the Green Room, and available. It didn't matter what I wanted, because he answered the phone in the middle of the first ring. Right about then, I was wishing we hadn't gone to the matinee of the Christmas play that afternoon, and Pete and I were both sitting in the audience, impossible to get to right that moment.

Stanzer wasn't happy with the news I passed on to him. I wasn't happy to pass on what he had found out after the matinee performance that afternoon, while the rest of us were preparing for the party. He gave me the gist of it, and when he started expanding on the technical details, I told him to wait a second, and passed the phone to Gordon. I relayed what he said to our new partner in solving the mystery.

"Stanzer spent a few hours with the Malones, trying to get more info from Toby. He's pretty sure Toby was programmed, with psychological techniques as well as drugs. The easiest analogy is to say he was set up like a remote-controlled bomb. The Malones have gotten a lot of hang-up phone calls in the last week, since he short-circuited. Stanzer thinks they were attempts to refresh the programming verbally. Whoever is pulling the strings has to be getting frustrated, since Toby never answers the phone and never goes anywhere alone."

"What'd you do, that someone would be after you like that? Takes a lot of work for all those tricks. Seems it'd be easier to do it all himself, instead of getting others to help," Hartman muttered. He divided his attention between me and Gordon, who said a lot of "uh huh" and "makes sense," and nodded. His eyes narrowed and his mouth flattened a little more with every minute that passed.

"We think I'm more like a convenient target than anything else," I hedged.

No way was I going to admit that someone might just know about my broken superpowers, and had targeted me for extinction because of them. If I confessed, I would have to demonstrate, to keep from being dragged away wearing a new jacket with sleeves that tied in the back. Right then, my brain was just too tired to demonstrate what little superpower gifts remained to me. I was pretty sure Hartman was just as skeptical and no-nonsense as his black Darbyville uniform suggested.

"What else did this Stanzer tell you?"

"His contacts are still analyzing the contents of the black bag of gas we found. They're pretty sure it's the same stuff that got Toby last week, but it degrades once it hits the air, so there's a lot they're missing out on."

"Probably too late to lecture you on using common sense and working with the authorities." The next moment, he nearly knocked me out of the chair from shock when he gave me a genuine smile.

"Yep. But believe me, if this ever happens again, you guys can handle everything. I'll head for Canada for a long vacation."

Of course, I lied. Our reasoning for not getting the authorities involved in this problem still held. I didn't want to end up on a vivisection table or running mental mazes so some egghead scientists could analyze my talents. No offense, guys, but I figured I had a legal right to live as normal a life as my wheelchair allowed, thanks very much.

Besides, I was a guardian, and guardians stayed in Neighborlee. Revealing what I was and what I could do, even by accident, could betray all of us.

When Gordon finished, he and Hartman stepped aside for a low-volume conversation, conferring on all the technical info Stanzer gave him. I got back on the phone with Stanzer, who had one more thing to tell me. The Hounds, his personal bodyguards, were finicky guardians. They didn't protect those who took stupid risks and needlessly exposed themselves. However, Stanzer was sure they would protect me against all attacks, if I wanted to put myself under his protection.

"I get the impression from them that they like you," he added, laughing a little. That sound showed me more than the rest of the conversation just how tired he was. I almost wished I had invited him to the Trek party, too. He probably would have fit right in. Too bad he was in the play, and couldn't take off once his part was finished. There was that curtain call he had to show up for, after all.

"Thanks," I said, "but you don't want me camping out at your place. The guys will tell you I'm a lousy roommate. Besides, your building isn't wheelchair accessible."

"Hey, I'll have a talk with the landlord and get him to make renovations."

We laughed together, promised to look for each other in church, and I hung up. Needless to say, I wasn't really in a party mood when the three of us left the furnace room and rejoined the others. Sundeep, our ship's doctor, wanted to know what was going on.

"Nothing too serious," Hartman said as he headed for the door with Gordon. "Don't worry about it. Nice seeing you again, Lanie."

"Don't take it the wrong way, but I hope we don't meet again for a long time," I had to say. Hey, it was in character. My friends would have been worried if I hadn't smarted off.

"I won't." He laughed, saluted, and stepped outside. Gordon went with him. I wished I had super-hearing, to catch the rest of whatever they were talking about.

"Would you believe I was stopped for drunk driving last week?" I said.

Nearly everybody laughed. Mandy, Pete and Daniel didn't. Mandy probably knew because Gordon couldn't keep much of anything secret from her. Pete knew the truth. I didn't want to think about why Daniel didn't laugh.

~~~~~

Winkies swirled down at me from the tip of the cross that hung at the front of the sanctuary over the baptismal, during the offertory Sunday morning. They spun around me, sitting on the far left aisle end of the second-from-the-front pew. That pew had always been our family's pew since Pastor Rocky and the original congregation of Neighborlee Gospel Church had bought and refurbished the Wickslow Chapel. When I came back to church, my first Sunday out of the hospital, I found someone had chopped three feet off the end of the pew to make room for my chair. All I needed was a plaque on the back of the pew in front, designating it my reserved parking space.

I watched the winkies dancing in the beams of colored light angling down from the stained glass panels near the ceiling. They spun around me and I thought I felt tiny flicks of cool energy when they lighted on me and leaped up into the air again. I flinched when several pale blue ones and a dozen green seemed set on a suicide course for Chief Tanner, who was waiting for the offering plate to come down the row from the inner aisle. Several winkies went through his face while most veered away. I didn't really look to see if they made it out the other side. Chief Tanner didn't seem to notice anything. That was good to know, I suppose. I made a mental note to check with Angela to find out why the winkies had followed me to church. How long could they show up throughout town before other people started to notice? And just what did that say about the level of energy remaining for the defenses of our town?

Then the silent alarm on my Jeep went off, just before Pastor Rocky asked us to bow our heads to pray. Kurt had tied the alarm into my cell phone, so the vibrator went off in my pocket. Yes, technically that was disobeying the instructions to turn off all electronics when we entered the sanctuary, except for those who had their Bibles on tablets, but I knew God would forgive me. I knew for a fact that parents who dropped kids off in the nursery
~~~~~

left their cell phones on, in vibrate mode, in case the nursery workers had to contact them during the service. Protecting my Jeep and solving the mystery and helping Toby surely mattered as much as a colicky baby, right?

I waited until everybody had their heads bowed, then did a quick three-point turn and wheeled down the aisle. The new carpeting in the sanctuary made it a little harder than usual to push the wheels, adding new traction, but I didn't mind. I got to the door out of the sanctuary before Pastor Rocky said amen, without making a bit of noise. I didn't even get a raised eyebrow from the ushers who were sitting or standing along the back wall, eyes closed and heads bowed. Considering how some of them had great instincts for catching kids who weren't with their parents and were about to act up, before the kids made a move, that was saying something for my stealth.

Once out in the main hall, the carpet was flatter and I could move faster. I got to the door that opened onto the parking lot in time to see a dark shape leap up from behind my Jeep, which sat in the first handicap spot next to the door.

And vanish.

Not dart behind another vehicle. I'm talking there-and-not-there, as in pop out of sight like a soap bubble, without moving in any direction.

Half a heartbeat later, that same dark shape popped into view about four lanes down the parking lot aisle. The absence of new tracks in the snow meant my enemy didn't have the ability to go invisible. He teleported. Was he limited to short distances?

The shape popped out again, and reappeared about the same distance, farther away. That supported the idea of short distances. Interesting.

Sighing, I slapped the control panel for the handicapped door and wheeled out. I remembered just in time that the doors were locked during services, except the one right next to the church office, where the custodian on duty could keep watch on things. People could get out just fine, but no one could get in undetected. We had suffered too many incidents of people walking in and helping themselves to coats and umbrellas and anything sitting on the shelves of the coat racks, to be as trusting and open as a church should ideally be. I didn't have a problem popping outside in my wheelchair for a few seconds without my coat, as long as I could get back in. I limited myself to sitting in the doorway with the back edge of my wheel holding the door open, while I tried to see if my visitor had done any damage to my Jeep.

Nothing was visible from where I sat. From the footprints left in the inch of snow that had fallen since we went inside for the service, Parker—if our theory was right and Jay Parker was part of the team—had only gotten as far as the right rear tire. Since it visibly flattened before my eyes, he had slit it, just like the last time. Hopefully, that was all the damage he did.

Kurt rolled into the parking lot while I sat there, trying to decide what to do. He was hooked up to the silent alarm on the Jeep, after all. What was the use of alarms if someone couldn't come running right away and take care of the problem?

He pulled up at the end of the wheelchair ramp, got out, and leaned against his open door, looking back and forth between me and the flat tire. He grinned, his shoulders just shaking a little bit, laughing silently at me.

"Got an extra coat?" That was the safest question I could ask.

"Nope. Go get your own, you lazy gimp. I'll still be working on this when you come back out."

"He teleports." I gave myself a good mental shove backwards through the door. I had the satisfaction of seeing Kurt's mouth drop open as the door slowly closed.

Kurt had the tire off when I got my coat back on and came outside again. This time, I remembered to snag a big wooden coat hanger, and used it to keep the door open enough that it wouldn't lock. I didn't feel like rolling around to the office door and explaining to Jennifer, the custodian on duty, why I had gone outside in the middle of the service. Jennifer was one of those earnestly righteous people, so busy making God happy, she forgot two important things. First, to *ask* God what would make Him happy, and second, to enjoy life. She took things so literally, it was nearly impossible to have a conversation with her about anything except keeping the church clean and in good repair.

She was good at her job, but she had an attitude about maintaining church security that made that chief of security from *Short Circuit* look like a cheerful, lazy, good old boy. If I told her I had gone outside because someone was breaking into my Jeep, I would spend half an hour, minimum, undergoing questioning. Nope. No time for that. Better to prop the door open and sneak back in unseen. That was if we finished with the Jeep before Pastor Rocky finished his sermon.

"He also gives off a static field, like Felicity," Kurt said, when I carefully slid down the wheelchair ramp and came to rest next to the Jeep.

Ice had built up despite the gritty layer of sand and salt laid down that morning. Common sense said to be careful and not trust in my telekinesis to save me from slide-crash-topple, or at least some mortal embarrassment.

He held up the tiny camera he had installed in the wheel well. There were eight of them positioned around my Jeep, attached to micro-miniaturized motion detectors that automatically activated when the engine stopped. He had already plugged the camera into a portable DVD player he had adapted for his own purposes. Kurt tapped a couple buttons on the auxiliary control panel he had built. A static-filled image rolled backwards on the screen, growing clearer, until we could see a dark figure in dark ski mask, bulky sweater, and gloves, down on one knee, pulling his hands back from the wheel with a knife in one hand. Kurt tapped the controls again and the picture went forward. We watched it four times through, while the picture filled with static and he slit my tire, then suddenly leaped to his feet and vanished, presumably at the point when I came to the door and startled him.

Kurt changed the tire while I put his equipment away in his custom-designed tool kit. As far as we could tell, Jay had only managed to slice my tire. He hadn't installed any bombs or tracking devices in my Jeep. I had enough time to think, and get to the point of being slightly amused that someone dressed all in dark clothes to go out on a snowy bright day. It wasn't like he tried to be invisible on a dark night, after all.

Or maybe he had something there. After all, nobody had seemed to notice him skulking around the parking lot. Even his teleporting in and out every hundred feet or so wouldn't have kept him totally invisible.

"Unless that's part of his talent, too?" I mused.

"What is?" Kurt grunted, tightening the last lug nut.

"Didn't it look a little weird to you, him dressed all in black —"

"Dark blue."

"Whatever." I stuck my tongue out at him. "He was just a little too much *Mission: Impossible*, and nobody noticed. What if he's invisible to ordinary people? Only freaks like us, and video equipment, can see him at work."

That got him. Kurt settled back on his heels, right there in the snow, one hand resting on the side of my Jeep. Slowly, he nodded.

"That kind of talent would make him very valuable to the military, wouldn't it?"

"Maybe he escaped his handlers?"

"The question is whether we want to help him stay free, or put him back into their clutches. Which hurts us more, and how much help do we owe him, as one of us?"

"Ugh. I hate philosophical discussions this early in the morning."

"Then what are you doing here?" He laughed at me and gestured at the sanctuary rising up behind me.

"Philosophy and spiritual things aren't quite the same."

"They are from where I'm sitting." He got to his feet and tossed the tire iron into the back of his truck.

"What we are, what we can do, makes me all the more sure there is a higher power. My ability to see pieces of the future tells me that there is someone watching, guiding, creating a pattern that we can't see right now, but we will see someday. A pattern that doesn't make sense now, but will make sense in the future."

"Okay, I can accept that. But how can you be sure it's … Him?" He hooked his thumb over his shoulder at the sanctuary again.

"It's kind of like getting an Equity job." I laughed when Kurt scowled at me. "You've heard the gripes from the kids who left WB's theater department and expected to become stars on Broadway within a year. The problem is, to get an Equity job, you have to belong to Equity, but the only way you can belong to Equity is to have an Equity job lined up."

"What does that have to do with you believing in this one, particular way to Heaven and illumination or whatever you want to call it?"

"You have to choose to believe before you can understand. And once you understand, you wonder why you couldn't believe before."

Kurt slowly closed the tailgate of his truck and leaned against it, his face thoughtful and weary. I could almost hear the gears and circuits whirring as he thought over what I had said. Every once in a while, he and Felicity and I had conversations like this. Maybe it was wrong for me not to press my friends more often on spiritual matters. Common sense said that if I cared about them, I should make sure of their spiritual conditions. But common sense also told me that pressing them would make them frustrated and possibly walk away for good. And I might lose forever my chance to say that one thing God had put me on Earth to say to them. I figured, I could afford to wait until the time was right.

"Okay," he finally said. "You have a point. I'm just not ready yet."

"That's fine. Just don't say no one time too many."

"How can we know when that is?" Kurt tried to grin, but his lips didn't quite stretch far enough.

"If I knew that, my foresight would be a lot more reliable, wouldn't it?"

"That's for sure. Okay, we're all set. We know a little more about the enemy than we did before. What do you want to do now?"

"I don't feel like dragging this problem into next year. I'm thinking we should pull the battle into our territory and on our schedule. We need to set a trap."

~~~~~

Tom Malone reported that Toby had tried three times Friday to get away, after they got him home and behind all the security Kurt installed in their house. Saturday, he tried eight times, drawing a blank when he came out of his trance or whatever had taken over his body. Sunday, he only tried four times. The previous week, his cell phone had rung nearly every hour, on the hour, with an "unknown number" display every time. The Malones took the cell phone away from Toby in the hospital and Tom kept it in his pocket, on vibrate, so Toby wouldn't know it was ringing. The cell phone had stopped ringing Friday morning. Tom was busy in Neighborlee business meetings until mid-afternoon, and when he checked, the phone had run out of power. That was when the home phone calls started. Toby's puppet master was desperate. Tom used a few connections with the phone company to arrange for calls to
~~~~~

be traced, but it would take time for that information to come in.

We didn't have that long. I wanted the problem over before the New Year. Heck, I wanted it over as a Christmas present. Since Christmas was that week, we were running out of time.

The security system Kurt installed at the Malone house took pictures of anyone who approached the doors. Motion sensor-controlled cameras came on whenever someone touched any of the windows. Five times total, a dark shape approached the windows of the family room and Toby's bedroom. All that activity stopped Sunday.

Stanzer had the fun task of keeping an eye on Steve Muldoon. Monday, he staked out a spot at the Sipping Post, across the street from the electronics store, and worked on paperwork and accounts, taking up the entire table with papers, his computer, and a carafe of coffee. In Neighborlee, people could see when you wanted to work. They didn't insist on sitting down at the table across from you, without asking, and then pushing aside your paperwork or even stacking it up after you had it all sorted out. They didn't assume that you'd rather gossip with them, and they didn't have a snit if you continued working when they interrupted you.

He kept Steve in his sights all morning Monday. He took a break from his work to do some window-shopping while the second member of the trouble trio ran out to pick up lunch for everyone in the store. With three shopping days until Christmas, they were understandably busy. All the shops in the downtown area of Neighborlee were busy.

Stanzer settled back into another shop when Steve came back from his errands. Scones Alone gave him a different viewing angle of the store through the big plate glass windows. He sipped tea all afternoon, continued with his office work, and kept an eye on Steve. At the end of the day, he was ready to close up his books for the end of the year and had a head start on his tax preparation. He later joked that he had tried every flavor of tea the English tea shop-themed bakery offered, but still hadn't been converted from his plain black coffee addiction.

# Chapter Fifteen

Steve looked like he was wiped out and dragging as he followed his father out to the truck behind the store at quitting time. We couldn't depend on Steve to stay home, just because he couldn't get together with Toby to run out and work some mischief. Not if Jay Parker was running around loose and impossible to locate. Knowing where Steve was would either help us in locating Jay, or limit the points of attack.

Kurt cleared things with Gordon and Chief Tanner at the police department. He let them know he was putting tracking devices on all the Muldoon vehicles, just so we could be warned if Steve decided to make a midnight run out to my side of town. The chief duly logged the report, checked with Gordon and the dispatcher to verify that mischief had been centering on my property, and asked for the report that Stanzer had ready and waiting. Chief Tanner was an easy-going kind of guy who didn't insist on micro-managing the entire town, but he liked to be kept in the loop.

He was on my side. While he didn't nurture a grudge or long-lasting suspicion against Toby and his cohorts, he admitted that since he had been there that night at the quarries when my back was broken, he was more ready to believe any charges against them. That was Neighborlee. No matter how weird the situation, people's first reaction was to want to believe what someone said.

All that being said, we were still pushing the letter and the spirit of the law when we set things up to keep an eye on Steve and Toby. By Tuesday morning, everybody involved was a little peeved that absolutely nothing had happened. Steve never tried to leave the house. Toby's blank spells and sleepwalking attempts to leave home died away completely. Either his programming was wearing off, or the control Parker had on his mind had lost its strength.

Tuesday morning, we put the plan into action. On Monday, Harry had complained to everyone at every delivery he made in town that he had to go on a long-distance pick-up for some out-of-town company, and would be gone until Christmas Eve. He let people know he had wanted to take Pete with him to let him earn some extra money, but Pete had come down with something wretched and was stuck at home, doctor's orders, until after Christmas. Then he let it be known he worried about how I would get around if there was deep snow and I needed something. Pete couldn't go out to run errands for me and Felicity was out of town until New Year's day. That last wasn't true, since Felicity was holed up at Kurt's place, but nobody knew that. Yet. Keeping those dogs quiet would be a chore and a half, but there was enough empty space around Kurt's place that the dogs had room to run off their energy. Since Felicity worked from home, she could stay home all day with her dogs and hide. That suited her just fine. Thank goodness she had all her Christmas shopping done. Otherwise, she would be in serious mental and emotional agony, having to keep away from the malls until the trap was sprung.

We laughed at how easily people in town bought the story that I was pretty much helpless, without my brothers to look after me or Felicity to run my errands. This, despite the fact I had been driving my modified Jeep for years, and getting my chair in and out of it without much help. People who didn't see me in action just assumed that wheelchair equaled total physical helplessness. We hoped Jay Parker, or whoever the real puppet master was, had also made that assumption. It didn't do much good to bait a trap if the bait had visible teeth and other means of self-defense.

Kurt would be close, keeping an eye on me as I went around town on errands, and so would Stanzer. Harry had plans to park his truck an entire county away, just in case Parker had someone watching the truck or had put a tracking bug on it. Then he would take a bus back to Neighborlee. The necessity of making me look like a defenseless little cripple meant my closest defenders had to be out of sight. That meant if someone really determined and skilled (say, trained by the military) came after me, there would be a delay before my defenders showed up.

I had my telekinesis, plus the upper body strength necessary to propel my wheelchair. Plus forewarned equaled forearmed. I was in good shape. At least, I hoped so.

Tuesday morning, when I set out to hit the *Tattler* and work ahead on the next few issues, because of the holidays changing the normal schedule, I felt perfectly calm. That didn't mean I didn't have my tense moments. Such as when a car backfiring brought up visions of a sniper taking me out from a rooftop as I wheeled my chair up the snowy ramp to the *Tattler*'s door. Or when I caught a shadowy movement from the corner of my eye, and paused to look all around. That assurance that God would take care of me didn't stop me from looking into dark spots or checking the snow for signs of people messing with my Jeep. Reliance on God, Mum and Pop had always taught us, meant being responsible for our own lives and not taking stupid risks. It was one thing to trust God to protect us when we raced into a burning building to rescue a trapped child. It was another thing altogether, a combination of arrogance and stupidity, to do a trapeze act without a net or training, and expect God to keep us from breaking our necks.

When I finished up at the *Tattler* and had done some last-minute shopping in town, I decided to take advantage of the cleared sidewalks to roll up the street to Divine's Emporium. Maybe it was the snow and sense of Christmas miracles and magic, but I always expected to go through a doorway at Divine's at this time of the year, and find myself in a snowy wood, watching Mr. Tumnus trot down the lane with Lucy on his arm. Divine's was a totally welcoming place at Christmas. I needed to visit there.

Besides, it left me out in the open for a good twenty minutes, breaking the routine my unseen shadow expected me to follow. If Jay Parker did want to hurt me, whatever brain damage made him turn to the Dark Side might just nudge him to forget what Divine's Emporium was capable of, when one of Neighborlee's own was in danger. History had proven that anyone who went up against Angela and Divine's Emporium regretted it.

I just prayed that same protection extended to anyone within sight of the olive and gold walls, and the cheerful green and gold Christmas lights that decorated the windows and gutters and trim.

I took my time heading through town, stopping to woolgather in front of the Spindelmutter building that would one day be a spa. I wondered if the owner would live upstairs. For a few heartbeats, an image of the spa filled the dirty glass and brown paper that blocked the big display window of the empty store. I stared greedily at the candles and offers of massages and facials, hoping for a glimpse of the future owner.

Because of that, I almost missed the blip in the real-time reflection. Part of that could be blamed on the snow glare and dirt, but how hard was it to see a figure dressed in dark blue (I still held out for black) sweater, pants, gloves, boots and ski mask?

My stalker was there for a heartbeat, staring at me, then gone again. Checking on me and my progress through town, or trying to figure out why I wasn't heading home? Maybe he had booby-trapped my Jeep, and was upset that I hadn't gone *boom* yet. Well, he was in for a surprise today. And disappointment.

I pulled out my cell phone and tapped in the code that let me call Kurt's cell and Felicity on Kurt's home phone, at the same time. Nice, having someone who knew how to override circuitry and programs and make gizmos do things their makers never intended.

"Hey, Pete. Just checking in," I said when first Felicity, then Kurt had both answered. What was the use of being stealthy about everything if I let Parker know who I was really talking to? Besides, using the wrong name would signal to them that I wasn't alone. "I'm doing some window shopping, heading up to Divine's. I'm going to be late getting home. Maybe three, four hours. Don't wait dinner for me."

I figured, if my stalker knew I wasn't expected home right away, he might be encouraged to strike now, while conditions were good for him.

"I saw something just now," Kurt said. "Was that him, popping in and out again?"

"You got it."

"I'm going to Divine's," Felicity said. "You want me to watch for you, or come meet you?"

"No hurry. I'll come to you." Hopefully she understood what that meant. It wasn't like we had worked out coded language for situations like this. "Stay where you are. It's nice out here, but if you leave that nice warm house, your doctor and I will both pound you. I'll be fine."

When I put my cell phone away, I made a show of adjusting my gloves and tucking my coat in tighter around me, so the ends wouldn't drag on the wheels. Nothing worse than dirty, slushy clothes, with spots worn through them. My hunch was that if Parker was going to attack, he'd do it on the long stretch of open sidewalk next to open field, leading to the dead-end where Divine's sat. That would work out just fine. Kurt would have plenty of visibility to watch me. Felicity would get to Divine's before I got to the street corner, and then she would be only a few running steps away, inside the shop.

No matter what Parker tried to do, it would take time. He would have to stop in one place long enough to aim and fire, if it was the worst-case scenario with my name on a bullet. He would have to stay in one place if it was a physical attack. If he was going to throw me in a car and kidnap me, that would mean driving up behind me, again giving my backup some warning.

Just as there were multiple scenarios for what he could try against me, there were just as many chances of success, and failure, on my part. Not a fun thing to remember. I wondered if the comic book superheroes ever had these logistical problems. Or did they just jump in and fight the battle and worry later about things like extreme physical injury and pain? Of course, a lot of them had regenerative powers, or were invulnerable to begin with. That was cheating, as far as I was concerned.

At long last, I turned the corner and started down the long strip of empty sidewalk toward Divine's Emporium. Angela had done a nice job with the decorations this year, very classy, elegantly simple, with big red velvet bows and green metallic ball ornaments the size of my fist decorating the wrought iron fence in front of the building. All those teeny gold and green lights trimming the building itself. And big pine wreaths dripping with red bows and gold ornaments.

Ten feet along the sidewalk. Twenty. One turn of the wheel equaled five feet traveled. Made it easier to keep track of distances that way.

Black filled my eyes, along with a stinging tingle along every square inch of my skin, whether it was covered or bare. I gasped and blinked as Parker popped into view right in front of me, close enough for my footrests to ram his shins. He snarled and cursed and swung with both hands clasped, swiping me out of my chair before I could brace and grab onto something. I went down into the snow. He laughed and pulled out a small, shiny black gun that looked uncomfortably like something from *Stargate SG-1* had mated with a gun from *Men in Black.*

Laughing was the wrong thing to do, along with knocking me out of my chair. Some people made the mistake of thinking that when gimps were out of their chairs, they were helpless, kind of like turtles turned onto their backs.

Parker took his time flipping on the power or whatever those switches controlled on his gun, making lights blink green and blue. Before another light could come on, a steady red dot the size of the tip of my pinkie, I had moved.

If I ever decided to go public with my talents and get a costume to hide my identity, I planned to wear all green and call myself the Lizard. I climbed up Parker faster than a tree lizard in the Amazon jungle. I had all that upper-body strength going for me, after all.

He yelled and let out a curse. Before the sound was out of his mouth, I had a good tight grip in his collar. Then I leaned back to give myself some maneuvering room, nearly pulling him off balance. Swung with my free hand. Clocked him right in the nose. I didn't know if that satisfying crunch came from his nose bones or my finger bones. Right then, I didn't care.

I threw myself away from him before he could go down, with a mental shove to get myself sprawled across my chair. In a matter of a few seconds, and some gymnastic moves that would make Nadia green with envy, I was back in my chair and loaded for bear.

Parker didn't drop his gun, and nearly clocked himself when he slapped both hands across his face to cup his bleeding nose. He dropped to his knees, roaring in pain and shock. He had blood in his eyes, literally and figuratively, when he put his hands down and raised that gun again.

"Don't you dare!" Felicity shrieked, from the front porch of Divine's.

The gun answered with a shriek of its own, spitting sparks, as her gizmo-killing talent went into overdrive. Smoke erupted from the muzzle and two seams on either side, and the stink of ozone and melting polymer burst through the cold air. Parker swore again and threw the gun away. He lunged at me, hands bent like claws.

I threw myself out of my chair, propelled with brain power as well as nicely toned arm power, and head-butted him right under his ribs. He *oofed* nice and loud and staggered backwards. I held onto him this time and went down with him, on top of him.

Kurt showed up then, accompanied by Gordon, with his handcuffs swinging. So that was what took him so long showing up. He wanted official reinforcements. I could probably have taken Parker in a few more rounds, but my head hurt from that last impact. Besides, we had to look out for Parker's mental state. He was already mental, but things could only get worse if a poor little crippled girl kept beating the snot out of him without breaking a sweat.

Stanzer showed up just about the time Gordon finished slapping the cuffs on Parker and tried to haul him upright.

The one fear we had when we made our plan was Parker just popping out, away, when we tried to haul him into custody. He wove and wobbled on his feet and his eyes crossed, meaning he was stunned hard enough to kill his teleporting ability. How long would that last? We would worry about that later.

Was it cruel of me to hope I had clocked him hard enough to knock a few circuits loose? Or maybe Felicity had scorched him hard enough to keep him in one place?

"You can still fly," Parker mumbled, through a face full of blood and melting snow.

"What do you mean, 'still'?" Kurt demanded, and neatly yanked Parker out of Gordon's hands.

"I saw her. The night we took the trucks. I saw her fly to get Toby off the truck. Her powers jumped to me when she got hurt." The most pitiful expression of relief and shock mixed crumpled his face. "Does that mean I'm normal again?"

My usual response to a question like that was to say there was no such thing as "normal," except a town in Illinois. Kurt glared at me, which made me think he could hear that particular retort bouncing around in my head, begging to get out. I kept my mouth shut, of course.

"You can't fly, Jay." Stanzer grasped his arm to get his attention. I admit, that was probably a smart move. Parker's eyes moved back and forth in his head so fast, I was worried they might pop out of his skull at any moment. "Nobody can fly. You were hallucinating that night and you're hallucinating now."

"But I saw her—"

"I was the track and basketball coach, remember?" I snapped. That got his attention focused on me. I wondered just how long he had gone without sleep, to be so shaky, his attention zipping around like that. Or maybe someone had him on some powerful drugs. "I was an athlete in high school and college. Of course I'm going to be able to jump up onto that truck, to try to free Toby.

Adrenaline lets you do a lot of things you ordinarily couldn't do."

"Yeah. Look at the *Incredible Hulk* movie. That's what they thought made people strong, when it wasn't gamma rays," Gordon offered. He cringed a little when Kurt and Stanzer both glared at him.

"Sorry to interrupt this philosophical discussion, but I really think Lanie needs to get inside. She's soaked." Felicity yanked on my shoulder to help me get seated more securely in my chair, then grabbed the handles and turned me around so fast I almost fell out of the seat again.

Angela had my vanilla chai waiting when Felicity pushed me up the shallow front steps and through the front door.

The three of us settled at the little wrought iron bistro table by the front counter. With my coat and gloves off, most of the wet was gone. I could put up with the wet spots on my pants, especially with it so toasty warm in Divine's. Besides, I didn't want to waste time changing into whatever emergency clothes Angela might have lying around, and let my drink get cold.

"My hero," I said after the first long, deliciously scalding gulp.

Angela just smiled and shook her head, her deep blue eyes sparkling like the lights on her enormous, ceiling-scraping tree.

"Okay," Felicity said. "Spill. I know I missed the good stuff."

"We saw plenty from the front window," Angela said. "If you ever give up working for the paper, I think you have a great career as a professional wrestler."

Felicity and I looked at each other and burst into semi-hysterical giggles. Angela knew all about our daydreams about ridiculous costumes and stage names.

Stanzer and Kurt joined us before I finished relaying what had led up to that battle in the snow. Angela produced more hot drinks for them, just about the time they walked through the front door. I was sitting right there and didn't see exactly where the ingredients came from. For all I knew, she had a matter-transmitter or a replicator hidden behind the tall marble counter where she had the cash register and the coffee machine, and it conjured up all the drinks ready-made and steaming. I much preferred that explanation to the common sense explanation that she had a small refrigerator and one of those nifty little coffee makers that made a dozen drinks at the touch of a button.

We learned a little more from Kurt and Stanzer. Parker had developed diarrhea of the vocal cords while Gordon left him in their custody, handcuffed, and went to get his truck. He babbled, confessing everything he had done to my Jeep and my house, everything he had tried to do, and all the things he had planned if he didn't manage to capture me that day. Kurt went chauvinistic and over-protective, and refused to share any details, other than to tell me I wouldn't have been comfortable or happy.

Since Jay Parker didn't get his grubby hands on me, what did that matter, anyway?

"From some of the things he said," Stanzer said, "he was working for someone. He got some equipment from Muldoon's, just like you thought, but the gas in that little bladder and some of the really fancy spying equipment came from someone else. His boss. Someone who believes Parker's story that you had psychic powers or you're an alien or something unusual, and when you were injured, some of your powers went to Parker."

"Some?" Angela tipped her head to the side in that way she had that reminded me of a very inquisitive bird. "Not all?"

"So they must have wanted to get hold of me to do some experimentation." I shook my head, immediately rejecting that idea. "If it was someone that powerful, why didn't they just come after me themselves, instead of sending Jay and Steve and Toby? They did send all of them as a team, right?"

"I got the idea that was the plan," Kurt said. "Some of what Parker said was a little…incoherent would be a good word."

Angela got up from the table, gathering up all our empty mugs. "I'm very glad you three didn't vanish like the other gifted children who were in the orphanage. Neighborlee needs its guardians. It's too bad Jay Parker's talents manifested so late, and in such strained circumstances. He could have benefited from your guidance. *If* you had known what he was and what he could do. Now… I'd be a little worried about what will happen if the wrong people in the outside world take him seriously."

She looked at me as she said that last part, and an image of Col. Hayward came to mind. I had no idea if Angela put him into my thoughts, or he just naturally appeared there. It made sense, though, to think of him. We would need help, especially if Parker's puppet master was military, which seemed pretty logical.

"The way he was babbling and shaking when Gordon loaded him into his truck, I doubt anybody's going to take him seriously for a long, long time," Kurt said.

We could only hope.

Just to be on the safe side, though, I left a message for Col. Hayward on the voicemail number he assured us was secure. I made it as cryptic as possible. Just to be on the safe side.

God, I firmly believe, is pleased with those who don't take stupid risks. With anything.

Which meant we sat and discussed how to deal with Parker when his head cleared enough he could use his teleporting trick again. Kurt was of the opinion that Parker was so convinced that my flying ability had transferred between us, he wouldn't even try to teleport to escape. Stanzer offered to ask for a Hound to keep watch on Parker, to prevent him escaping.

That led to an interesting half hour or so, learning about the Hunt and the Hounds of Hamin, and Stanzer's search for the other members of the Hunt. Part of the reason he had worked so hard to buy that six-story building he owned was to have a place for them to settle, when he found them. If he ever found them. They had all been children when they were sent from their homeworld, through a dimensional rift, to sanctuary on Earth. He had grown up, and so had many of them. The youngest would be in high school now.

"I think this is a job for Athena and her crew of geniuses," Angela said. "If all the members of the Hunt have arrived in the same way that John did, there are enough telltales and similarities to help identify them. Or at least sift them out from among all the other children found in strange circumstances. Starting with those scars on your wrists."

"Once we get things settled with the Zephyrs and bring them home," Stanzer said, with a nod to me.

~~~~~

That was Tuesday.

Wednesday, I woke in a panic, realizing that I had one day until Christmas and practically nothing done on my arm-long list of Christmas baking.

Felicity and I spent the entire day in the kitchen. Pete and Harry helped out, borrowing mixing bowls and cookie trays and pans from neighbors, washing dishes, and carrying the finished
~~~~~

goods out to the screened-in porch to cool. Nothing like having a walk-in freezer when we most needed it.

We turned off the ringers on the land line and our cell phones, so we didn't know Stanzer called until the answering machine started recording his message. He apologized, but the Hounds hadn't responded to his request for help and Parker was gone. He hadn't teleported out of the jail cell, though.

Four men with enough paperwork to choke two mules had come to the police station just before noon. They were the intimidating types in sleek, dark suits, with chiseled features and the sense that the Liquid Metal Terminator would emerge from them at any moment. They knew the right names and had dozens of papers with all the right signatures and whisked Jay Parker out of the Neighborlee jail. Despite the best efforts of Sgt. By-the-Book Schacker to keep the suspect in custody.

That was the bad news.

The good news was that Parker had undergone two interviews with the city counselor and the department's psychotherapist. Stanzer knew just what buttons to push and strings to pull to get us the transcripts of those interviews. I had a right to know what he said, after all, since I was the intended target.

Stanzer came over and sat in a corner of the kitchen where he would be out of the way, and read us the transcript while the four of us kept moving, mixing and cutting and baking and packing away cooled cookies in gift boxes.

A lot of what Jay Parker said was raving and rambling, but our unique perspective let us read between the lines.

The mental control of the threesome had been handled by someone using drugs and sleep deprivation, and a lot of other techniques that bordered on torture.

Stanzer had already read the report, and he thought ahead to call the Malones and the Muldoons, to warn them, in case someone military came along and tried to confiscate the boys. They were to call Gordon and Chief Tanner if that happened, and if either boy started acting strange. Neither family was very happy, but at least the warning seemed to come in plenty of time for Steve Muldoon.

Jay Parker could teleport himself short distances, nothing farther than fifty yards per leap. That was it. No telepathy, no levitation, no ability to go through solid objects, no super-speedy healing. It was almost funny, how the two interviewers tried to talk reason into Parker, to get him to realize his talent was just in his imagination, most likely a result of the mental torture he had endured. I said almost funny. I was relieved that they didn't believe him for one second, especially when he kept insisting he got his talent from me when I was injured on Senior Prank Night.

Yet at the same time, these people lived and worked in Neighborlee. Why didn't they believe a little bit?

I could see how he got the idea that he had absorbed my talent. The shock of the accident that night had pushed him to teleport without realizing what he had done. Since he watched me until he got sent away to boot camp, and I most definitely didn't "fly" again, he thought he had inherited my talent.

The guilt eating at him all these years must have been horrific. He talked to the wrong military head-shrinker, who sent him to someone just twisted enough to believe Parker's ravings. When they investigated Toby and Steve to find out their side of that night's events, they must have decided to put the trio together, with Parker nominally in charge. It really was rather clever of this unseen, powerful person in the military, to divide up the attacks among Steve and Jay, and put Toby out front where he would attract all the suspicion. Only, as we proved, he was not quite clever enough.

All my problems started when the person in charge of the trio decided to test his puppets, and test me. He set them loose with vague instructions to find out if I had some other powers or had healed in the intervening years, against all odds. And if so, to bring me in for examination.

Excuse me? If I had demonstrated some really drastic superpowers, like teleporting or mind control or whatever it was he wanted to confiscate, what made him think anyone could capture me?

Yeah, I considered the age-old means of control: threatening my family and friends. Anyone watching my brothers long enough would figure out quickly enough that trying to use them against me was a losing proposition. Pete and Harry could create more trouble than anyone trying to use them as pawns could handle. Think the old story, "The Ransom of Red Chief."

"You think …" Pete looked a little queasy for a moment. I knew his cast-iron constitution, so it wasn't a result of taking samples of every batch of dough, every finished cookie and dipped pretzel and piece of candy.

The rest of us paused in our different tasks and Stanzer looked up from the last page of the report. From where I was sitting, it looked like some printouts of pictures of Parker sitting in his jail cell.

"What if they're the ones who took Mum and Pop?" he finally said. "They didn't vanish from something freaky that happened, they didn't trigger something, investigating all those electro-magnetic lines of force or whatever. What if those people who sent the guys took Mum and Pop, first?"

"That makes too much sense," Felicity said. A few pink and green sparks swirled up from the ends of her hair. She swallowed hard and sat down and took a couple deep breaths, visibly fighting to be calm. "Your folks were looking after us all those years we were figuring things out. We still go to them. Maybe not as much as we go to Angela, but … yeah, they're like our advisories. Our mentors. Maybe these jerks think your folks are our leaders."

"Then they have to know by now Charlie and Rainbow are pretty ordinary, and they don't have any gifts," Stanzer said.

Harry snorted. "Have you met our parents?"

"You know what I mean." He shrugged and offered a grin.

That seemed to break some of the thickness in the air, the chill settling in. I could breathe a little easier.

Stanzer gave us the copy of the report to go over later. He said he would stop by the church to talk to Pastor Rocky and by Divine's, on his way home. To report, to ask for special help and any insight or advice. We appreciated that. He offered to let us stay in his building, where he could be sure the Hounds would protect us. I thanked him, but we felt very safe between Kurt's security system and our own talents.

Before Stanzer could even start to argue, Chief Tanner called. He wanted to check on me, after the ruckus the day before, and to let us know that a number of our friends in the police department didn't like how the whole situation with Parker had been handled. They had volunteered to double patrols in our neighborhood, until we had some answers.

"Neighborlee does take care of its own, doesn't it?" Stanzer mused, once I got off the phone and reported the gist of the call.

"In more ways than one," Felicity said.

He left a short time later, with a big box of cookies. The four of us settled down to finish our chores and depressurize after everything that had happened. Despite proof that the weirdness that seemed to protect Neighborlee wasn't always reliable, we felt safe. We just knew, with no solid proof beyond our sense of "that's just the way it is," no one was going to pull up to my house in a windowless black van in the middle of the night, to snatch us out of our beds, and whisk us away to some super-secret underground lab for a lifetime of testing.

Maybe it was just the magic of Christmas that made us so sure. Maybe it was exhaustion. We had gone past the point of "enough."

That left us only one big challenge: finishing the holiday baking before four. It was Christmas Eve, after all. Even though Mum and Pop weren't home, that didn't mean we would skip the Christmas Eve service at church and all our other traditions.

Felicity brought in the mail for me before settling into her place to prepare for a romantic, quiet Christmas Eve with Jake. I really hoped she was going to get a ring.

I got a big, battered, padded envelope.

Addressed from Bermuda.

In Pop's spiky, strong handwriting, and his signature neon purple ink.

I nearly dropped the envelope four times before I could get it open, and then I dropped the DVD case twice. Finally, I shrieked for my brothers.

"It's from Mum and Pop," I explained, and held out the case with shaking hands.

Hey, it had been a rough couple of weeks. I was entitled to some shaking, right?

Pete turned on the TV and got the channel switched. Harry pried open the case and nearly dropped the disc as he slid it into the little drawer, which seemed to take forever to slide into the player. We settled about four feet away from the screen, with the volume turned up loud so we could hear it over the thudding of our hearts.

The static cleared to show Pop sitting on the beach, his extremely hairy, pale legs exposed by the ugliest pair of purple and orange plaid Bermuda shorts I had ever seen in my life. Nice to know nothing had changed in the short while they had been gone. Mum scurried into sight from behind the camera and settled down on the sand next to him. She wore a crown of pink and yellow flowers that matched the sarong she wore over her bikini. When I got to be Mum's age, I wanted to have her figure.

"Hi, kids," Mum said, as she snuggled up against Pop, with his arm tight around her. "We've found a few leads that are just blowing our minds. Chances are pretty good, if we follow up on every one of them, we're not going to make it home for Christmas. We're sending this package by a slow boat from China, literally, to make sure that the wrong people don't get their hands on this. We've formulated some theories that could be pretty dangerous if they got into the wrong hands. Believe us, Lanie especially, you do not want the wrong people finding out about this. The rest of this disk has all our notes and documentation, so if we don't make it home, someone can figure out what we did and where we went. What we're guessing at is out of this world. In more ways than one." She giggled and spread her arms wide. "Hugs and kisses, kids. We love you more than anything in this world, or the next."

"Say your prayers and look after each other," Pop added. "Pray for us. But I know I don't have to remind you, because I know you are. I don't know how we managed to end up with three kids who are more grown up than us, but I guess that's God's sense of humor, right? Remember we love you."

"And if we don't come home," Mum said, "don't be sad. We're all going to end up together, no matter what. See you there, or in the air. We love you."

Harry hit the pause button, and for a long time, we just sat there, staring at the picture of our parents.

All things considered, it was a great Christmas after all.

**END**

# Neighborlee, Ohio

*(Title, Original Title, Release Date)*

**Confessions of a Lost Kid** (Growing Up Neighborlee) 05/20
**Semi-Pseudo-Superheroes** (Dorm Rats) 07/20
**Virtually London** (London Holiday) 09/20
**Living Proof (that no good deed goes unpunished)** (Living Proof) 11/20
**Night of the Living Proof**, 01/21
**Quitting the Hero Biz** (Hero Blues) 03/21
**Bride of the Living Proof**, 05/21
**Shrunk: The Exile of Maurice** (Divine's Emporium) 07/21
**Return of the Living Proof**, 09/21
**Allergic to Mistletoe** (Have Yourself a Faerie Little Christmas) 11/21
**Dawn of the Living Proof**, 01/22
**Angela's Knight** (Divine Knight) 03/22
**The Living Proof Gets the Blues**, 05/22

# ABOUT THE AUTHOR

On the road to publication, Michelle fell into fandom in college and has 40+ stories in various SF and fantasy universes. She has a bunch of useless degrees in theater, English, film/communication, and writing. Even worse, she has over 100 books and novellas with multiple small presses, in science fiction and fantasy, YA, suspense, women's fiction, and sub-genres of romance.

Her official launch into publishing came with winning first place in the Writers of the Future contest in 1990. She was a finalist in the EPIC Awards competition multiple times, winning with *Lorien* in 2006 and ***The Meruk Episodes, I-V***, in 2010, and was a finalist in the Realm Award competition, in conjunction with the Realm Makers convention.

Her training includes the Institute for Children's Literature; proofreading at an advertising agency; and working at a community newspaper. She is a tea snob and freelance edits for a living (MichelleLevigne@gmail.com for info/rates), but only enough to give her time to write. Her newest crime against the literary world is to be co-managing editor at Mt. Zion Ridge Press and launching the publishing co-op, Ye Olde Dragon Books. Be afraid … be very afraid.

www.Mlevigne.com
www.MichelleLevigne.blogspot.com
@MichelleLevigne

Also by Michelle L. Levigne

*Guardians of the Time Stream*: 4-book Steampunk series
*The Match Girls*: Humorous inspirational romance series starting with **A Match (Not) Made in Heaven**
*Sarai's Journey:* A 2-book biblical fiction series

*Tabor Heights*: 20-book inspirational small town romance series.
*Quarry Hall*: 11-book women's fiction/suspense series
***For Sale: Wedding Dress. Never Used***: inspirational romance
***Crooked Creek: Fun Fables About Critters and Kids***: Children's short stories.
***Do Yourself a Favor: Tips and Quips on the Writing Life.*** A book of writing advice.
***Killing His Alter-Ego***: contemporary romance/suspense, taking place in fandom.
*The Commonwealth Universe*: SF series, 25 books and growing
*The Hunt*: 5-book YA fantasy series
*Faxinor*: Fantasy series, 4 books and growing
*Wildvine*: Fantasy series, 14 books when all released
*Neighborlee:* Humorous fantasy series
*Zygradon*: 5-book Arthurian fantasy series